PENGUIN BOOKS

The Homestead Girls

Fiona McArthur has worked as a rural midwife for many years. She is a clinical midwifery educator, mentors midwifery students, and is involved with obstetric emergency education for midwives and doctors from all over Australia.

Fiona's love of writing has seen her sell over two million books in twelve languages. She is the author of the nonfiction works *The Don't Panic Guide to Birth*, *Breech Baby: A Guide for Parents* and *Aussie Midwives*.

She lives on an often swampy farm in northern New South Wales with her husband and some happy cows. She's constantly taking photographs of sunrise and sunset and loves that researching her books allows her to travel to remote places.

fionamcarthurauthor.com

FIONA McARTHUR

The Homestead Girls

PENGUIN BOOKS

PENGUIN BOOKS

UK | USA | Canada | Ireland | Australia
India | New Zealand | South Africa | China

Penguin Books is part of the Penguin Random House group of companies
whose addresses can be found at global.penguinrandomhouse.com.

Penguin
Random House
Australia

First published by Penguin Random House Australia Pty Ltd, 2015
This edition published by Penguin Random House Australia Pty Ltd, 2016

1 3 5 7 9 10 8 6 4 2

Cover design by Nada Backovic © Penguin Random House Australia Pty Ltd
Text design by Samantha Jayaweera © Penguin Random House Australia Pty Ltd
Cover photographs by: Woman: Joshua Hodge Photography/Getty Images;
Background: Auscape/UIG/Getty Images; Plane: Bruce Miller/Alamy
Typeset in Sabon by Penguin Random House Australia Pty Ltd
Colour separation by Splitting Image Colour Studio, Clayton, Victoria
Printed and bound in Australia by Griffin Press, an accredited ISO AS/NZS
14001 Environmental Management Systems printer.

National Library of Australia
Cataloguing-in-Publication data:

McArthur, Fiona, author.
The homestead girls / by Fiona McArthur.
ISBN 9780143573852 (paperback)
Subjects: Royal Flying Doctor Service of Australia--Fiction.
Country life--New South Wales--Fiction.
Female friendship--Fiction.

A823.4

penguin.com.au

MIX
Paper from
responsible sources
FSC® C009448

To the Royal Flying Doctor Service:
their incredible flight nurses, flying doctors and outreach
clinic care providers; the control room coordinators,
the mechanics and the pilots who get them there safely,
and to those who raise funds to help support this
incredible service. You are all heroes.

PROLOGUE

Today, Layla had a jellybean up her nose. Last week she'd pushed a pebble in her ear. Dr Billie Green patted the arm of the worried mother because this so reminded her of her own daughter, Mia, as a little girl, when she'd vied for attention in their busy life. But it was pointless to wish that her sixteen-year-old daughter was as adorable as she'd been all those years ago.

Flipping through the sterile packets of instruments for the long-nosed artery forceps, Billie tried not to wonder just what Mia was up to right at this moment as she tilted this little girl's face to the light.

Before her previous patient, Billie had called home and the house phone had rung out. Sometimes it was hard to keep up with her daughter, this was the problem with being a single parent, and the unanswered call meant worrying that maybe Mia was out doing something she shouldn't be.

Focus on the job at hand, she reminded herself. 'Okay, sweetheart. Hold still and I'll get that yucky thing out of your nose.'

With one hand on the tiny chin and the other on the instrument, Billie directed the metal forceps towards the offending object, her lips twitching at the sight of the red-bean-smeared nostril. After initial resistance, the jellybean slid out with a final firm tug. Success. Billie's eyes met those of the mother and they both released pent-up breaths and grinned.

'Thank you, Dr Green.' The mum scooped up her daughter and hugged her with relief.

Billie winked at Layla, then she bypassed the lolly jar that she used when she needed to bribe nervous young patients and chose the rabbit hand print. 'Stamp?'

'Pwease.'

'Good choice. No more nose poking.' Layla solemnly shook her head and held out her hand for Billie to brand with the bright-coloured bunny outline. They all looked at it—it was pink and perfect, like a tiny tattoo on the white skin.

Layla's mum hugged her close once more. 'Say thank you to Dr Green.'

'Fanks.'

Billie rubbed the fine strands of blonde hair on her patient's adorable head. 'You were such a good girl. If only every little girl could be so easy.'

Including her daughter. She flicked another look at the clock—nearly eight p.m. She showed them out of her consulting room and there were no more patients waiting. Someone else was, though.

'Dr Green?' Billie's pulse rate jumped as the man in the blue uniform straightened off the wall of her office and stepped forward.

'Yes?'

Gruffly but not unkindly, he said, 'I'm Sergeant Hill. A word with you in private.'

'Of course. Come in.' She looked across at the receptionist, who raised her shoulders in a worried shrug. They'd find out soon enough.

As soon as she'd shut the door she asked, 'Is my daughter okay?'

'That would be Miss Mia Rose Green?'

'Yes.' Cold terror flooded her. It *was* Mia. Now Billie struggled to contain the fear that closed her throat. An accident? Blood, broken bones? Molested? Her father? 'Tell me?'

'Your daughter's detained at the police station. Though she'll be released into your care as soon as you come to collect her.'

Relief sagged her shoulders until other implications sank in. Trouble, then. Better than physical harm, although she still dreaded the answer to her next question. 'What's she done?'

He sighed and she could tell he hated this. Probably had kids Mia's age as well. 'Were you aware it's high school muck-up tonight?'

'No.' She hadn't been or she'd have made sure someone had stayed home with Mia. The local kids had been getting rowdier every year. Last year's high-school-leaving students had painted the town toilet block iridescent yellow and stuck feathers all over the concrete walls. And the local McDonald's sign had mysteriously flown to the top of the school auditorium. The authorities still didn't know how they'd managed to get it there.

'Your daughter was a passenger in a car that we apprehended this evening. The driver and his passengers accosted a security guard, wearing balaclavas to obscure their faces. They were brandishing toy guns.'

Billie plonked inelegantly into the chair behind her desk. Mia was grounded! And just who had she been riding around with in a car at night? Then the true horror of how she could have been hurt if the security guard had been armed sank in. What if they'd done it to a police car? They could have been shot!

The policeman went on. 'Your daughter's fortunate. No charges will be laid because of her age, but we've taken a statement from all of them. The nineteen-year-old driver will appear in court.'

She'd bet it was that creepy Jensen who'd been turning up late at night wanting to see Mia. 'Who was driving?'

The policeman avoided her eyes and she had the feeling he was the kind of man who would want to know who was driving if it had been his teenager in the back seat. 'I'm not at liberty to say. But you can ask your daughter when you come to the station.'

My word, she'd ask her daughter when she came to the station. Billie checked the clock on her office wall again. Her evening clinic would finish in three minutes anyway. 'I'll follow you in my car.'

She thought she sounded calm—hopefully the policeman couldn't see the steam coming out of her ears—but her car keys dug into her palm as she followed him out and closed her office door with a forceful click. She rolled her eyes at the receptionist as she went past but didn't see her response because she was thinking, *How many times have I told you to choose your friends wisely? You wait, Miss Mia, you are in so much trouble. I'm getting you away from here before you make the same mistake I did.*

ONE

A month later and twelve hundred kilometres away on a drought-stricken sheep-and-cattle station in far western New South Wales, Soretta Byrnes scanned the distance through her kitchen window. The paddock stretched away down the hill: the greenish blue of the saltbush, red dirt, and maroon rocks poking through the cracked soil and dust. She wanted to throw on her boots and head out again, check the ewe she was worried about, just potter around on the quad with the dogs before it got dark to make sure the troughs were still filling with bore water. But she needed to make tea.

It was days like this that she missed Gran the most. It was as if the house had lost its heart. Oh she used the cedar oil, kept the floorboards shiny, did it for the comfort of hearing Gran's gentle voice in her head saying, *Just fifteen minutes a day and your house is a home*. But a house wasn't a home without people, and hopefully the horizon would yield a small dust ball, two quad bikes and her grandfather before sunset. It was a long way home from their joint boundary with the next-door station in the dark.

Peripherally she heard the *creak*, *creak*, of the windmill as it pumped water from the hard ground, but this afternoon her skin prickled with premonition instead of the subtle calming effect the pump's cadence usually had on her. Even the grand old homestead, a home she and her grandfather both had rattled around in since her grandmother had died, felt claustrophobic.

It was her twenty-second birthday today. 'Lucky I'm not precious,' she murmured and swiped a date out of the packet in the door of the fridge. Maybe she could make scones and put a candle on top?

Grandad might like that and she was almost at the sing-and-dance stage of trying to cheer him up. Maybe she had it wrong and he'd remember it was her birthday, breeze in and say, 'Pretty yourself up, sweetheart, I'm taking you all the way into town for dinner.' Highly unlikely. Not that she blamed him.

In the last eighteen months they hadn't seen any decent rain, the dams were dry for the first time in years, and her grandad's dream of climbing out of spiralling debt had shrivelled into dust, along with the grass in the home paddock and the weaker sheep. Mustering feral goats was the only thing keeping them going.

She had this mounting dread he'd do something silly like put the place on the market if the rain didn't come soon. The spectre of depression, an evilly charismatic black wraith, had touched other drought-stricken families, and, for the first time, she worried about her own grandfather.

Lately he barely spoke to her.

Soretta glared at the empty fridge until the roar of a quadbike coming up the track lifted her head and she moved to the creaking screen door to step out onto the verandah.

The one backpacker who hadn't abandoned them had been known to be a little reckless, but there was something unsettling about the speed of this approach and the hairs on the back of her neck waved again uneasily.

Klaus jumped from the quad almost before it stopped. 'Boss down. Hit an anthill on the quad bike. He landed on a mulga root. Lots of blood.'

She clamped down on the gory picture that sprang immediately to her mind. 'Where?'

'Next-door boundary. We use that holding yard for this muster. Near airstrip. Phone smashed. You get the flying doctor.' Klaus's usual florid face was pale and sickly with shock and stress.

This was bad. Soretta felt the panic flutter in her throat and she squashed it down, too. It would have taken forty minutes for Klaus to get to her. Her grandad had been alone that long. 'Go back to him. I'll bring the utility.'

Klaus nodded, jumped back onto the bike and roared away.

Soretta jerked open the screen door and sprinted up the hallway to the phone on the wall. Her grandad was injured. Klaus's words were screaming like neon lights in her head: hitting the ground at speed, speared by a mulga root, lots of blood. Even Grandad wasn't invincible. He'd be all right. He'd better be all right. He was all she had in the world.

Daphne Prince glanced out the window of the office as the aircraft lifted off with the flight crew from the next shift, and narrowed her eyes as it disappeared into the sunset. Another night on call for any emergencies until they came back, but that was okay. The control room at Broken Hill would phone her at home until seven the next morning. She loved her job, was falling in love with the country even though she'd been a city girl her entire life, and she was fiercely proud of the whole Flying Doctor Service she'd joined. For one thing, having to deal with emergency medical situations with very little help had certainly brought her out of her shell.

'Don't suppose there's any more of that coconut slice?' Rex was holding his hand out dolefully like Oliver Twist. 'Please, ma'am, is there more?'

'Nope. I think you've eaten it all, Rex.' She grinned at the hopeful expression on the pilot's face. Just looking at him made her feel warm inside. She had no expectations, but passing time with the delightful Rex was no hardship. Besides, she had nothing else to go home for.

At least she'd found a job she loved. She might be vertically challenged or suffering from duck's disease, as her ex-husband had told everyone—even here she had the nickname, Legs—but it was useful being small when you were crawling around inside a tiny aircraft for most of your working day.

Tonight was a shame, though. She'd been looking forward to meeting the new female doctor and now it was likely she'd be called out. The doctor and her daughter would have arrived by now to share the other side of the duplex Daphne lived in. It would be good to have another woman around here. There was more than enough testosterone with the boss, Rex, and the other nurses and pilots all being male.

The Mica Ridge base didn't take calls twenty-four hours a day, they were coordinated from Broken Hill, but Daphne and Rex were on call until the team came back. With Morgan here as senior doctor, the base had an extra person during office hours, and with the new doctor his load would be lightened, too. Maybe Daphne wouldn't be needed tonight and as soon as the others returned she'd be able to relax.

The phone rang and Daphne scooped it up. Heard a strangled, 'Come on!' on the other end and instantly recognised the stress of an emergency.

She heard a deep breath as the caller collected herself. 'Daphne. Thank God. It's Soretta Byrnes from Blue Hills Station.'

Daphne switched the phone to loudspeaker so Rex could hear and prepare as she listened and wrote swiftly. *Seventy-year-old male. Impact off high-speed quad bike.* Lord she hated those quad bikes, Daphne thought.

Impaled by mulga root. Daphne winced. *Abdominal wound. Extent not seen by caller. Back paddock Blue Hills Station. Closest airstrip adjoining station. Large blood loss.* She looked over at Rex who stood to study the map.

'I'll switch the phone through to Morgan and let him know we're out,' Rex said. 'Just over ninety k. Landing in forty minutes.'

Daphne relayed that. 'Don't move him without a spine board. We'll move him when we get there. Can you try to meet us at the airstrip with the utility and we'll transfer the gear to him?' The caller agreed and hung up and Daphne scooted out from behind the desk. They'd need extra fluids, pain relief if he was well enough, extra sponges for a pressure bandage, and battery packs for basic life support equipment. Rex was gone and pre-flight checks would be well under way by the time she scooped her essentials and headed out the door to the plane. This was always the hardest part. Trying to imagine scenarios, pre-empt disaster, prepare for every eventuality when, really, you couldn't.

She walked as fast as due care would allow; Morgan would skin her alive if she slipped and fell because she was hurrying too much. By the time she'd stowed her extra gear, Rex was pulling the door shut behind her and she held her breath as he squeezed past into the cockpit. Best part of the day really, Rex squeezing past. She smiled to herself then switched back into rescue mode.

Listening to the whirr of the engines as they began to warm, she willed Soretta to stay calm. And willed Soretta's grandfather to stay alive because if he did his part, they'd do theirs.

Soretta wasn't going to move him, but the bleeding wouldn't stop and she decided if they were very careful they could put him on the board that stayed strapped to the back of the ute for emergencies like this. If she didn't move him, it could be too late by the time the plane arrived. It was an agonisingly long time later that she and Klaus finally had her grandfather in the back of the utility. They were nearly there now, but her grandfather's white face glistened with shock and pain as they bounced as gently as Klaus could navigate the potholes, over the rough track to the airstrip on the neighbour's property.

Soretta's face felt tight, petrified like the piece of mulga that had caused such damage, as she settled the blanket around her grandfather's bony shoulders and tried to keep from crying.

One of the hardest things she'd ever done was shift her grandad onto the stretcher board and she hoped she'd done the right thing. His pale face, the beads of sweat as he'd tried to hold back the groans of agony, and the way the bleeding had continued to seep around the wad of dressing she'd held had warned her there was no other option. 'Hang in there, Grandad.'

'Sorry, hon.'

His voice was so damn thready. 'Don't you dare die!' She heard the squeak in her tone as she fought down the panic.

The drone of a plane caught her attention, and she held her breathe as she watched it and prayed like she'd never prayed before. Mentally, she hurried it onto the ground and willed the door to open. Soretta sucked in a breath as her head began to swim. It was okay, she chanted to herself. They'd be able to get him to help before it was too late.

'You were a beautiful baby.' Her grandfather's hoarse whisper held a smile. 'Now you look like your grandmother. Even more beautiful.'

No! That sounded way too much like goodbye. 'Save your strength,' she said, fiercely. 'We're nearly there.'

And then they were coming around the end of the airstrip as the plane taxied towards them. She turned to her grandfather to tell him but his eyes were closed. For a horrific moment she thought he was gone, but then she saw his chest rise as he drew another ragged breath.

Klaus jolted the utility to a stop, but her grandad was unconscious and didn't notice. Soretta willed him to stay with her.

The hatch of the plane lowered, the steps followed, and then there was Daphne. Calm, kind and brilliantly efficient as she hopped down onto the ground and sprinted with her kit across to them. Soretta had never been so glad to see someone in her life.

Soretta eased back as Daphne skidded to a halt beside them. She saw the flight nurse's quick assessing glance that, despite its speed, seemed to encompass her granddad from head to foot. How did she do that?

'I had to move him.'

'I think you did. You did the right thing.' Daphne gently lifted

Soretta's hand and the wadded dressing she held clamped against him. She sucked air in through her teeth at the jagged, seeping wound. 'Good job,' she said.

Soretta didn't know if she was talking to her or her grandfather but the relief of handing over responsibility made her head swim again.

Daphne went on in that quiet, steady voice, and some of the rigid tension in Soretta's neck eased a fraction. 'I'll just reinforce this, strap it down more firmly so it won't shift in flight, and get a couple of intravenous lines in.' Daphne shot her a look. 'Can you hold this again firmly while Rex rolls him so I can slip the bandage under?'

Soretta hadn't even noticed the pilot had crouched down beside them. 'Of course.' It was done swiftly, much more securely than Soretta had been able to manage, and then a bag of intravenous fluids was thrust into her hands.

'And this, sweetie. Just hold it up when I say.' Within seconds two bags of fluid were raised over her grandad.

Fifteen minutes later Soretta sat quietly in the spare seat in the tiny aircraft cabin and watched Daphne struggle to keep her grandfather alive as the pilot revved the engines.

Twin IV lines ran fluid into his veins on each wrist. Oxygen blew into the mask on his face and the compression bandage on his stomach had finally stopped seeping. But still her chest felt leaden with anxiety as she listened to the increasing timbre of the plane's engines as at last they began to take off.

Billie Green made the turn into the main road of the outback town and breathed a sigh of relief. She was finally on her way to achieving her dream of joining the Mica Ridge Flying Doctor Service. This was something she'd been planning to do since she was a child.

Mica Ridge, the next biggest town to Broken Hill on the border of New South Wales and South Australia, was a long way from boys in balaclavas, or the past she'd worked so hard to forget. But here, with the Barrier Ranges to her back and the Menindee Plains in front of her, she could feel the sense of impending doom about her daughter seep away. It felt good to come back to the place where she'd grown up. And it felt safe for Mia.

Eighteen years, a daughter and her medical career later, she was returning stronger than when she'd left Mica Ridge as a heartbroken orphan. A lot of that had to do with the elderly aunt who'd believed Billie could do anything, no matter what obstacles appeared. And there had been obstacles.

Billie guessed she needed to practise her aunt's kind of faith in Mia because obviously trying to protect her daughter from the world wasn't working. Today, even during Mia's time as a learner driver at the wheel, she had bombarded Billie with her tirade against moving. Mia had been like an angry bee trapped against the glass as she'd railed bitterly about being uprooted from her friends and familiar surroundings. Her daughter's quite impressive stamina had lasted most of the trip yesterday and today. She'd only been diverted when one of the families of emus had run beside the car or one of the majestic wedge-tailed eagles had soared from the side of the road. Two days of a narky Mia and Billie's head had felt like it was going to explode.

Billie could see Mia's black hair swivelling as they both got out of the car so Billie could drive through the built up area.

Apparently Mia didn't think it was a built up area.

'You have to be kidding me,' she heard Mia mutter.

'What did you expect?' Billie said mildly as she met those green eyes which everyone said were so beautiful, and so unlike Billie's blue ones, then watched them widen with horror at the stark contrast a country mining town was proving to be to cosmopolitan Sydney.

Billie lifted her eyes to the skyline for strength. Felt the squeeze of homecoming again. She'd loved those peaks. Apparently, Mia wasn't appreciating the last rays of the sun that tinged the clouds pink and fairy-flossed each jagged ridge rising from the creviced rocks, drawing in the tourists.

They drove off again, and at this time of the day, with the quiet streets of tiny restored miners' cottages and the magnificent heritage buildings from a long-gone mining boom, Billie could see there might be little to excite a teenager. But Billie saw the banks of roses everywhere—how could she have forgotten they bloomed so magnificently out here?—and they were in front of every civic building and every yard as if the hot dry world was just what they'd ordered.

Peace settled over her. There was so much more to this place than Mia knew.

'I can see why you haven't been back since you were my age.' Mia said.

'No you don't.' *I would have come earlier except you kicked and screamed so much about leaving Sydney.* She didn't say it again. Or comment on Mia's chequered last year. 'The schools are good and outback people are amazing.'

A snort. 'What people?'

Billie suppressed a sigh. 'You'll see.'

As if to support her words, as they drove further down the one wide main street they began to see movement under the huge overhanging verandahs outside the shops. Saw tourists peering into an old-fashioned department store turned into an art gallery, an early 1900s legal firm refurbished and morphed into stylish apartments with scalloped wood and marble ledges, people taking photos of the magnificent clock tower of the post office, and the austerely elegant police station that loomed in a circle of glowing Peace roses.

Then the biggest pub came into view. A grand old lady with upstairs verandahs circled in white lace railings, while downstairs tables spilled out onto the wide footpath under a trellis covered in green-leaved grapevines. Beckoning travellers to share the oasis in the heat.

Even Mia gave a grudging nod.

Billie smiled with relief. It was even better than she remembered. 'See? Not what you expected after the arid land of the last few hundred kilometres.'

'Not as big as Broken Hill.'

'But just as good,' Billie said, remembering the sometimes not-so-friendly rivalry between the two towns.

Mia sat up a little higher as she spied a posse of six-packed cowboys leaning on their four-wheel-drive utes, whip aerials, dish-sized spot-lights and rear-mud flaps all bigger than necessary. They all had akubra hats glued to their heads in expectation of a good time in town.

Billie remembered them. The boys from the bush. She bit back the smile so her daughter couldn't see her amusement.

At the end of the main block there was a shopping centre where once there'd been a horse paddock, and they began to see more townsfolk. Families with toddlers. Elderly couples moving towards the caravans parked at the side of the road. Smartly dressed business-women, testimony to a town that had reinvented itself as an artist's mecca and a hub of tourism.

Her daughter offered a seemingly reluctant, 'We'll see.' But her neck stretched sideways as she watched the young men disappear in the rear-vision mirror and the bracelets on her wrist jangled as her hand went unconsciously to her black ponytail.

Billie sighed. She hadn't moved Mia here to fall into the same traps she'd been heading towards in Sydney; she'd hoped her daughter would dive into her studies again with a new school and a clean record, but she guessed change had to come from within.

But there was always hope. Her aunt had always said, 'Anyone could make mistakes,' and Billie's blunders had been monumental.

She turned left towards the Flying Doctor Base, away from the direction her parents' house lay, if it was still there. Those memories were for another day and a quiet moment, but she would go there soon. Lay to rest the gnawing feeling of needing to say good-bye to her late childhood, which had been left so abruptly.

No, today was for the shared housing on the outskirts of town they'd been offered as an easy transition. She didn't think they'd be there long. Billie wanted a more permanent place to live. She wanted to finally put down roots, think of a life for herself as a woman, not just a mother, because soon Mia would finish school. Maybe she could purchase a property with an overseer close to town. The utopia of waking up to no neighbours, no passing cars, a vista to restore her soul, seemed almost within reach. Good grief. Where had that come from?

'Where's the school?' Billie's least favourite tone grated in Mia's petulant voice.

Billie snapped back into parent mode. She was good at that. 'Halfway between here and that pub you were so interested in.'

'Who, me?' But there was a reluctant smile from Mia and Billie relaxed a little. The surly princess act had been getting old.

She checked the house numbers and pulled up outside a modest grey-painted duplex, sensibly constructed with a concrete block that looked more depressing than welcoming, the whole yard encased in a running blank wall of brown colour-bond fence. She bit back a sigh. 'We're here,' she said brightly.

Mia looked at the uninspiring duplex and concreted yard. 'Goody.' She rolled her eyes.

Oh, dear. There had been a lot of similar places in the last ten years. 'Let's get unpacked. We've got a big day tomorrow.'

Mia's response was a hunch of her shoulders and a snort. 'You've got a big day. You'll be doing what you've always wanted to do. I'm doing what I'm told.'

'Nice change. How about we unload the car and sort our gear?' Billie's mild comment seemed to have the desired effect because Mia slid from the car and opened the hatchback. They always travelled light. Her rule for so many years. Imagine if she changed that? Let herself accumulate possessions instead of constantly being aware that they'd be moving on?

Billie peered under the lid of the tin mailbox at the head of the path and lifted out an envelope with her name on it. She smiled wearily. 'We have a key. Good start.'

TWO

Daphne shrugged the tightness out of her shoulders and waggled her head to loosen her neck. A fifteen-hour shift wasn't going to stop her calling in to make sure Lachlan Byrnes and Soretta were okay.

They'd rushed Lachlan straight from the plane into an operating theatre and an hour ago he'd been holding his own but still in recovery. The nurses thought he'd make it, but it would be a while before he'd be back riding quad bikes again. Though he probably would. At seventy, the accident he'd had would have killed a lesser man. A testimony to what a tough old boot he really was.

Daphne had picked up noodles and fried rice for a late supper, and a plastic bottle of iced coffee because the girl looked half-starved. Daphne was sure Soretta was doing the workload of three men out there on the station. She'd also picked up a slightly stale iced cupcake and one candle. Some birthday the poor girl had been subjected to. A fact she'd discovered when she'd asked Soretta how old she was. Daphne had no doubt that if the birthday girl hadn't been so shaken by the accident she'd never have told her that.

She nodded to the nurse at the desk, and thought wryly how already they were used to her dropping back to check on patients she'd brought in. A yawn crept up on her and she bit it back as she knocked quietly on the doorframe of the waiting room. She glanced at the plastic swing doors into the operating theatres and recovery to her left, but they hung silently in the deserted corridor.

Soretta jumped up and then her face fell when she realised it wasn't someone to tell her about her grandfather.

Daphne watched the effort Soretta put into trying to smile and felt her heart contract. To hide the fact that she'd seen it, Daphne put the carry bag of food on the table, but she couldn't ignore what came naturally and she stepped in to put her hands around the young woman's back and give her a brief hug. After a few seconds Soretta relaxed and hugged her in return. She wasn't very good at it. That was okay. Daphne was.

Then Soretta stepped back. 'Daphne. You didn't have to come.'

'Of course I did. Have you heard anything?'

Soretta lifted her head as though it weighed as much as one of those boulders that crowned the ridges outside of town. 'He's in recovery. And he's alive.'

'They make them hardy out here.'

Soretta almost laughed but it turned into a sob. Her hand flew to her mouth as if it was the absolute worst noise she could have let out.

Daphne's voice lowered until it was almost a whisper. 'You're allowed to cry, you know. I won't tell anyone.'

Soretta sniffed it all back and set her mouth firmly.

'And studies suggest tears are endorphins so when they soak into your skin they make you feel better.'

Soretta sniffed again and then, despite herself, she did smile weakly. 'You're a beautiful lady.'

Daphne looked away. Compliments about her looks made her uncomfortable. To be honest, any compliments made her uncomfortable because she didn't believe them, but that wasn't Soretta's fault. She'd held onto lots of hang-ups from childhood. 'Not so sure about that one but I did bring food. Have you eaten?'

A shake of a red ponytail. 'I couldn't.'

'Try now. He's in recovery and would probably prefer if you didn't faint when you see him.'

This time Soretta produced a real smile. Peered into the white plastic carry bag and sighed. 'Chinese? Yum.'

Daphne pulled out plastic plates, knives, forks and two serviettes. 'I'll set up while you wash your hands.' They both looked at the blood caked under Soretta's fingernails.

Soretta's smile fell and she nodded before turning to the sink in the corner of the room. When she came back everything was laid out on the table and the smell of hot oyster sauce drifted in eddies between them.

'Dig in. I've brought enough for both of us. You can debrief while you eat. We didn't have time to talk about the shock you must've had.'

Soretta's pale brows drew together. 'I need to give you money for this.'

Not happening. Daphne patted her pocket. 'I've got a bill right here for you.'

She saw Soretta blink, saw the smile peep out again, and felt the warmth expand inside her. Soretta was a good girl.

'Okay. I won't try to pay you. But I owe you one,' she said with a nod that promised this outback girl did not forget favours. Ever. 'Thank you.'

'My pleasure. Now speak.'

They both sat, and haltingly, with more pauses at the beginning until it started to come out in a rush, Soretta told of Klaus jumping off the bike with news of the accident and how she'd found her grandad, his face white like the ghost gums that had surrounded him, softly moaning with agony, seeping blood into the red earth. How ghastly it had been moving him. His groans and gritted teeth. Her glancing at the sky for help.

Daphne resisted the impulse to squeeze Soretta's hand. 'You did well. I know it must've been hard to move him. Normally it should be avoided, but this time it was the right thing to do so we could take off again almost straight away.'

Soretta's eyes stared into a corner of the room and Daphne knew she was back in the lonely paddock again. 'That plane landing was all I wanted to see.'

'Waiting is the worst,' Daphne said quietly. 'At least the strain of organising the transfer to the strip gave you something to do while we were coming. Another reason it was a good thing you moved him.' Risking paralysis from a spinal injury versus bleeding out with the delay. It had been a hard decision for the young woman, Daphne thought grimly.

The young woman shuddered. 'At one stage I thought he'd gone. Then I saw his chest move. If you hadn't been as fast as you were he would've died.' Her voice cracked on the last word and Daphne wondered how many times Soretta had repeated that to herself over the last few hours. *He would have died!* That was the problem. Reliving the fear.

'You're going to have to let that go and concentrate on the fact that Lachlan didn't die. He's still holding up a bed so we'll take his tenacity and run with it.' She paused to let the words sink in.

She needed to reach the panicked centre of Soretta's shocked brain. 'Will there be anyone at the station when you go home? Do you want to stay with me in town while you visit your grandad in here?' She thought about the new doctor and her daughter at the other end of the house. Soretta wouldn't be a bother to anyone.

Soretta looked up. Her chin set stubbornly. 'Thanks, Daphne, but once he's stable I'll go home and come in the afternoons. Get home before dark. There's only Klaus—our backpacker from Germany. I've got the dogs and the horses. And a couple of lambs in the laundry.'

Of course she would. 'So the three of you have been running the station? What happened to the other help?'

Soretta shrugged, philosophical. 'The Swiss contingent left soon after the satellite dish blew off the roof in the dust storm last month. They'll do without a lot but they won't do without the internet.'

It was a big property. Somewhere around a hundred thousand acres, Rex had said, though to others around here she guessed it was mid-sized. A lot for three people. 'Can you get the dish fixed?'

She shook her head. 'Not until it rains. You know the old story. Asset rich, cash poor, and a drought.'

So Lachlan would be lying in bed here stressing about the station for the next month or two. 'So there's a lot on both your minds?'

Soretta hesitated. 'I really need a cash-paying job. But I need to be on the station.'

Tricky. 'What can you do?'

Another shrug. Daphne guessed Soretta was capable of doing anything a man could do. 'Farm stuff. Muster with the quad.

Maintain the troughs and the pumps and sort the sheep and cattle. Fence.' She grimaced then brightened. 'I can do accounts.'

'That's good.' Encouragement was all she could offer. Nobody around here had much to add up with the drought going on.

Daphne scooped a fork full of noodles into her mouth and her stomach rumbled. She'd missed lunch. Thought briefly of the extra padding around her waist and mentally shrugged. This was a mercy dash. She had to eat with Soretta. And everyone knew carbs were more comforting. 'So accounts and farm work. But these are all things you need to do at home, too?'

Soretta nodded glumly. 'We only need a small cash flow to stop us going backwards and pay for minor expenses. Just for food and a way to attract casual labour until mustering. The last lot of feral goats we mustered brought in enough to pay the bank for this month.'

Daphne watched her pause for a minute. Then Soretta sighed and shook her head, making a strand of hair fall in her eyes. 'At the moment I need my grandad to be able to walk out of this hospital in one piece.'

'Let's start with that one,' Daphne agreed. Later they could brainstorm. Between them they might come up with some solutions.

They finished the Chinese food and Daphne cleared away the packaging. Then she reached into her bag and drew something out carefully. 'I have something small I'd like to share with you.'

She sat the cupcake with the candle on the scarred coffee table. 'Although you probably don't feel like it, we still need to celebrate your birthday. Because you are the light in your grandad's life and without you being here he wouldn't be. So celebrating your birth is a must.'

'Thank you.' Soretta stared for a minute, blinked and then gave Daphne a watery smile.

'The next year is going to be your best yet.'

Soretta raised one disbelieving eyebrow. 'I'll hold you to that.'

When Billie let herself into the control centre of Mica Ridge Flying Doctor Service nobody noticed her for a minute. It felt like the room wasn't big enough to fit her in as well. She'd been sitting dressed at the side of the bed since five this morning, ready to go, and now her belly twisted with nerves.

How did you approach your dream job come true? Something you'd worked towards for years, and always kept at the back of your mind.

Her palms felt sweaty and she wiped them down the side of her trousers as she glanced at her surroundings. There was a circular workstation with a computer screen opposite and she knew that most retrieval calls came in via the ordinary telephone during the day.

Most of those calls would be logged on the computer and fielded by the doctor on duty, and on the days she wasn't flying to an outlying health clinic to provide much-needed chronic care, that would be her. Then it would be her decision in an emergency whether a nurse and pilot would fly out to assist or if the situation required a doctor as well. She knew that most of the time the nurses and pilots were frontline and she'd be at the end of the phone.

There was no hospital visiting involved, but there was a little consulting room on the base where a doctor could follow up a patient they'd seen at an outlying clinic on a rare occasion when a patient came to town. And, of course, the two doctors would take turns to be available if one of the nursing or ancillary staff fell ill. She could manage all that.

It was a much smaller base than Broken Hill, which ran differently with its admin centre, eight doctors and sixteen nursing staff. They only had two aircraft at Mica Ridge and the maintenance was across at the Hill.

She saw the colour-coordinated daily roster board with the other doctor's name, and there was hers, as well as a column for the flight nurses and for pilots, and any extras for the outreach clinics of the day.

Across the room a group of four staff in flight uniform, three men and one woman, stood talking. Apart from them stood a tall, hulking, black-haired commander in a white shirt with the insignia of the MRFDS. The other doctor and station boss, Morgan Fraser. He filled a whole corner of the cramped room as he stood in front of another computer desk.

One look was enough for Billie to see he wore authority so easily it didn't require effort as he spoke firmly into the phone.

She switched her attention back to a small, dark-haired woman in the same blue trousers she was in, who split from the group and came across. She looked about Billie's age, maybe a couple of years younger, around thirty. For some reason, probably the smile, Billie thought of Pollyanna.

'You must be Dr Green. Lovely to meet you.' She gave a wide, genuine grin that touched Billie unexpectedly.

The woman held out her hand well before she reached Billie. 'I'm Daphne, the nurse manager, but also one of the flight nurses. We missed each other last night.'

They shook hands briefly. Billie met the friendly brown eyes and felt the unaffected warmth in them. Daphne was one of those people you liked on sight.

'Call me Billie.' One responsive face was all it took. Her belly settled to a gentle flutter.

Daphne said, 'I hoped to meet you last night, but we all get used to things cropping up. Did you find everything in the flat?'

So Daphne had set things up. 'Yep. All sorted. Thanks for leaving the key. And the milk and bread.' She studied her surroundings again. 'Have you been up all night?'

'On and off. Just came in for a retrieval in the early morning. There's an accident-prone cook out at Pallinup Station, between here and Broken Hill. Accidental Al, we call him. Shot himself with the nail gun trying to knock tin cans off the fence in the dark. Punctured an artery in his leg.' She grinned. 'That's not something that happens much in the city. Rex and I are going home now for a few hours, but I'll introduce you around first.'

So Daphne was the motherly type. She was young for that, but there was something about her thoughtfulness that spoke to Billie. She had the feeling Daphne had needed to find big-girl britches in the past. Billie had learned to rely on herself, too.

As the others came across Daphne said, 'We'll have to catch up later.'

'I'll look forward to it.'

'This is Rex.' There was an extra 'tada' in the introduction that she didn't think Daphne actually noticed, and Billie felt her mouth twitch.

Rex just smiled. A tall, sandy-haired man, he had tired lines at the sides of his eyes that looked like they would turn into laughter lines if he had enough sleep. He shook her hand calmly. His hand was big and capable, like him, and she warmed to him, too. Rex would be a good man to have beside you in an emergency, she decided, just by the look of him.

'I'm the senior pilot,' he said. 'We've exceeded our on-call time. Welcome to the mad house.'

She said again, 'I'm looking forward to it.' It didn't look too mad at the moment. Except for the expression on the face of the big guy growling into the phone, taking up emotional space as he continued his phone discussion.

He must have sensed her look because he lifted one long finger her way and raised dark eyebrows in acknowledgement at least. She nodded back before she looked away from him to smile in the general direction of the other two, who began to cross the room towards her.

Rex waved and left, and Daphne turned to introduce the new-comers. 'This is Hector, the other pilot, and Michael, a flight nurse like me. They'll look after you.'

'I'm not as pretty as Legs, here, but I'm way taller.' Michael grinned. He pushed back the mop of dark hair falling over his fore-head. 'Welcome, Doc.'

As Billie smiled at Michael's harmless compliment to the nurse, she noticed Daphne wince at the teasing, hesitate and then shrug and look away.

Daphne said to no one in particular, 'Well, I'll leave so I can come back. Have a good day.'

They watched Daphne leave. 'Michael's not as easy to get along with as Daphne,' Hector murmured. He was mid-height and wiry, like he enjoyed sport and was probably very good at it, blond and blue-eyed. He grinned at Billie and sized her up. 'Hi. Hope you like it here.'

The vibe was good. Professional and genuine, which was a huge bonus on a first day. All the flutters in her belly went to sleep.

'We're going to leave you, too,' Michael said. 'Our first clinic starts in an hour and it's forty minutes' flying time.' He glanced across the room. 'Morgan said you're staying on base today to get used to it all?' He grinned again. 'I've bet him five bucks you'll get called out.'

The man called Morgan loomed up beside her and she suddenly felt as though she was going to start shrinking, like Alice in Wonderland down the rabbit hole as he towered over her. That was weird.

She hadn't noticed him move, which said a lot for his agility for such a big guy. It might pay to remember that. She didn't like men who could sneak up on you.

'Welcome.' He held out his hand and the shake was firm and no-nonsense, but for some reason she wanted to check she didn't have a smudge on her nose. He did 'Boss' very well. Made her neck prickle.

'Morgan Fraser. We spoke on the phone. We'll walk out to the aircraft and hangar as the others leave. Then cover how the base runs and what we expect of our medical officers.'

His voice was deep and slow, not drawling, but measured as if nothing would send him into a real flap. But there was an undercurrent that switched on her warning signals; he had the sort of voice that was viscerally attractive in a macho kind of way, not suggestive, just sexy, like she'd always imagine phone sex would sound—not that she'd tried it.

Spare me, she reprimanded, and reminded herself she wasn't going to risk allowing men back into her life for at least two years. She straightened and wrenched autonomy back from his easy hold.

'Sure. Let's go,' she said, as if it was her idea. She couldn't help the tiny spurt of independence that reared its head. She could take orders but she didn't have to like it. It had been a long time since she'd felt like a schoolgirl and she wasn't going to start now with Captain Seductive.

Morgan raised one eyebrow and she had the feeling they were at a stand-off. Except she sensed he was amused.

'All right then,' he said as she followed him outside. 'As you know, FDS planes never have a patient without a nurse. Ever. The cabin, equipment, satellite phone etcetera is the nurse's responsibility and when a doctor comes along they still run the show, we just oversee and make decisions regarding the patient.'

Billie nodded. At orientation they'd talked a *lot* about cabin safety.

Morgan went on as if she'd disagreed. 'It's her or, in the case of our male nurses Michael and Grant, his cabin, and even if there are two doctors, which happens sometimes, it's the nurse's responsibility during the flight to make sure the safety briefing is given to all patients, teams, escorts and so on. They ensure the patient is secured adequately – we have harness type seat belts on the stretchers, capsules for bubs, a "pedimate" to secure a child to the adult stretcher, or the humidicrib for a neonate. The pilot always asks the nurse if everything is "all secure" prior to take off and landing, too.'

Billie had forgotten to feel annoyed. She looked at the aircraft in front of them and glanced at the blue sky above. When she looked back at Morgan she nodded again. This was so much bigger than her ego. Or even his. Maybe she could get on with this guy after all. She could feel the smile stretch her face and he smiled back. He understood.

By the time Billie let herself back into the house late that afternoon, she knew she was in the right place. She resisted the urge to hug herself with glee. If Mia's day had panned out okay then they were laughing.

Now that she thought about it, she hadn't spent as much time as she'd thought she would worrying about her daughter, mainly because there was so much going on at the base.

Morgan she found challenging, but she'd met challenging men before, although perhaps not quite like him. He ran a tight ship, and apparently he'd been in the army before becoming a doctor and she guessed that this was a good place to be multi-skilled when lives depended on them all.

She'd spent the day re-reading the induction manual, taking phone calls from outlying stations, and referring those whom she diagnosed as needing medication.

Then there'd been one or two patients from outlying areas who had seen the doctors at an outreach clinic and were in town for the day, so she'd seen them, too.

It was like holding her usual surgery except she couldn't see the patient. As their doctor, Billie could hear their voice and read the corresponding number on the body chart that identified the area of the pain or problem. It was funny how much even inflection in the voice could tell her when it was all she had to rely on. She made sure she confirmed diagnosis and advice with Morgan until she became used to the way he did it. She'd gained the impression Captain Seductive appreciated that. She doubted he'd appreciate her nickname for him, but at least it made her smile.

And for these outback families their pharmacist lived in a box. The 'Medicine Chest in the Home' concept was an excellent system when the logistics of dashing down to the chemist possibly hundreds of kilometres away just wasn't on. One person in the household held the keys to the chest and the responsibility for being accountable and replacing stock. This was a necessary precaution when addictive drugs were part of the inventory and you couldn't have just anybody waltzing in and peering into the lolly shop. Then there was the fact that the accountable person would have to know how to give an injection if needed in an emergency. Station families had many responsibilities that people in towns didn't think about when they could just pop into a hospital or a doctor's surgery. Or a chemist.

Tomorrow she was going on her first outreach clinic. Like most of the FDS services, they flew to towns too small to have doctors or dentists and who relied on the monthly visits provided by the flying doctor. Early diagnosis drastically improved outcomes for these families. Outback health problems were shifted to the back burner because it was so time-consuming to get advice.

This was preventative medicine at its most needed and tomorrow she'd get started. But that was tomorrow, and Billie unlocked the front door of the grey residence with some trepidation about whether her daughter had enjoyed her own day.

Mia bounced into sight munching on something. 'Mum! You're home!'

Phew. Mia looked okay. 'I am. How was school?'

Mia's eyes skittered away. 'Actually not too bad.' Billie's initial relief was tempered by a suspicious thought. *Has she already met a boy?*

'So the teachers were good and you were happy with your classes?'

She received a vague nod and then a small shy smile. 'The people are nice.' So she had met a young man. She hoped he was young. It was the older ones you had to watch out for. She wished someone had told her that all those years ago.

Billie resisted the urge to put her hands on her hips. 'Did you meet any girls?'

Mia shrugged. 'Of course.'

Billie gave in. 'And what's the interesting new boy's name?'

'Trent.' She said it quickly, and then she caught the look on her mother's face and blushed.

Billie raised her eyebrows. 'Trent the gent.'

'He's in my year.' So Mia knew that her mother was wary of seniors. She must have made her feelings clear at some point. At least Mia seemed to have listened to something she'd said. 'How was your day?'

Well this boy sounded better than someone three years older, like the hellion in Sydney. And it was nice that Mia had asked about Billie's day. 'Interesting.'

Billie felt her daughter's scrutiny and there was definitely cheeky humour glinting back at her.

Mia tilted her face. 'And what's your new man's name?'

To her own surprise she almost said, Morgan, and then stopped herself. Instead she said, 'Funny girl. Did you get to meet Daphne today?'

Daphne had been banned by Morgan from coming back again for another twelve hours. He'd discovered she'd spent hours at the hospital with one of the patient's daughters and he'd said she had to sleep. Billie had been privy to that phone conversation and had winced for the kind-hearted woman.

'Yep. She knocked just after I got home from school. Seems nice. She can cook. I'll show you how well.'

Mia grinned, waltzed into the tiny kitchen and lifted the lid on a glass jar of enormous chocolate-chip biscuits, lusciously piled on top of each other, and reached in to take another one.

'That's very sweet of her. How many have you had?'

Mia grinned. 'Three. They're great.'

'Stop then.' Billie felt the last of the tension fall from her shoulders. She hadn't seen Mia this friendly for a long time. And her work was worthwhile and exciting, and despite the challenging boss, she couldn't wait until she climbed into that plane tomorrow.

THREE

Daphne had heard the new doctor come home and she had to stop herself from knocking at the door as soon as Billie would have put her car keys down.

'They don't need you barging in like a busybody,' she muttered and winced at the echo of her ex-husband's voice. She'd only wanted to offer food, and anything else she could do to help, after a family next door had suffered a tragedy, but his derision still hurt.

She switched the kettle on for another cup of tea she didn't want, to distract herself from the rumble of voices through the wall, and deliberately picked up her iPad to scan the local news. She'd see Dr Billie at work tomorrow. That would be the best way to start. Give them time to settle in.

Daphne scanned the digital news and saw the small column devoted to the farm accident yesterday. Soretta had looked tired this afternoon, and Daphne wished there was something she could do to lighten the girl's load. Make sure she ate a decent meal, for one thing. Or offer an ear to listen to her concerns.

Soretta's grandad was still heavily sedated from the pain relief he needed and it wasn't surprising that she was stressed.

That wouldn't be helped by being bowed down with the financial responsibility of a floundering property. Maybe she could zip out to the station on her days off. Take over the housework so Soretta could concentraté on the farm.

It wasn't the first time Daphne had done that. Some of her best weekends since she'd moved to Mica Ridge had been when a station family had all come down with some nasty lurgy and she'd been dropped off to be nanny, cook and bottle washer. Had been in her element cooking up and freezing food, cleaning houses and minding children, until the parents had been able to walk.

The hard part of that idea, of course, would be getting it past Soretta who, like most of the locals around here was fiercely independent. But Daphne understood that. She hadn't asked for help herself when her world had imploded.

A gentle knock sounded at the door and Daphne jumped. Visitors? She wished. Probably a door-knock appeal. She picked up her purse and began counting her change. But when she opened the door it was the new doctor from next door and the smile that greeted her warmed the cold loneliness like a ray of afternoon sunlight.

'Daphne. Hope you don't mind me knocking, just wanted to say thanks for dropping in on Mia. And the biscuits.'

Daphne could feel the heat in her cheeks. It was nothing. 'You're welcome. She's a lovely girl. She's tall like you.'

Billie sighed. 'The rest of her is totally different. She's a challenge and a joy.'

There was something there that made Daphne want to comfort the woman. Which was stupid. 'I'd know her as yours any day. Would you like to come in?'

'Thanks. For a minute.'

Daphne gestured Billie to one of the lounge chairs and watched her sink gracefully into it. Daphne had never mastered being graceful and she tried not to be envious of the other woman's social ease.

She saw her glance around. 'Your flat is lovely.'

Daphne appraised the room. It was better than it was originally. For a plain box of a flat she'd made it homey. She'd always been able to create ambience with furnishings. It was her inability to satisfy fathers and husbands and create the family she'd so desperately wanted that she had trouble with.

'I try.' She pushed thoughts of herself away. 'So how was your first day?'

'Fine.' The word held a world of relief. 'Everyone does a great job out here.'

Daphne felt the pride expand in her chest. There were other types of family and she was finding them in her work. It seemed Billie felt it, too.

She nodded happily. 'I'm glad you think so. What made you come out here to work?'

Billie hesitated. 'I've had the dream for a while. I used to live here as a little girl before my parents died. Was always going to come back. It just took longer than I anticipated.'

Daphne wanted to ask: How old were you when they died? Who looked after you? but held herself in, just chewed her lip instead before she said, 'Well, we're glad to see you now.' She saw Billie visibly relax because she hadn't asked nosy questions. Maybe she was learning to step back after all.

Billie asked, 'And how long have you been here?'

'Six months. I came from Canberra. Grew up in the suburbs.

My father was a politician and so was my ex-husband.'

It was now Daphne's turn to dread the questions that would come, but she guessed it was best to get them out of the way. Like the sting of lancing a boil. Just what she needed. Yuk. Except she didn't have to.

Billie smiled almost as if she knew the story. Which was silly. Nobody knew the story. 'I'm glad you moved here for my sake, too, then.' They smiled at each other and what awkward tension was left seeped away.

The next morning at the base Morgan was the first person Billie saw when she opened the door. He looked ridiculously athletic and she wondered if she needed to think about joining a gym or something. Her inappropriate half scanned the taught thighs in beige trousers and tight shirt sleeves and decided he was more like one of those guys who hung out of a helicopter by his feet and scooped you up from a sinking ship. He really didn't look like any of the doctors she knew.

That sneaky ember she'd warned herself about glowed in her belly and she doused it with a cup of common sense. 'Morning.' She almost said 'Captain', but she bit her lip to hold back the smile as he raised those black and moody eyebrows. So the man wasn't slow. She'd thought she'd hidden her amusement well.

'Something entertains you?'

Well obviously. 'Just glad to be here, boss.'

'Passed the first test, then,' he said with an easy smile that startled her, and which was way harder to ignore, then he turned back to the large schedule board that stood on the easel in the corner of the room. 'Let's see where we'll send you today.'

There was no guess work involved. The roster was made for the month, with clinics and delegations and teams. She'd already seen he was the type who had everything planned and allocated before he'd leave the previous day, and as she followed his silent stride across the room the flutter of anticipation skittered across her belly.

Today she'd fly. Could put all the flight physiology she'd learned into practice. Have her first glimpses of the browns and oranges of the landscape below from her aerial vantage point. She'd meet her first outback community as they dropped off the other health workers and flew on to their own clinic.

'I'll send you with Daphne on the last drop. She's replacing one of the clinic nurses today who's off sick. Generally she does retrievals. You'll do the chronic GP clinic while she runs the immunisation and antenatal checks. Boorenji is one of our furthest clinics. Start you off easy.'

She narrowed her eyes, lifted her head, prepared to say she didn't want easy, when she saw his smile.

Morgan was way ahead of her. There was another unexpected twinkle in his eye that disappeared quickly. 'Don't worry. There is no easy. They're all unique challenges. I imagine the hardest part will be prising Daphne away at the end of the clinic. She does tend to want to mother everyone.'

Billie could see that. 'She's a treasure.'

No such flowery stuff for Morgan. 'She's an excellent clinician.' Then they both glanced towards the door as Daphne entered, juggling a big plate of biscuits and two hot coffees in her hands.

'Morning, Morgan. Morning, Billie.'

*

The health clinic at Boorenji was held in a converted shipping container with a high corrugated-iron roof built above it to allow the hot still air to breathe around the box. The air conditioner hummed energetically in the middle between the two consulting room ends and puffed cooler air towards the exterior doors, where it was sucked out and beaten into submission by the heat outside.

Daphne helped Billie settle into her GP clinic which held a tiny desk, two chairs and a fold-up examination bed similar to those carried by a masseuse for home visits. There was enough equipment to achieve rudimentary examinations, plus a hand-held i-STAT machine for quick blood tests. But she thought perhaps the communication of medical history might prove problematic with the heavy dialect of the local people, so different to Billie's experience.

Outside the structure, standing and sitting under a tree were a dozen candidates for the doctor, two younger station women with their children for Daphne herself, who'd brought folding chairs with them, an old jackaroo with bowlegs and a chest infection, and two Aboriginal elders sitting on haunches against the backdrop of desert. All were good-naturedly waiting their turn or being nudged to the head of the line for various reasons.

On Daphne's end of the container, it was immunisation day and children clutched their mother's hands or necks and buried their faces when Daphne called the next victim through for a weigh on the portable scales, an immunisation needle and finally a juicy mandarin from the bag she'd stowed in the plane that morning for rewards.

Barbara Tomkins's daughter, Gwyn, was here for her four-year-old injections. Barbara's family had been one of the ones Daphne had dropped in to nurture when they all came down with chicken pox. Gwyn was happy to see Daphne, and she didn't even cry when the second injection went in.

'Aunty Daphne will need to come and have a fun visit one day. Won't she, Gwyn? And we won't let her lift a finger.'

'No fun in that, Barb.' Daphne smiled at the mum and the stoic child, whose huge dark eyes were glued to Daphne as she clutched her mandarin. Daphne opened the door to let them out.

The next patient was ushered to the front of the line outside Daphne's door by a determined older lady. One look at the younger woman as she grimaced and dropped her hand to her big belly and Daphne smiled. She tried not to be too excited that she'd have the chance to do a bit of midwifery for a change. Not too much, but a little would be very nice.

'Come in. Sit down.' The young woman sidled past, eyes down, chewing her lip, but she didn't sit. Too uncomfortable, maybe? Daphne smiled at the older lady. 'Are you her mum?'

'Aunty May. This's Belle. She's too early. Didn't want to come but I made her.'

Maybe six weeks, Daphne thought and glanced again at the noticeable but not huge pregnant belly. 'Lucky you did, I'm thinking. When is your baby due, Belle?"

'End of next month.' Aunty May nodded and the clinic chair groaned in protest as she lowered her bottom into it and crossed her arms in front of her ample bosom. She'd effectively blocked the door and Belle wasn't going anywhere.

So six weeks early. Daphne glanced at the bed and wondered

how she'd get Belle up there so she could feel her belly. Find out the baby's position, because if it was early it could quite possibly be breech.

Belle groaned.

'Are you in labour, Belle?' Silly question. Another contraction caused a small moue of distress. Yep! They'd have to fly her out. ASAP.

The girl raised wild eyes to Daphne. 'Gotta push.'

Daphne straightened. This was a whole new ballgame. She recognised the look and so didn't need to ask if she was sure. Well, then. Her voice gentled even more. 'Don't be scared.'

The girl's eyes skittered to her aunty's. 'Gotta push. Now.'

Daphne stepped to her left and opened the communication door between the two consulting rooms. Poked her head in. 'Looks like we're having a baby in here, Doctor. About thirty-four weeks.'

Without waiting for an answer Daphne turned and grabbed a pair of gloves and the only two towels she had within reach. She put one on the floor in front of Belle and slung one over her shoulder so she could use it to wipe the baby when she needed to.

'Do you want to lie down?' Daphne inclined her head to the bed and Belle shook her head vehemently just as Billie opened the door.

Without turning her head Daphne said, 'Can you turn off the air-conditioner please. Prem baby.' And then, 'Did you want to do this, Doctor?'

'I'll watch and help if I'm needed.'

'The Syntocinon's in the emergency box in the fridge. You could draw that up.' Having the injection ready for after the birth would be good. They didn't need the mother to have a bleed as well.

Daphne shot Billie a reassuring smile before she returned her attention to the girl. 'Why don't you lean on the back of this chair, Belle, and just do what feels right. It's okay.'

Belle gasped, then shook her head at the sensations that were building.

Daphne put her hand very gently on Belle's shoulder. Smiled at her. Her voice was just above a whisper and very calm. 'It's okay. Let me help get your knickers off and you can have your baby. If we have time I'd really like to try to listen to your baby's heartbeat.'

But when she looked into Belle's face she saw that there was no time for anything. She was pushing. They'd probably be listening to this baby's heartbeat on the outside.

A sudden gush of water splashed the floor between the girl's legs, mostly caught by the strategic towel, and Belle jumped at the sensation.

Daphne glanced quickly at the colour of the liquid and met Billie's eyes in relief, because the water pooling on the towel and floor was, reassuringly, faintly pink.

Billie nodded. They were both happy the baby hadn't passed a meconium stool before birth, because there was more chance of respiratory problems after birth if the amniotic fluid was green with meconium.

The girl planted her hands on the back of the chair, sank slowly to her haunches above the wet towel, closed her eyes and squeezed with a low growling moan that meant business.

And then it happened.

Daphne hurriedly crouched too, gloved hands waiting under the other draped towel, and almost missed the catch because the baby shot out so fast, but she deftly gathered the tiny wizened body as it tumbled into the towel on the end of a snaking purple umbilical cord.

'Well caught,' Billie murmured.

Daphne smiled to herself as she rubbed the thick protective coating of white vernix from a little screwed-up face so the sticky eyes could blink slowly as if still unsure what the heck had just happened. Then finally he opened his mouth and made a scratchy mewling cry that slowly strengthened into an indignant protest.

'Good,' said the quiet, satisfied voice of Aunty May from the corner of the room.

'I hear you guys had an exciting day.'

Daphne had been called out on another retrieval, this time to a man with chest pain, after they'd come back from the emergency flight with Belle and her baby. Billie was checking up on blood results from some of the patients she'd seen today.

Morgan had finished what he'd been doing at his desk and crossed the room to her workspace to lean against the wall.

Billie looked up, and up, at him. She wished he wouldn't tower over her because it made it hard to concentrate. She resisted the urge to stand as well, but it might have shown in her face because he put one big arm out and lifted a chair as if it was a box of matches and sat it across from her desk. Sank into it, lounged back and studied her. At least it wasn't so crowded when he sat down.

What had he said? Exciting day. She thought about the tiny mewling baby and the surprised mum and couldn't help the smile that flooded her face. It warmed her heart. 'Very. It all happened pretty fast. I was still looking around for cord clamps but had no idea where they were.' Her brow creased. 'Daphne didn't seem in a hurry to cut the cord.'

He nodded. 'Good. A lot of mums are anaemic out here and baby gets extra red blood cells from the placenta if you don't rush to cut the cord. Waiting for it to stop pulsating is a good thing. There's an interesting research paper with evidence that the blood flows back and forth until the newborn's body shuts it down at just the right moment.'

She might have read that somewhere. Boy, did she need to brush up on the latest obstetric trends. She'd spent most of her pre-start time on snake bites and chest pains. 'How much extra?'

'Anything from seventy to a hundred and fifty mils of blood. Makes a huge difference to childhood anaemia, and it's especially good if a baby is six weeks premature, like Anthony was.'

The baby boy's inquisitive eyes appeared in her mind and she smiled again. 'I can't believe how alert he was. He did so well on the flight coming in.'

He ignored that. Instead, he was piercing her with his black eyes as if he'd found a fault he wouldn't tolerate. She was distracted for a second. A man's eyes couldn't be black. They must be the darkest brown.

Whoa there. Stop it. She blinked herself back to the real world and he went on. 'You don't sound as confident with neonates as I expected. You said you had your Obstetric Diploma.'

'Just the experience in maternity. I did that in a semi-rural hospital. It was more antenatal bloods and occasional caesareans than actual high-risk birthing practice. The paediatric registrar did the babies. But they were mostly low risk.'

'You must have had some babies that needed resuscitation?'

'Sure, but any really sick babies were shipped out, and apart from the required number of normal births I was mostly dealing with the paperwork and getting the lay of the land. It was fun but there wasn't quite enough experience, even though what was there was good. After that I went on and did ophthalmology for three months.'

He lifted his head at that. 'The eyes have it?' he quipped. 'That'll be handy.'

'It requires vision,' she said, tongue in cheek.

He gave her one of those real smiles and somewhere down in the pit of her stomach that tiny coal of long slumbering heat flick-ered again.

No! She turned her head away. Mentally pinched out the flames like the smouldering wick of a candle. 'Anyway. I'd better get this report done or I'll be off late and my daughter will be home.' That was the idea. No men until Mia was safely at university.

He sat back and studied her. With leisurely thoroughness. A confident, meticulous assessment that warmed her belly again even while it raised her hackles. 'Your daughter's name is Mia?'

She couldn't think of one work-related reason he'd needed to remember that. Mia's age could impact on Billie's work. Mia's health or behaviour maybe. But not her daughter's name. So it was a personal question and she hadn't expected anything personal from Morgan. He gave off that 'work is for work' vibe and she'd thought it was only her who'd found the other person distracting.

'Yes, that's right. Daphne met her yesterday with cookies.'

He stood up. 'Daphne's cookies. They'd go over well. A tough act to follow.' Then he walked away and she felt vaguely unsettled.

When she was ready to leave, Billie drove home via a different route. One that took her up towards the houses nearer the ridge that looked over the town, to where her parents had had their neat three-bedroom bungalow with the big tree that somehow didn't seem so big now that she was a grown woman.

She sat outside in her car and stared at the house she'd lived in with her parents. Obviously a young family had moved in. A scooter lay on its side outside the front door on the path, and there was a new shiny plastic swing on the tree she could remember having an old rope and tyre on.

The memories were all good and the unsettled feeling Morgan had left her with disappeared and in its place was a sense of homecoming, belonging, and finally some peace. Coming back here, with Mia, this was not just another new town. This was where she would settle.

In central Mica Ridge in the Hair For You beauty salon, Lorna Lamerton put the new donation tin for the Mica Ridge Flying Doctor Service on the edge of the shelf. Then she straightened the black plastic hairdressers' shawl back into place. 'What have I missed this week?'

The young cockney stylist straightened Lorna's head and met her eyes in the mirror. 'They say there's another new doctor at the Flying Doctor Base.' She flicked her chin in the direction of the tin. 'We all know you're interested in what goes on there.'

A new doctor? A pang of too-familiar grief for her husband stung until she shook it off. They'd been lucky for all the wonderful years they'd had. Not so lucky with the downward spiral of Alzheimer's in the last two. She let the breath sticking in her prickling throat ease out carefully.

Lorna concentrated on the news. 'Male or female?'

'Female. Has a teenage daughter, I hear. Grew up in Mica Ridge but left years ago when her parents were killed. Apparently they were school teachers.'

Lorna straightened. Green. The name sprang into her mind with startling clarity. The past always did. It was the present that got somewhat muddled. She remembered a lovely couple, both of whom taught at the primary school, and they had one sweet daughter. The town had been devastated. Her husband had been very upset because the ambulance had picked him up on the way to the accident but there'd been nothing he could do. Too little too late. The girl had gone to a relative in the city.

Lorna did love to catch up on the local news and nowadays that only happened at the yearly Christmas cake fundraiser for the MRFDS or at the hairdresser's.

She so enjoyed having her hair washed and set, it was the best part of her week since she'd lost her husband. She missed years of chatting, hearing about people's lives at the surgery, and being the person people turned to. Being useful! When dear Wallace had passed on, she hadn't had the energy for her old life because she'd been so exhausted from caring for him until the end. Then That Woman had married her son and moved in to look after her.

Humph. All she'd needed was a good sleep for a month and she would have been fine. Mentally she snorted. Now she wasn't encouraged to invite people to drop in and she missed the interaction she'd had as The Doctor's Wife. Lorna was beginning to feel something she'd never felt before—old and useless. And she didn't like it one bit.

She dragged her mind back to the conversation. 'Always good

to have a new doctor. Can you remember her first name?'

'No, sorry. Don't know her name.' The girl pulled back a new part line to touch up the roots.

Lorna would miss this dear girl when she moved on. Like most of these young adventurers, she'd hear of a new town to visit and set her sights on a new quest. Backpack away. Lorna wished she could do that. Just disappear. She wished she could move out to one of those one-horse towns and be the nurse again.

Like she'd been fifty years ago when she'd met her husband. Doing something worthwhile. Constantly alert for the next crisis. Dealing with the impossible until help arrived. Riding through storms on horseback when the roads were too bad to drive, to help deliver a baby or splint a bone. She'd done some exhilarating things in her time. Maybe she could go somewhere really remote. She wasn't young but she'd be better than no resources.

Who was she kidding? She was too old now. Only able to raise pitiful sums of money to help the local Flying Doctor Base. Too old to be employed, too old to be a help rather than a hindrance. And wasn't that drummed into her every day. In the nicest possible way.

Humph. She'd always said she wasn't going to be one of those grannies who minded the grandchildren and tidied the house, but she would have eaten those words these last two years if she'd had the chance. And with her son's wife apparently putting motherhood off until Lorna was dead, she had no choice anyway.

'Lorna?' The young girl paused as she painted the purple dye along the silver roots. 'You okay there?'

'I'm fine, dear.' Silly old fool she was. 'Just wool-gathering.'

'Wool-gathering?' The hairdresser tilted her head and glanced again at Lorna in the mirror. Smiled that genuinely interested smile.

'And what would that be?'

Wool-gathering? A lovely phrase. Diverted, Lorna explained. 'When the sheep brush along the fences, little tufts of wool get caught on the wire, and on tree branches and sharp rocks, like the boulders we have on the ridge out of town. If you were to go along and collect these, you'd be wool-gathering.'

The girl nodded with keen attention. 'Someone told me yesterday there were two million sheep along the Darling. For a shallow brown river that's a lot of livestock.'

'True. Though there's less now with the drought.' Lorna thought about it and a picture with wool-studded fences floated into her mind. 'Imagine all the tiny bits of fluff caught up with twigs and leaves.' She smiled, accepting her own foibles. 'And it's like my mind. Collecting little thoughts and things that stick in my brain and come out in a clump for me to unravel. You do more of it as you get older, probably because of all the trails old people have travelled.'

As long as she kept her wits, unlike poor Wallace.

The girl shook her head vehemently. 'You're not old!'

Lorna snorted. 'I'm eighty next week.'

'So what are you doing for your eightieth, Lorna?' The spiky-haired young backpacker leant down to add in her drawling Liverpool accent, 'Something naughty, I'll bet. You're the youngest eighty-year-old I know. There's a wild life in you yet. Run away with a younger man and have your wicked way with him.'

Lorna spluttered and laughed. It wasn't even patronising, like her daughter-in-law would have been if she'd said something similar. It was genuine. Encouraging. Warm like the young woman who'd said it.

'Don't know about the wicked way.' Lorna was too old to blush, but she grinned roguishly. 'But you're sweet.'

Lorna wondered. Was bumped gently out of her resignation. Not about the sex. Lord, no. But was she too old to run away from home?

FOUR

A week after they'd arrived, Mia Green decided that moving out of Sydney may not have been the worst thing that had happened to her. Her new friend, Trent, had a motorbike and her first glimpse of the out-of-town dirt racing track was the most exciting place Mia had ever seen.

They'd come straight from school, ducking into the back garage at Trent's house and wheeling the motorbike up the street so his mum didn't hear it start up. Both riders under age, an unregistered bike, and a quick blatt through the back streets until they hit a dirt track was just the sort of clandestine adventure Mia loved.

She knew who wouldn't like it, but what her mother didn't know wouldn't hurt her, and Mum didn't finish work until five. That gave Mia ninety minutes to get from school to home and a lot of fun could be had in ninety minutes.

'Can I try steering?' They'd stopped after fifteen minutes of going around and around the rough bush track, skirting straggly gum trees, leaning precariously around rocky outcrops until she'd laughed out loud, and finally rolling to a stop under a spotted gum to take off their helmets.

Trent checked his watch. 'It's pretty powerful.' He shook his head. 'Maybe tomorrow.'

'Just a quick go,' Mia wheedled.

He frowned at her. 'Have you ridden a bike before on your own?'

She was tempted to lie but decided against it. 'Just as a passenger.'

He shook his head decisively. 'It's getting late. We'll see tomorrow.' Trent was firm and Mia actually didn't mind that. There was something pretty cool about a guy she couldn't manipulate easily. A challenge. She smiled to herself. But she'd get her way.

Trent dropped her off at the end of her street in case her mother was home early, and they went their separate ways. She felt like skipping except she was far too mature for that.

Mia passed the white house with the gabled roof that she'd decided was her favourite and waved to the old lady with purple hair sitting on the front verandah. Lots of people at her school in Sydney had purple hair. But not old people. She glanced again at the lady and couldn't imagine ever being that old.

Her world was pretty darned good, actually. She wondered if her mother would buy her a bike if she asked. Her mood flattened. Doubt it. That would be considered too dangerous. The downside of having a doctor for a mother. Or one of them. She turned into the front path and almost ran into Daphne coming the other way. Stinker.

'Hello, Mia.' Daphne caught the flare of dismay in Mia's eyes and thought, *Where have you been?* Billie's daughter quickly lowered her lashes and Daphne wondered if her mother knew Mia wasn't coming straight back from school.

'Hi, Daphne. You going out?' The tone was nonchalant and Daphne suppressed a smile. Little minx. She'd sounded totally unconcerned. As if the thought that Daphne might mention it to her mother never crossed her mind. She wouldn't, unless she was asked.

Her shift started at seven a.m. and finished at three-thirty pm. Billie ran on the doctor's roster, left and finished an hour and a half later, so wouldn't be home until five p.m.

Daphne put aside her concerns but she didn't put them away. She'd keep an eye out.

She changed the subject. 'I'm visiting a young friend. Her grandad had a station accident and she comes in to visit in the afternoons. That way she gets home before the roos get too thick on the highway.'

She saw the girl nod. A flash of compassion crossed her face and Daphne was pleased to see that Mia had her mother's empathy. 'Hope her grandad feels better. See you, then.' She waved.

Daphne watched her turn and hurry up the path to the side door. Probably wanted to wash the red dust off the back of her legs and uniform before her mum came home. Daphne wondered what young Mia had been doing and hoped it wasn't something Billie would hate too much.

She turned onto the footpath and strode along the street towards the hospital. She imagined it would be challenging to have a teenage daughter, and realised Billie must have been very young when Mia was born. She was probably used to challenges.

Daphne would have loved a daughter. A family of any kind. It had always been her dream, but she was getting to the stage where it looked less likely. In fact, sometimes it felt totally impossible given she was thirty and there was no man on the horizon except her doomed attraction to Rex. The problem was she didn't fancy anyone else and Rex liked to tease her but didn't think of her in that way.

She saw Lorna Lamerton sitting on the verandah and remembered that all families had their moments. She'd met her at one of the MRFDS fundraising meetings and Lorna had invited her to the annual Christmas pudding-making week coming up. She was really looking forward to that.

The older lady seemed to be spending more time sitting on the verandah these days. Daphne had dropped in a week ago and they'd had a cup of tea overlooking the street. Talking about the time Lorna had been a nurse all those years ago. Fascinating stuff.

Daphne had the impression Lorna didn't see eye to eye with her new daughter-in-law, though she hadn't said as much.

Daphne waved and Lorna waved back. That woman had a few tales to tell. Daphne made a mental note to drop in again one day soon because the company suited them both.

When Billie arrived home, Mia was already showered and a load of washing was in the machine. Impulsively she hugged her daughter. Life was pretty darn good.

'I'm so pleased we've moved here. You were never this organised in Sydney.'

Mia blushed. 'Um... I'm getting older.'

'That you are.' Billie couldn't help sharing her excitement. 'We delivered a baby today. Out in a tin shed in the middle of nowhere.'

As she said it she corrected herself. 'We were there when a baby was born.' Daphne was right. They hadn't delivered a baby. Belle had done all the work.

Mia looked up. 'Wow! That's pretty cool. Can I tell . . .' a slight hesitation, 'the kids at school tomorrow?'

Or one kid. One particular 'male' kid? 'Sorry. Probably not. Patient confidentiality.'

Mia turned away. 'Okay.' She turned back. 'What was it like? Watching a baby be born? It must be gross.'

Billie laughed, remembering. It was different to any delivery she'd seen in the past. 'Quick. Slightly scary if I started to think what would happen if the baby didn't cry. But he did. And was fine. So then it was just amazing. Not gross at all.'

She tilted her head at her daughter, who seemed to be glowing and happy and more animated than she'd been for months. 'I didn't think 'gross' when you were born.'

Mia looked at her. 'Thanks, Mum.'

It was a look she hadn't seen on her daughter's face before. 'What for?'

'An honest answer.'

'I try to be honest with you all the time, Mia. And I hope you'd want to be honest with me.'

'Sure.' There was a pause. 'Can I have a motorbike?'

'No!'

Mia shook her head in disgust. 'That was brutally honest.'

Billie ran her fingers through her hair. Okay, maybe that had been a reflex bark. 'We live in town. Maybe if we had some land around us.'

Mia rolled her eyes. 'Well that's not going to happen.'

It might. 'Did something happen at school today?'

'Nope. Nothing ever happens.' Then she turned away and walked into her room.

Billie sank down on a chair. What had all that been about? How had she handled that so badly they'd ended up not talking? Billie thought with a tinge of unease that maybe she was missing something and then sighed. She was tired. It had been a big day.

She remembered during her aeromedical training they'd mentioned how fatigue could sneak up on you until you became accustomed to the different pressures of the aircraft. It had been interesting to be reminded about the added stresses of air travel on patients and staff alike. Today had been a hot one and the aircraft had taken a while to cool down after they took off. They'd had to monitor Anthony's temperature. Not too hot and certainly not cold.

It was all so different to road ambulance transport. There were medical adjustments you didn't normally think about. Having to fly lower for head and abdominal injuries, managing the extreme heat in the cabin until the air-conditioner kicked in after take-off, and working with headphones constantly, even while carrying on a conversation with the patient. And the rubbery legs sometimes when you climbed down from the plane.

She could see how it could be physically demanding to edge around the patient, accessing equipment and IV lines and monitoring equipment, all the while in the air. Especially if the patient's condition deteriorated. Hence the reason to be well set up before the plane left the ground.

Daphne did it all the time. Had done most of the organising today. Billie was beginning to think she was lucky the doctors only went out when more help was needed or to clinics.

She thought about today's baby and her spirits lifted. Boy, she loved this. The unpredictability of it. The genuine need and appreciation of their patients for the service they offered. This was what she wanted to do. And the people were great. Daphne was great.

Her thoughts drifted back to Morgan.

How on earth did his shoulders fit in the aircraft?

Billie grimaced. She didn't need to complicate it all by having a stupid attraction to her boss, but it was a long forgotten feeling to suspect she was admired as a woman and not just a doctor. Was she so wrong to want to bask in it for a change? As long as she stayed in control it was fine.

'I'm sorry, honey. But I've asked the real estate agent to come out and value Blue Hills. I think we should sell.'

Looking at her grandfather as he lay in his hospital bed, Soretta didn't know what to do. Her brain felt so full of words that she wanted to cry. There were so many thoughts she needed to clarify, but the impending disaster and loss of what was, for her, heartland, was swirling so thickly in the shock of the moment she couldn't make her mouth work.

That her grandfather was putting their home on the market after four generations in their family sat like a lump in her throat, and a thick black coat of hopelessness settled around her shoulders.

She wasn't used to feeling like this. Vulnerable. She'd never been in a situation where she couldn't fight her way out. Even those first three months at boarding school when the last thing she'd wanted to do was to live five hundred miles away from her home, she'd accepted that it was what her grandparents judged was the best thing for her. So she'd gone as asked. Refused to let it get her down when Year 7 girls all around her had cried with homesickness and despair, had concentrated on working hard and building her agricultural and business skills to make her grandparents proud.

She'd hidden the homesickness that never really went away and put in the structured hours of homework the school had mapped out, while the other girls had slipped out and made mischief and caused mayhem in the boy's school across the road.

Thankfully, she'd flown back to Mica Ridge in the holidays and thrown on her jeans and boots and headed out into the paddocks as fast as she could. God, she'd loved getting home for holidays.

She'd missed her horses. Missed her dogs. Missed the sunrise out in the paddock before the heat and mustering, fixing fences, kicking around in the old Landrover. But it had all worked out well because she'd taken over the business accounts and tried to stay on top of the latest agricultural trends after her gran had died.

Yes, at the moment they had a drought, but there were always droughts. Yes, there was only her and Grandad, but she'd thought they were doing okay. Or would be as soon as the rain came. The wild goat harvest had been good. Her sheep were healthy. She didn't ask for much, didn't need anything she didn't have, just wanted to keep the life that she and her grandad loved. And she had no idea what she would do if they sold.

'Oh, Grandad,' was all she could say.

By the time Daphne arrived at the hospital, only slightly puffed from the long walk, her roaming thoughts were interrupted by the sight of Soretta, ahead along the corridor, despair in every line of her body. Soretta was known for greeting the world eye-to-eye.

The young woman's back was facing her as she leant the side of her head against the corridor wall, shoulders bowed, and Daphne's stomach dropped. Not Lachlan, she prayed, and hurried forward.

'You okay, Soretta?' She spoke quietly as she put her hand gently on Soretta's shoulder and the young woman lifted her head. Her eyes were weary but not damp.

'Daphne. Hi. I'm fine.' She looked anything but fine until she pulled herself back to a normal facade.

'Your grandad okay?'

'Physically, you mean?' Soretta gave a half-strangled laugh. 'The doctor says he's slowly healing. But it's going to take at least weeks in here, if not months.'

Daphne had suspected that would be the case. 'How are you managing out at the station?'

'I'm doing good.' Her tone was all defiance. 'But apparently not good enough to stop Grandad thinking we need to sell.'

Daphne could see the hurt in her eyes. 'Did he say that today? When you arrived?'

'It was the first thing he said. If the rain came he'd be fine. We could sell some lambs for a decent price and start the cash flowing again. But we're scraping the bottom of the barrel now. I don't have enough to pay Klaus. Grandad's decided we'll lose all the sheep and the station anyway so we may as well sell now.'

Daphne tried to lift her spirits. 'He's probably worried about you working too hard.'

Soretta shook her head despairingly. 'He's never worried before.'

'Sure he has. He's just been there to make sure you didn't overdo it. Now he can't physically be there. It'd be hard for a man like your grandad to watch his granddaughter do his work.'

She saw Soretta consider that and take it on board. She looked even less happy. 'I guess.'

Daphne didn't know what to say. 'What can I do to help?'

Soretta shook her head at the magnitude of the problem. 'You do enough just by coming to visit.' She glanced around at the grey hospital corridor. At Daphne. 'I don't know why you bother to come after a day of flying all over the country in a hot aircraft.'

Daphne saw the look Soretta gave her. No doubt her hair had slipped into 'bad hair day' hours ago. It had been uncomfortable today, but she was used to it now.

'I know you've had a huge day at work already. I heard the nurses say you brought in a premature baby today. You're marvellous.'

Daphne could feel the heat in her cheeks and she brushed the compliment away. 'I'm just one of the team. Everyone does a good job.' She paused. Changed the subject back to where she wanted it. 'But I'd like to be on your team, too.'

There was a pause. When Soretta didn't answer she tried again. 'So cash is the problem. And a little would help?'

Soretta's head jerked up. 'I'm not borrowing money.'

Daphne smiled. Of course she wouldn't. 'I wouldn't offend you by offering.' Though maybe she could just move out to the station and offer the rent she was paying here to Soretta.

'I was wondering if you'd thought about renting out part of the homestead? Even if you were looking for people like me? I'd love to live on a station instead of in town. You could put all those extra rooms to good use, like a boarding house.' Daphne had thought of this yesterday.

'A boarding house?' Soretta stared, and Daphne felt like saying, it's not that mad an idea. Then Soretta said, 'Why on earth would anyone want to do that? Why would you?'

She wanted to help. Loved helping. But she also wanted to experience for herself what it was like to live on a station. 'I've been lonely,' she told Soretta. 'And I've always wanted to live on the land. That's why I came out here in the first place. You're alone and we get on well. I wouldn't bother you and it could work for both of us. Think about it. The money might be enough to at least pay the backpacker's wages and stop you slipping further into debt. It might even buy you time with your grandfather because you wouldn't be alone out there. That's probably part of the problem for him.'

Daphne saw the flare of hope rise and then die in Soretta's eyes. 'Except, I couldn't let you pay anything. You've already been so good to me.'

Daphne shook her head. 'I pay rent where I am now. And it's a dingy, dreary place to live.' She thought of Billie's dilemma. About Mia's lack of supervision after school. The doctors had their rent paid but Billie might still think it was a good idea. Mia might even be safer on a property. 'Maybe even the new doctor and her daughter would like to come? Imagine if you had three boarder rents coming in.'

She'd actually run the idea of living out of town past Morgan yesterday and he'd raised his eyebrows. Commented on her strange ability to seek out lame ducks and the fact that the wildlife could be a problem if she was driving in dim light. But reluctantly he'd agreed that it was on the perimeter of permissible. While the homestead itself was not far out of town, the station boundaries stretched back to the South Australian border for another hundred kilometres, so the house was just close enough on this boundary.

After hours she needed to be on base within twenty minutes so they were ready to fly forty minutes after the call came in, though often the pilots had the aircraft ready sooner.

'The homestead is under the limit allowed so I can still do on-call from there.'

'It's a nice idea.' Soretta ran her fingers through her hair slowly as she thought. 'But Grandad would never agree.'

'If he didn't then of course that's it.'

They were both silent until Daphne said, 'But you know, I'd almost be away more than in.' She thought about on-call again.

Realistically, call-outs happened a couple of times every week. 'If it did look possible, would it disturb you if I come in and out some nights?'

Soretta frowned. 'Of course not. The spare bedrooms are at the other end of the house from ours.'

Soretta glanced down the corridor towards the room where her grandfather lay, her gaze troubled. 'I'll ask him. At least it's something different to talk about. He's asleep at the moment.'

'Then I'll go and you think about it. But only if it seems like a good idea.' She waved the brown paper bag she held. 'Can I leave these savoury muffins with you?'

Soretta laughed. 'Take them off your hands, you mean? Because they're being a nuisance in your house?'

Daphne was pleased to see a different face to the one she'd witnessed when she'd first arrived and she felt her heart expand with relief. She so admired Soretta.

Soretta never complained, but it wasn't much of a life for a young woman running a station single-handedly. It was a big job for anyone, and knowing now that it could be in vain must be soul-destroying. Just maybe, another person's company around the house would help as much as the little cash it would bring in.

She hoped Lachlan saw that. If he didn't . . . she might just have to visit one day when his granddaughter wasn't here and help him see it!

FIVE

'It sounds like a perfect solution, Daphne.' Lorna was sitting forward in her chair with the Royal Doulton teapot suspended in the air. Daphne had called in after the hospital because Lorna had still been sitting on the verandah when she'd walked back past.

Lorna sighed. 'That poor girl.' Her hand started to shake with the weight of the pot and she grimaced in annoyance before putting it down.

Daphne didn't comment. 'I think the no-frills station lifestyle could be fun, Lorna, I've never lived on the land. And apparently the homestead is quite large. It'd be a nice change from town.'

Lorna nodded enthusiastically. 'I remember the homestead. It's huge. Almost like the lodging houses we used to have in my day. Originally there were two families living there and after a couple of really bumper years they added a lot of rooms. If she could get a few hundred dollars a week it could make all the difference. And you say the new doctor and her daughter might be interested?' Lorna took a delicate bite of her scone. 'I envy you all.'

'I haven't actually broached the subject with Dr Green yet, but maybe it could work out well for her, too. Maybe not,' Daphne said.

'But I'm going out the day after tomorrow to talk to Soretta, have a look, and see if it could work. I'll go before lunch, before Soretta comes in to the hospital to see her grandad.'

Lorna sniffed. 'I always said that duplex you're in now was too poky for staff. Our flight nurses and doctors deserve better.' Lorna put her cup down. 'When you go,' she hesitated and Daphne tilted her head to pay attention. 'I don't suppose I could come for the drive with you. Get out of the house?'

Daphne's mouth twitched. They both loved company. 'I'll mention it to Soretta and I'm sure you could. Nice for me, too, to have someone to drive out with.'

Lorna sat back with a happy sigh. 'You're very kind. I haven't been out to Blue Hills Station since Lachlan's wife went into labour with Soretta's father nearly fifty years ago.'

Daphne laughed. She could just picture Lorna arriving with a bag at the homestead, ready to help. 'I keep forgetting you know these places so much better than I do.'

Lorna smiled with the happy memories. 'A lot has changed since my day. Not least being able to get into a car as comfortable as yours and arrive in less than fifteen minutes.' She grinned. 'You know, my husband's old black saloon is still in the garage out the back. I keep threatening to polish it up and go for my driver's licence again. I won't let them sell it.'

Lorna sank back with a reminiscing gleam in her eye. 'But in those days, half the time the roads were so bad we rode horses to get through. I rode the most cantankerous horse that day. The darned thing knew only two speeds: flat out or dawdle. Took me two hours to gee it up out there.'

Daphne laughed and shook her head. 'I'll remember that when

I think about complaining about the heat in the parked aircraft next time we take off.'

Two days later, Daphne, with Lorna beside her in the passenger seat, drove the nine kilometres of tarred road to Blue Hills with purple Paterson's curse and yellow native bushes that were in flower at the side of the road.

Daphne thought it looked like native jasmine, very pretty, but it was probably a weed like Mr Paterson's bush.

The heat haze shimmered in the distance. Trees seemed suspended in air above the earth in the gap where the mirage lay on the horizon.

'Look at that emu, Lorna,' Daphne said. 'He's totally unconcerned by the heat. He's just munching at the side of the road. Smart Alec.'

'Cheeky blighters, emus.' Lorna scanned the paddocks. 'I always forget there are very few trees out here. Those that pop up close are stunted and small. Look at those few cattle huddling with their heads in the shade and their rumps out to the fierce sun.'

Daphne slowed the car as the gates to the station appeared. They grinned at each other before Daphne steered up Blue Hills Station's twin strips of dirt driveway and the women craned ahead to the homestead on the hill.

Commandingly situated with the long dry paddocks arrayed like a dehydrated swathe in front, the house stood with the blue stone hills in the distance, the peaks turned up like a ruffled collar behind the house.

The homestead, silvered by the years, was surrounded on all

sides with covered verandahs, secret spaces of shade depending on the direction of the sun. In every direction the paddocks disappeared into rock- and saltbush-strewn lots.

Across the yard a windmill rasped slowly in the gentle hot breeze as the car pulled up. When Daphne opened the door she thought fancifully that the *creak*, *creak* from the windmill sounded a lyrical welcome as she got out.

Then Soretta opened the screen door and came out to welcome them up onto the main verandah. Daphne looked across to check Lorna had her seatbelt off but discovered the door open and her travel mate walking with sprightly energy towards the steps.

Soretta met her at the top. 'You must be Mrs Lamerton. Daphne tells me you came here to help deliver my dad?'

Lorna nodded. 'Now that is a true story. I didn't imagine one day I would meet his daughter in the same place.' She'd reached the top without using the rail, or losing her breath, and shook Soretta's hand with enthusiasm.

Daphne suppressed her smile. She was a goer, that Lorna, she thought, as she carried a plate of scones, kicked Lorna's door shut, and followed the older lady's example and hurried up the stairs. They all paused and turned to look back over the dry paddocks and the driveway.

Daphne said, 'It's wonderful, Soretta.'

Soretta's gaze rested on the dry paddocks in front of the house. Drifted across to the empty dam. 'It can be. You should see it when it's not in drought.' Her eyes skimmed every direction as if her heart was breaking. 'I don't want to lose it.'

'Of course you don't,' said Lorna. 'I think this boarding-house concept is a wonderful idea to bring in some income.'

*

One hundred kilometres west of Mica Ridge another wind-mill pumped water from the hard ground in the red afternoon sun. Barbara Tomkins, lean and sun-browned like all her family, absently folded the clothes from the swaying wire and ran over in her mind the jobs she needed to complete before nightfall.

Barb flicked a glance at the darkening horizon, looking for the men from the camp. Lifting a corner of her apron, she mopped the bead of sweat on her brow, until a sudden gasp from her four-year-old daughter, who was sitting in the shade, spun her around.

'He bite me!' Gwyn's lip dropped as she stared at the twin red marks on her hand and sick horror exploded in Barbara's brain as the words sank in. Her worst nightmare. The men weren't in yet and she was alone.

Dropping the basket, she frantically scooped Gwyn from the play rug, scattering homemade farm animals and tiny fences, while the unmistakable slither of a snake disappeared under the tank stand.

'Shit. Shit.'

Her daughter whimpered as Barbara bolted for the back steps of the verandah. 'Stay still. Don't move.' Of course Gwyn began to cry and struggle in response to the fear in her mother's voice.

Immobilise the limb. Bandage, bandage! Barbara spotted the fruit bowl where her husband always kept the wide roll of elastic bandage and she sat her daughter on the table. She picked up the wooden spoon she'd left there earlier when she'd been making the dough. With a superhuman effort she tried to make her voice more reassuring. Even tried a wobbly smile that didn't fool either of them.

'If you sit really quiet, it won't sting as much, and Mummy needs to wrap it up with this spoon to keep it still. Can you do that?'

A trembling nod and a tear glistened at the edge of those huge eyes that were so like her father's. Barbara couldn't contemplate a reality of Gwyn not being there, but the sickness of deep fear coiled in her belly. 'Mummy's going to ring the flying doctor. Then Daddy.'

The colour suddenly leached from Gwyn's face as her eyes rolled back and she began to shake.

In Mica Ridge Flying Doctor Base the phone rang and Billie reached for it. It had been a slow day for her, though not for Daphne who was off late, and she picked it up with excess energy. 'Mica Ridge Base. Dr Green. Can I help you?'

'Doctor. Thank God. It's Barbara Tomkins from Golden Ridge Station. My daughter's been bitten by a snake.'

Billie switched the phone to loudspeaker and wrote swiftly as the words poured from Barbara. *Gwyn, bitten by unidentified snake five minutes ago.* Her stomach tightened. Had she seen that name on the immunisation list last week?

She quickly switched her mind back before she missed anything. *Bandaged hand. Splinted. Already vomited. Pale. Shaking.* Not good.

'That's fine, Barbara. You're doing everything right. Firm bandage, not too tight, enough to compress the lymphatics but not the blood flow, that's good. A splint is good. Try to keep Gwyn calm. Maybe even lie down with her. Hold on and I'll give you a time to expect the aircraft.'

She shot a look across at Morgan and Rex. They'd moved swiftly to stand in front of the large map pinned to the wall and were working out the direction and flight distance. Daphne arrived back from re-checking the aircraft drugs and took in the situation in a glance. Billie saw the moment Daphne's face paled and Billie realised this was the family she'd stayed with.

Morgan turned to watch Billie and his gaze narrowed. 'I'll come with you and Daphne. It'll be tight for space but there's enough room. You'll still be in charge of the medical decisions and Daphne will ensure the aircraft cabin is secure as always, but you might need help.' He nodded at the phone. 'Thirty-five minutes tops. We'll be on the ground around five p.m. Get Barbara to drive to the strip with the child when we fly over the house. It's best not to move her until just before we get there.'

Rex strode from the room to start his pre-flight check of the aircraft and Daphne disappeared in to the medical supply room to gather extra equipment. Morgan picked up another phone as Billie repeated the instructions to Barbara. Then Morgan said, 'Tell her I'm onto the consultant at the Children's Hospital in Adelaide and he'll connect us with a venom specialist from his end.'

Barbara listened as Billie repeated the information. Her voice cracked as she lost some of her control. 'Hurry.'

Billie mentally hugged the woman. 'Hang on. We're on our way.'

After she hung up, Billie followed Daphne into the supply room while Morgan made the next swift call to the consultant and arranged a call-back number on the satellite phone in the aircraft, then he nodded as they reappeared with the extra equipment.

'There's a strong chance we'll need to intubate or, failing that, we'll put the LMA in and Daphne will be managing the rest. While she's experienced at placing the laryngeal mask and either bagging or connecting the ventilator, I can be the extra hands when you need help. Daphne will sort us all into the best spots.'

Despite her pale face, Daphne's voice was calm as she explained. 'Adelaide will have the antivenom ready when we get there.' She didn't say that there was a chance they wouldn't get there in time, but Billie understood and grabbed the extra paediatric resuscitation kit Daphne thrust into her hand before she took off at a brisk trot after Rex. Barbara's daughter could die if they didn't get out there fast enough.

As Billie glanced around to see if she'd forgotten anything, Morgan had switched the base over to Broken Hill. She shot past him out the door and heard his 'Slow down,' as she came out into the afternoon heat. Billie obediently slowed her pace to a safer hurried walk and followed Rex up the steps into the plane.

Thankfully, the pilot had finished his meticulous walk around. That was a bonus. With summer here, there'd be plenty of light for hours of flying yet.

Daphne secured the cabin once everyone was seated. They'd removed the second stretcher in case Morgan needed to be in the rear of the cabin on the way back but for now Morgan had climbed up beside Rex. Billie couldn't help being thankful they had him along as well. Once they were in the air she and Daphne began to go over the protocols for treatment on arrival. Then Billie quickly re-read the instructions on paediatric treatment for snake bite in case she'd forgotten anything. She stole a look at her watch and winced at the thought of Barbara waiting for them.

*

Half an hour later Barbara Tomkins heard the sound she'd been straining for in the distance: the drone of a plane. 'Thank God.' She eased herself off the chair.

Her daughter had twitched uneasily in her arms for the last twenty minutes and Barbara prayed as she picked up her bulging shoulder bag.

Gwyn had been limp and her breathing shallow while they'd waited, but Barbara had hesitated to try to rouse her in case she shifted Gwyn's tiny hand and pumped more of the venom around her small body.

She'd given up trying to reach her husband. She'd left a note but he'd eventually find the missed calls and contact her. Goodness knew where she'd be tonight; not that it mattered as long as Gwyn was okay.

She didn't allow herself to contemplate anything worse or her brain wouldn't remain calmly sensible, which was the most important thing.

She heard the plane pass over the house and she picked up her keys to the spare truck and hurried out with Gwyn in her arms.

Driving with Gwyn's head in her lap, she sent a silent thanks that her husband had made that cattle grid over the landing strip paddock and she didn't have to open a gate. She parked just as the plane touched down and chewed her trembling lip, fervently pleading with God to let the flying doctor save her baby.

Billie took one look at Gwyn's condition, another quick look at Morgan, and decided to intubate right away.

They moved inside the aircraft to be out of the sun, and without the second stretcher there was room for Morgan and Daphne to put an intravenous cannula into each of Gwyn's arms. Billie drew up the drugs for rapid intubation.

In the quickly increasing heat, Billie held the laryngoscope in her left hand, visualised the vocal cords, and, without taking her eyes off the airway, held out her right hand as Morgan handed her the endotracheal tube to slide in. All the while she could feel Morgan's quiet confidence in her and, surprisingly, she drew strength from that. They barely spoke as all members of the team, despite their relative newness together, anticipated the needs of the others. Then it was done. Gwyn's airway was secured. Billie inflated the cuff, took the CO_2 detector from Daphne to check the position of the airway, and then handed her the tape to secure the tube. They connected the bag. Morgan squeezed the Air Viva bag and Gwyn's little chest rose and fell with the movement. Everyone in the cabin seemed to breathe out at the same moment.

Morgan's murmured 'Well done,' came from somewhere in the background, making her eyes sting. Billie heard Barbara's sob from behind the pilot's partition, and her fingers trembled involuntarily in response. She blocked the sound out as she concentrated. Daphne had the ventilator to connect as soon as Morgan disconnected the Air Viva bag. They all glanced at the monitor and Billie added a sedative to the IV lines

'Let's get this young lady to Adelaide,' Morgan said quietly.

Daphne rose from the kneeling position and rearranged everyone until she was happy with how they were seated and belted. Billie was in the doctor's seat, the perfect position to watch the airway, at the top of the stretcher where the little girl was safely strapped in by the special pedi-mate child's harness. Rex had added the extra adult seats from the wing locker and Morgan was positioned to the side of Gwyn's abdomen. Daphne was in her usual spot facing backwards towards the cabin with her back to Rex on the other side of the partition, and Barbara had been extricated from the front to sit next to Morgan and could reach across and touch her daughter at an angle.

Billie saw Daphne check equipment and that IV lines were in place with pressure bags to allow them to run during the flight.

'Everything secure?' Rex asked.

'Cabin secure,' Daphne said.

That flight was the worst of Billie's life. By the time they'd handed Gwyn over to the specialist in intensive care, and made sure Barbara had been connected to the social worker to find somewhere to stay, it was almost seven o'clock. Her hands, now that they were allowed to, were shaking uncontrollably. Travelling back to Mica Ridge from Adelaide, Morgan manoeuvred Daphne up beside Rex and he sat in the back with Billie.

After a few minutes of flying his voice broke the silence between them. 'How do you feel about the care given at the scene?'

Billie blinked. That was all she could think about. It seemed Morgan knew she was rehashing. She took a breath, and seized the opportunity to talk. She knew it would lessen the chance of it keeping her awake later tonight. 'I thought the intubation went well, though my hands were a little shaky at times.' She spread her fingers and grimaced at their steadiness now.

'The intubation couldn't have been better.' Morgan's quiet words did a lot to settle her nerves. 'You, the rest of us, and Barbara, did everything we could to save Gwyn.'

Billie's stomach plummeted. 'Do you know something we don't? Is Gwyn still fighting?'

He smiled at her. 'Last I heard she was improving slowly. There were positive signs she'll win. What I'm saying is that if you do that well in all your retrievals the majority of our patients will survive. Some won't, but you can't do the impossible. And your best is outstanding. Welcome to the team, Billie.'

Billie's throat felt tight with the unexpected release of tension his words allowed. Eventually she could speak and, as they flew into the darkening skies, she and Morgan went over the details of the retrieval until all her questions were answered: what they'd done well, what they could have done better, what they'd do next time. By the end, while she was emotionally exhausted, her mind was quiet.

They didn't arrive until late. Billie got her wish to see the town glowing with fairy lights, the multi-orange lights of the mines glowing like decorations, and she fell silent as they circled over the well-lit Mica Ridge. For the first time she had a moment to think of her daughter, hoping that Mia was keeping up her end of the bargain and doing the right thing unsupervised at home. Thank goodness they weren't in Sydney.

The next day Daphne kept them updated with Gwyn's battle in Adelaide and after the last instalment at 3:30 p.m. she left to go home. Billie and Michael had gone to retrieve a station owner with a suspected heart attack, but the trip had become complicated when his condition deteriorated en route and he required cardiac compression mid flight. By the time they'd handed him over to the coronary care team in Adelaide it had been another late night.

Morgan was still in the control room when Billie went in to collect her bag and he called her over to his desk.

'Good job. I just spoke to the hospital. Tom's critical but stable and on his way to theatre for a by-pass. His wife has arrived.'

'Thanks.' Billie shuddered. 'He was critical when I left and it's good to know he's stabilised.'

His eyes narrowed as if to see what she was really thinking—or see under her skin. She wished he'd look away because she felt raw and exposed after the harrowing trip and she needed to regather herself before going home. She'd had her run of intense emergency medicine over the last two days and she was feeling a bit fraught.

He said conversationally, 'How'd the resus go?'

Better than it could have. 'It was tricky with just Michael and I but he's good. Next time I'd be aiming to have my drugs prepared before take-off if there was a chance they might be needed.'

He nodded. 'Sometimes it's hard to gauge.'

'It's reassuring to have managed, I guess.' She thought about the harrowing ten minutes and the hyper-alert state she and Michael had been in after they'd managed to get him back and shuddered.

'You did well, Billie.' His voice lowered. 'Really well. I said it yesterday. We're pleased to have you on the team.'

It should have sounded patronising but it didn't. It sounded genuine. Proud, even. And the underlying relief for another patient making it into the higher level of care at the hospital showed how much he cared about their patients.

'I've got to get home.' It had been a traumatic day, cardiac compression and bagging in a small aircraft was hard work, but they'd kept him alive until they'd landed.

'I know.' There was something in his voice that said that wasn't all he knew. It was her turn to frown.

'Daphne rang. Mia had an,' he hesitated, corrected himself, 'a *slight* accident on the way home from school. Daphne said not to worry and she'd stay until you came in.'

Billie's eyes widened and she grabbed her bag. 'You should've told me that first!'

His voice was level. 'You need to debrief from work initially before the next crisis comes along. We're in a high-stress job.'

'Mia's accident is a crisis? Why am I still here?' She spun on her heel and headed for the door.

It was dark when Billie pulled up outside the dingy flats and all the lights were on in her side of the house. When she opened the door the smell of onions and tomato and possibly basil hit her nose, and she remembered for a second that she hadn't eaten for about six hours. 'Mia?'

'I'm here,' Mia replied in a small voice from behind the back of the lounge in front of the silent television.

Daphne appeared from the kitchen and smiled reassuringly at Billie. 'Spaghetti bolognaise when you're ready,' she said, then disappeared back into the kitchen.

Mia had her arm in a sling. No plaster so maybe it wasn't broken. She was lying on the lounge and Billie could see a graze down her other arm and left leg. Her heart squeezed.

She sank down on the edge of the lounge. 'Poor Baby. What happened?' And she hadn't been here!

Mia looked so lost and young, and for a moment Billie could see the unsteady toddler the first time she'd badly grazed her knee. Bewildered by the concept of pain and blood and needing Mummy's arms.

Billie felt her throat close up as she knelt down and hugged her daughter gently, all her love for the most important person in her world flooding out in a wave. Heightened no doubt because yesterday she'd spent a large part of her day with another mother who had very nearly lost her daughter. Sometimes she felt that no matter how hard she tried, she wasn't there enough for Mia.

Tears rolled down Mia's cheek. 'I'm sorry.'

'Sorry?' Billie's brow creased. No. These should be her words for not being around when she was needed. 'Don't be silly.' She stroked the hair back from Mia's forehead. 'What happened?'

'I stacked Trent's bike.'

Trent. The young man. Well, accidents happened. 'Trent has a pushbike?'

Mia shook her head and Billie sat back. 'A motorbike?'

Then Billie remembered yesterday's wish list. A vision of her daughter's hair—and fragile skull—flying free as she risked life and limb. Fabulous. Not. 'You've been riding someone else's motorbike? This Trent?' She could feel her face heat so she took a breath. And then another one. She tried not to think how hurt she was that Mia had let her down again. And hoped she'd had a helmet on. She also tried to remember that her daughter had probably had a shock from the accident. And had been waiting all afternoon to break the news. But it was freaking hard. She took another breath before she trusted herself to talk.

She said in a level tone, 'I had a big day too. Yesterday, a four-year-old girl was bitten by a snake and almost died. Today I had to ventilate a man in an aircraft until we landed at the hospital. I thought the both of them were going to die for most of the way.'

She looked at her daughter—battered, bruised, tense and

wary—and sighed. 'I'm glad you're not too badly hurt. I'm also sorry I couldn't trust you to not get up to mischief while I was at work supporting us both.'

She stood up. Closed her lips on more of what she shouldn't say. Instead she said, 'I'm going to have something to eat,' and strode into the kitchen, where Daphne was waiting.

'Thank you, Daphne.'

Daphne shot her a sympathetic glance and then looked away. 'I hope you don't mind that I've taken over your house.'

Billie gave a bitter laugh. 'Feel free. I'm not doing such a great job.' She crossed to the stove and lifted the lid. A billow of fragrant steam rose to meet her and rich red meat bubbled.

Billie eyed the dish of drained spaghetti. 'You,' she said with heartfelt appreciation, 'are a champion.' When she looked at Daphne, she seemed to be squirming under her mild compliment. 'Food will help enormously.'

Daphne smiled. 'I'm glad.' She inclined her head towards the lounge. 'She's okay. Probably sprained her wrist so I put it in a sling. It was swollen but I don't think it's broken. She's got good movement.'

Billie nodded. 'I'll have a look later when I've eaten and cooled down. I might be a bit unsympathetic if I touch her now.'

They smiled at each other and Billie couldn't believe how good it felt to have Daphne there. It was like old times with her aunt before she died. She'd missed the company. The shared adult conversation. And poor Daphne was copping it.

'Did she come home on her own?'

Daphne shook her head. 'Trent came with her. Knocked on my door. He was shaken. He seems like a nice boy. Must be a reasonable young man because he was more worried about Mia than the bike they'd dragged here, which looked terminal, to my untrained eye.'

'We'll probably have a visit from his parents, then.' She put her head in her hands.

Billie could hear the sounds of Daphne dishing up her plate as she spoke. 'I'm not a mother. But at least I could see she was worried about upsetting you, Billie.'

She lifted her head. Daphne was right. And Mia wasn't badly hurt. Just shaken. It could have been a whole lot worse. She sighed and thought about the retrieval today. 'Tom from Jinda station arrested mid flight today. We got him back.'

Daphne sucked in her breath and put Billie's plate in front of her with a clatter and covered her mouth. 'I know the family well. I've been out there for one of the stockmen.'

Billie nodded. 'One of the station hands met us on the airstrip. His wife was away.'

Daphne looked pale. 'How is he now?'

Billie pulled out a chair. 'Sit down. Alive. Critical but stable.'

Daphne was shaking her head. 'Morgan didn't say that's where you were when I rang to tell him about Mia.'

Morgan wouldn't. He was a professional. A calculated professional. One who could hold information until he deemed it right to impart. She'd known a calculating man before. Note to self. 'Are you astonished he didn't tell you?'

Daphne glared out the window as if she could see him. 'No. Probably not. No useful reason for me to know, he would've thought.'

To her surprise, Billie found herself defending him. 'You're on your day off. And you've had a big week, too.'

But Daphne wouldn't be diverted. 'How terrifying for his wife.' She checked the clock. 'I'll ring them tomorrow in Adelaide and see if they need anything. Thank goodness I have another day off.'

Billie finished the mouthful of truly incredible pasta before she spoke again. 'He's stable. I think he'll come through.' In an effort to distract her, Billie asked, 'So what did you do today, before my daughter brought her dramas to you?'

Daphne blinked. Rubbed her forehead as if to think. 'Oh. I drove out to Blue Hills Station and looked into boarding there.'

Billie felt her stomach sink. Daphne gone from next door? Funny how disappointed that made her feel. 'Move out of here?' Were they so bad to live next to? *Knock it off, Billie.* This wasn't about her. This was Daphne's life.

'It was mainly to help out a young friend. We flew Lachlan in the day you arrived. He's lucky to be alive. His granddaughter is doing a great job even though she's only twenty-two. The drought's making it tough to make ends meet on the station.'

Billie could hear the concern in Daphne's voice. This was important to her. 'Is anyone else there with her?'

'A German backpacker, a thousand sheep, and a pack of kelpies,' was the dry reply.

Billie raised her brows. 'A lot to manage. No wonder it's tough. And she's on her own?'

'If it rains she'll be fine. For the moment she's having trouble week to week and I've offered to be a boarder. I've always wanted to try living on a station and never had the chance. This one's close to town, and it's a huge house. Plus it'd bring a little extra cash and company if she wants it. Like an extended farm stay.'

Billie tried to sound enthusiastic for Daphne. 'We'd miss you.'

She looked at Daphne's face and caught the embarrassment and telltale spread of colour up her neck. Her new friend really didn't take praise well.

Daphne looked away. 'I'm sure you won't.'

Billie looked down at the food in front of her before raising her eyebrows again. 'Um. Yes. Of course we will. Though it sounds right up your alley and I'll still see you at work.'

'I've checked out the distance,' Daphne said hesitantly. 'Morgan said I could do on-call from there. The actual homestead is just under 10 kilometres out of town even though the property runs almost to the South Australian border.' There was another hesitation before she said, 'You never know. You and Mia might be interested in moving out of town as well, one day. There's a school bus that goes past the door and it would mean Mia wouldn't have the after-school time lag.'

As if relieved to get it all out, Daphne stood up and bustled away to put her own plate in the sink, then washed it vigorously. 'It's none of my business, of course,' she said over her shoulder, 'but I thought I might as well run the idea past you.'

Billie thought about it, and was surprised by how much the idea appealed. She'd wanted to try station life, and she wouldn't need a manager if it wasn't her station, and Daphne would be there. Before she could say anything, Mia's voice called from the lounge.

'Mummmm.'

Billie stood up as Daphne dried her hands and prepared to leave. 'I'll go next door. If she needs to stay home tomorrow I can drop in and check on her every now and then.'

Billie put her hand out and touched Daphne's shoulder. 'Thank you. For looking after Mia, for everything.' She waved to her half-eaten plate. 'It's just what I needed to retain my sanity.'

Daphne looked ridiculously pleased and Billie wondered just what the past had done to this woman, who was possibly the kindest person she'd ever met.

The next morning Morgan stopped Billie as she walked past him to put her bag away. 'How's Mia?'

She glanced at him coolly. He'd known she would be upset and withheld telling her until he decided the time was right. Well, he had no right. 'Bruised and sorry for herself. She's staying home today.'

His voice was level but she had the feeling he knew he'd blotted his copybook. 'I thought you might have called in sick to stay with her.'

She looked at him. Lifted her chin. He wasn't the only professional around here. 'Thought of it but she's sixteen. And I didn't want to let everyone down.'

He nodded. Didn't say thank you. Did she really need him to? 'Daphne mentioned she was thinking of moving out of town. Renting a room on a station,' she said.

'Hmm.' His expression didn't change. But then it didn't change much that she noticed any time except when the sudden smiles surprised her. She didn't like him, remember, she told herself.

'I was thinking I might try that, too,' she said.

'Hmmm.' Still no expression.

Well, that wasn't very helpful. Did he think it was acceptable for her to add 10 kilometres to her drive to work? But he hadn't said no either.

Billie decided to ask Daphne if she would take her out to meet Soretta. If that went well then Mia could lump it along with Morgan.

SIX

Soretta and Billie hit it off right away. They both believed in getting things done and agreed to give it a one-month trial period.

Mia wasn't happy. Which was an understatement.

'I cannot believe you are doing this to me,' she said when Billie told her the news. 'Again. Are you trying to ruin my life?'

Billie tried not to react. 'I'm trying to stop you doing that.' She was happy with the calmness in her voice.

Mia was anything but calm. 'By incarcerating me on a drought-stricken, desolate sheep farm where I won't even be able to wash my hair because they won't have enough water? It'll be a hundred degrees out there!'

Billie's temper strained at the edges. 'Soretta says there's still enough tank water. You just have to be careful with it.'

'Oh goody. And, what's more, I'm not coming home on the school bus like a baby.'

'You have to. Daphne doesn't always get off on time.' It was becoming more difficult to keep her voice level.

Mia folded her arms across her chest and Billie noticed that her daughter's shirt buttons on her uniform were bulging a little. The thought sent a pang of nostalgia through her and her anger drained away. She had to accept that Mia was turning into a woman in front of her eyes. A bolshy, cranky when thwarted, woman.

Mia said, 'I'll wait for you to arrive and pick me up from school.'

'I might not get off on time either and two hours is too long to wait anyway.' Billie closed her eyes for a second. 'You can go in with me on the days I work but you'll catch the bus home. But I'm afraid that's the end of the story. Starting on Friday.'

Mia glared at her. 'You'll regret this.'

Billie took a deep breath. Let it out slowly and said in a very quiet voice, 'I hope not. But if it doesn't work we'll come back here.'

Moving out to Blue Hills Station only took a week to organise. Thankfully, it fell on the Friday rostered day off so Billie even had a three-day weekend to settle in.

Morgan had arranged with the powers that be that one of the town flats would remain as an on-call backstop for the nights on-call. Which would be good as well if staff were too tired to drive home after a call-out.

He demurred when Billie tried to thank him. 'It's something I've been thinking about for a while. And not just for you and Daphne.'

Liar, Billie thought, because she could see the concern in his eyes. But maybe he had a point. She could imagine a close shave with wildlife, especially at dawn and dusk when her reflexes were likely to be half asleep.

But she wasn't going to think about work this morning. Or her boss. She was thinking about her days off and her new place of residence.

This move would be the perfect way to see if she really did want to live on the land, as opposed to being forever an in-town person. And she didn't have to buy a high-maintenance place to find out.

Tonight would be their first night at Blue Hills Station, with the only downside being Mia was not excited, to say the least. But Billie got that. Maybe they had moved way too often. Hopefully, this would be a turning point for both of them.

Daphne and Billie drove their cars out to Blue Hills as soon as Mia left for school and Billie could see Daphne's smiling face in the rear-view mirror as she led the way.

It was a peaceful drive. They didn't pass a single soul, and had wide open spaces on each side of the road. The sun behind them, Billie felt like a pioneer heading into the distance with purple flowers and waving yellow grass flashing past and the open plains ahead of her.

When she turned into the station gate and started up the rock strewn driveway, Billie felt the surge of excitement, like a wave of new adventurous spirit she'd been waiting to unleash. She couldn't keep the smile off her face. She braked close to the verandah steps so they could unload. She'd find out where to park later.

Daphne pulled up next to her and they grinned at each other as they got out.

Soretta, dressed in well-worn jeans, a workman's shirt with the sleeves rolled up and socks, pushed open the screen door and gestured them up the steps. 'Welcome, ladies. I'm afraid I have to run away, but make yourselves at home.'

When they got to the top step, she flashed them a smile as she picked up one of her boots. 'Something's come up over at the yards. But I'll be back later to answer questions.'

Billie blinked, but Soretta on a mission was unstoppable and obviously she had no doubt they'd manage fine on their own.

'Have fun shifting stuff,' she said. 'I'm on my way out to move sheep to another paddock.'

Billie was still processing this when Soretta added, 'I had a brilliant idea last night.' She pulled on her boot. 'Grandad and I don't use the lounge rooms between our rooms and yours, just the kitchen and the dining room occasionally, so you can have a sitting room each in the middle.' She pulled on the other boot. 'Make them your own spaces, shift the furniture in any of your rooms. You'll see which ones are ours, so use any of the others. Only thing is, Grandad has the ensuite, so we'll all have to share the other bathroom.'

She stood up. Stomped her feet to settle them into the boots. 'If this boarding thing doesn't work, that's okay, too, but we'll see how it goes.' She glanced at her watch. 'Sorry, I didn't expect to do this today but needs must. I have to be early before Klaus gets tied up doing other things. He lives in the shearer's quarters over the hill. Call me if you need something urgent explained.'

She pulled her phone from her pocket, showed them the bars of reception, and put it back. 'My mobile works most times when I'm away from the house but not all the time. The number's stuck on the fridge. I'll be back at three to go see Grandad. The school bus gets here at four forty-five.'

She waved and trotted down the steps and strode across the yard. A minute later they heard the roar of an engine and then she came out of the shed on a quad bike, two kelpies jumping and skidding in excitement, as she puttered down the driveway until she broke right and steered across a paddock.

Billie shook her head at the dynamo that was their landlady.

Daphne seemed to think everything was as it should be. 'She's a doer, that Soretta.'

Billie dragged her eyebrows back down to normal and followed after Daphne, who'd now stepped inside and was standing in the central hallway.

'Ah, yes,' Billie murmured as she began to take in the lovely old home. In her brief look through during the week when she'd met Soretta, she really hadn't noticed much except the fact the house was out of town, and seemed large enough to not find themselves living in each other's pockets. Of Soretta, she'd decided she could admire her drive and stamina, and the rest she'd see how they went. Billie got on with most people and she just hoped Mia would settle in.

She hadn't missed the fact it would be very different to the featureless duplex they'd moved out of or that people would be coming and going. Which was a good thing for Mia.

With Soretta gone, and time to soak it in, now she saw the ceilings were high, pressed-metal and painted white. The hallway was divided by white painted wooden arches down its length where it gave way into rooms.

'The house is huge,' Billie marvelled quietly as they walked slowly down the wooden boards of the hallway, and she shook her head at the stained-glass bottoms of the windows shining multi-coloured light as the sun streamed through the eastern side of the house.

They peered into each of the seven bedrooms except Lachlan's, which was right at the end of the long arched hallway, and Soretta's that lay opposite.

They perused the available rooms, which were closer to the kitchen, and after them, the sitting rooms.

Each bedroom had its own latticed double door leading out onto the verandah and an outside chair and round table. Inside both of the high-ceilinged rooms was a wall of built-in robes, plus a colonial writing desk, a deep chest of drawers with mirror, and a wrought-iron double bed, stripped bare, with blankets folded on top. The furnishings were old but shone with years of polish applied with love.

The two sitting rooms were elongated rather than wide, and one of them was scarce of furniture, which suited Daphne and her belongings. The other was fully furnished and showed signs of more use. Both had huge bay windows with a window seat looking out over the verandah.

A couple of folded newspapers and an open book that Billie suspected had been there for a while lay on the side table in her sitting room. Both rooms had black metal fireplaces with tiled surrounds. Billie's had a wing chair pulled up in front of her fireplace and she could imagine being tucked up there on a cold winter's night with her own book. The ambience was a world away from the concrete rooms staring into the blank metal fence they'd just left.

The slow excitement that had been building all day expanded into a burst of anticipation. She had a job she loved. A safe place for Mia to come home to. And a connection with the land she'd always dreamed of, even if she'd really be a farm-stay renter. Finally, things were coming together the way she'd always hoped they could.

They tore themselves away from the sitting rooms and moved on to the enormous bathroom—with claw-foot bath that neither of them could imagine having enough water to be able to use, but there was nothing wrong with dreaming—a dark-green tiled shower with an old-fashioned bird-neck shower rose, and an oak dresser with an oval basin set into the wood. The separate toilet room sported washbasin and stained-glass mirror and was almost big enough to fit another bath.

Daphne shook her head at the elegance of the fittings. 'Soretta's grandmother certainly had a flair for interior decorating.'

'The whole place is beautiful,' Billie whispered as if a ghost might hear. 'I know her gran died, but what happened to Soretta's mother?'

'She died not long after Soretta was born. Her father was killed in a farm accident, so her paternal grandparents brought her up, but her grandmother died two years ago. Lorna told me Lachlan's never been the same since her death, which makes it harder for Soretta.'

Billie got that. The homestead showed all the signs of warmth and family and a woman's caring touch, but it must have echoed a little emptily with just Lachlan and Soretta in it. 'Well, her gran certainly created a beautiful home. It's perfectly maintained. How can Soretta keep it like this with what she does outside?'

Daphne smiled. 'I asked. Apparently, she spends fifteen minutes in a different room every day, cleaning and vacuuming lightly, early in the morning, so the task is built into her day, and she leaves the rest until its turn. That way she gets through the lot. She said she started it when her gran died because she felt close to her when she was doing it, and hasn't stopped.'

Billie shook her head. Homemaking wasn't her strong suit but she could appreciate the sense of a consistently doing a small amount. She'd always kept her current rooms clean and tidy and this would be an absolute pleasure to maintain. 'At least Soretta will have a few less rooms to do now.'

Daphne had chosen the room beside the minimally furnished sitting room on the left side of the hallway and Billie was very happy with the two rooms next to each other on the right.

They moved back into the hallway and her head shook in spite of herself. 'But it's still a huge house.'

Daphne had been right when she'd said there'd be room for more lodgers if Soretta wanted. The place could hold more than three families very comfortably if everyone pulled their own weight.

Billie smiled at the sudden image of Soretta dealing with anyone she considered slacking. Miss Mia might be in for a shock.

In the separate dining room the glory piece, a formal table with enough seating for twelve, was polished rosewood. The matching high-backed chairs, with a carver at each end, were regal. Billie could almost imagine the original settlers hosting dinner parties for men with curling moustaches and military jackets.

Back in the kitchen the table held seating for eight and the long scrubbed timber setting looked like it had seen generations of family life.

Rex was coming at morning teatime with a u-hire trailer full of Daphne's furniture. Billie thought again that Rex might be sweet on Daphne, but when she'd raised the idea discreetly with her new friend Daphne had blushed and denied it strenuously. Such was Daphne's embarrassment that Billie had backed away from the statement, but she still hadn't changed her mind. He'd been pretty quick to offer help, and hadn't taken no for an answer.

The two women spent the next two hours unpacking their suit-cases, stocking the food pantry in the kitchen while looking at the bare cupboards and each other in dismay, and generally settling in.

Daphne had brought her slow cooker, and before they'd gone too far she'd slipped in a corned beef piece to simmer away qui-etly in the corner of the kitchen to make sandwiches with later, and packed cakes and slices she'd cooked at the flat into empty round Tupperware containers, which Soretta seemed to have hundreds of.

'Love the idea of the corned meat.' Billie rubbed her hands together. 'I can see we'll have to come to an arrangement. Of course we can take it in turns cooking, but I need you to make the suggestions.'

Daphne nodded happily at the prospect. 'I love cooking and adore my slow cooker. It only takes a minute to start a whole meal that cooks while I'm at work.'

'I read that somewhere,' Billie said dryly. 'I never believed it,' she muttered.

The dogs barked, a farm sound and one they'd have to get used to. Mia had always fussed over other people's animals even though they'd never had a pet. In fact, Billie hadn't had one since her par-ents died. The dogs kept barking and she wondered if they'd drive her mad.

A few minutes later there was a knock at the door.

They both looked up. Oops. So barking dogs meant visitors. She must remember that.

Billie went to the door and looked out. A towering four-wheel drive, festooned with spotlights and bull bar and requisite kelpie chained on the back, was parked under the tree.

A tall, confident young cowboy, sporting a very rakishly tilted akubra, was coming up the steps.

'I'm Clem. Outback Internet Service.' The strapping young man had a delightfully slow drawl. He shifted his hat to one hand with that innate country courtesy she'd noticed time and again since she'd moved here, and carried a bulky toolbox easily in the other.

Billie pushed open the screen door. 'Excellent. I didn't think you'd get here today. Thanks for coming so quickly.'

He nodded, and she loved the way he put his toolbox down and automatically bent and slipped off his boots before coming in.

Once he was inside she waved him in to the dining room, where the wi-fi internet had originally been based. 'Second door on the left.'

He paused. 'Soretta home?'

Billie shook her head. 'She's sorting sheep at the yards.'

The young man nodded and carried his toolbox and equipment down towards the original but defunct internet connections and she turned back to Daphne.

Billie raised her hands in disbelief. 'That was quick. It takes weeks in Sydney to get a tradie. I checked with Soretta and she was happy if I put the internet back on for the house. I can't believe it might actually happen today.' In case Daphne thought she expected Soretta to pay, she added, 'My expense, of course. Mia wouldn't cope without it and I'm partial to the occasional download myself.'

Down the hallway the young man had begun a soft-whistled country ballad that floated up into the high ceiling. 'I remember what you said about the Swiss workers leaving and I'll ask him about routers and see if we can get it to the shearers' quarters for casual labour when Soretta needs it.'

Billie mightn't be much of a cook, but she could make things happen if all it took was a money and organising. It felt good to be part of a group enterprise.

She grinned. 'Might give that nice young man a chance to say hi to our landlady while he's here.'

The next vehicle to arrive was Rex's. The dogs barked, Daphne glanced nervously at the mirror placed strategically beside the back door, and Billie nodded to herself. Thought so. By the time the rattling trailer was dragged up beside the verandah steps the two women had moved outside to watch him pull up.

Except, unexpectedly, Morgan uncoiled from the car at the other side and Billie wished she'd taken a bit of time checking herself in that damn mirror. Nobody said he was coming.

He looked Billie's way and lifted his akubra. Another man who looked good in a hat. Apparently she was starting to develop a fetish for cowboys.

'Didn't know you were coming, Morgan.' Daphne sounded pleased and Billie suspected she might be a bit pleased herself, though it was hard to tell under the jumbling pros and cons of more-exposure-to-Morgan thoughts in her brain.

She considered the concept and decided to hell with it, she was very pleased. The more men, the better for shifting stuff. It was just the shock of seeing people she associated with work in her downtime. Nothing else.

'Said I'd give Rex a hand,' Morgan drawled.

Billie smiled, satisfied she'd given nothing away, and decided she'd stand somewhere with a good view. Nothing wrong with enjoying the eye candy working out.

'It also meant I could check just how long it was going to take you to get to work when I need you.' She'd initially looked guiltily away at her naughty thoughts, but this comment had her attention.

'Twelve minutes, I timed it.' She raised her brows. Thankfully, her voice sounded surprisingly cool and composed and she decided maybe she shouldn't watch.

Nah. Too good an opportunity. She leant back against the house wall and ogled for the hell of it.

Rex opened the rear of the trailer and jumped up into it, and Daphne's long lounge began feeding out into Morgan's hands.

Billie watched and the day just got better. She could feel the smile curve her lips as Morgan's biceps bulged and his back straightened when he took most of the weight until Rex jumped down. Then Rex backed his end, *nice end, Rex*, she thought, and flicked an amused smile at Daphne's rapt gaze. The men heaved it towards the verandah steps and inched up. That lounge looked very heavy.

She smiled across at Daphne, who still had that dreamy look on her face. Seriously, a crooked finger towards Rex would have worked a treat, but she had the feeling Daphne would take a while to get to that point. No doubt that was where the land lay, though. Maybe she and Daphne could have a good giggle about this later, and the thought of having a friend she could share this silly stuff with was a new shiny notion she hugged to herself.

Another magical twenty minutes and all was done. It was very short work as the two well-muscled men easily set Daphne's lounge and chairs and solid coffee table in her sitting room, then rearranged the remaining furniture good-naturedly for the third time. It was a novel experience to see how extra muscles could make house shuffling a breeze. Then it was over and suddenly the kitchen was a whole lot smaller as everyone sat down.

Morgan sat next to Billie, his big frame encroaching on her

space. His muscled leg grazed hers and gave off heat from his exertion, and far from repelling her, she actually enjoyed the subtle briny scent as he reached for a plate of sandwiches.

Daphne, of course, had produced a feast, including scones and cream, and presided over the big pot of tea with a beatific expression on her face. Someone was having fun.

Billie wished Soretta was here because it felt very strange to host a tea party in someone else's house, and it might have distracted her from the man beside her to see Soretta in action when there was company.

Daphne had sent a plate of scones with that nice young internet man over to the shearing sheds to share. He said he'd worked here once before and knew where they were located, and would check out the best way of setting up wi-fi over there.

Morgan's leg shifted against hers again and Billie almost rubbed back, but instead she inched her foot away slightly. In desperation to stay centred, she clutched at the idea that this was her home for a while at least, these were her people, and how she felt more settled since moving here than she had for a long time. The concept gelled into conviction. She concentrated on the reality of waking up here tomorrow, and the next day and the next, out on the land, distanced, and not just by time, from the past.

The concept of freedom from worry about what Mia was getting up to brought a joy to her heart and a smile to her face that she hadn't expected.

Suddenly everything was easy. She turned to Morgan. Unconsciously, she shared the new lightness she could feel expanding inside her. 'Thanks so much for helping us settle in and for moving the furniture.'

His eyes widened as she blasted him with her new found happiness and he looked startled for a moment. This was the most expressive she'd seen him since meeting him. 'And thank you,' he said gravely.

She looked around the table and then back at him, then cocked an eyebrow, confused now. 'What for?'

'The smile.'

'That wasn't yours,' she said without thinking, then blushed. Cripes. She sounded like an ungrateful wretch. 'I mean,' she drew a breath, 'you're welcome.' And reached across for a scone she didn't want to give her hands something to do.

Soretta drove back for lunch to see how the tenants were going and saw the car and trailer turning out of her gate and onto the road. Apparently she'd just missed the furniture arriving. It had been kind of Daphne to send scones across with Clem, and to sort the internet over there, too, which would help enormously with keeping transient staff.

The sun glinted off the new satellite dish on the roof of the homestead and a small portion of the weight around her shoulders lifted. Another bonus. Klaus was pleased at the idea because he had a girlfriend in Germany and she wasn't happy with his email silence. And the new satellite dish would make it easier to get the ear-tagging and mustering done like they used to, when they could entice staff for heavy-workload days.

She leapt lightly up the steps onto the verandah and when she walked into the house the aroma of cooked meat moistened her tastebuds and suddenly, ridiculously, she felt like crying. It was like

NINETEEN

The following Friday at the base was one of those silly days, Billie thought, that never seemed to end. A cook on one of the muster camps slipped on a pumpkin peel and split the back of his scalp open. They'd had to fly him out to Broken Hill for an overnight stay in the high-dependency ward.

A six-year-old boy on a remote farm had burned himself playing with matches in the shed and been lucky not to be trapped in the burning building.

Morgan had taken that message and sent her out with Daphne. She'd shuddered at the close call as they'd transferred the boy to Adelaide. It had always been her worst nightmare that Mia would leave a candle burning or play with matches. Morgan must have seen her distress because he'd been very gentle with her when she returned.

Then a three-year-old girl almost drowned in a trough and needed to be monitored overnight in hospital after her parents resuscitated her. Daphne had gone alone on that call but Billie had been on tenterhooks until they'd arrived back with the good news.

Billie's shoulders felt stiff from the tension and she caught Morgan assessing her as she rolled her shoulders. She knew she

her grandmother was here again. Which was stupid because neither of the smiling women were her gran, but still she felt a warmth she hadn't sensed for two years and she had to blink several times and hope nobody would notice.

She needed to remember that these women, one of whom she barely knew and the other she'd only known for a short time, weren't here forever, but it was nice to have feminine company again. Almost as if the homestead felt welcoming instead of a guilty burden she'd shouldered as she'd tried to shield her grandfather from their loss. And maybe now it would be less responsibility to maintain the house the way her gran had liked. That load would lighten and it would all happen while she'd be doing what she needed and loved to do: work out on the land.

SEVEN

Three hours later and 10 kilometres away from Blue Hills Station, Mia's mood was not improving as she sat on the school bus, surrounded by a posse of noisy children she didn't know. She glared out the window at the passing countryside and scratched at the healing scab on her arm from the motorbike escapade.

The landscape looked like the stinking moon. Stunted trees, outcrops of rocks, and dry paddocks with straggly sheep. Not one house. Until they rounded a bend and the bus slowed. Of course the bus driver knew where she was going without her telling him. She hadn't made a sign. Everyone knew everything around here. Stupid place. The bus jerked to a stop as she grabbed her bag and stood up.

'Blue Hills Station,' the driver said. 'Pick up at seven thirty-five a.m. tomorrow.' He grinned evilly at her shocked face. 'We don't wait for slackers.'

She wasn't getting back in the stinking bus. Her mother could take her in the mornings and she could come home with Daphne.

She started the walk up the drive, which was just as long as the walk she'd had back from school in the old house. Just when she'd been getting used to living in that dump of a town. And having fun in the afternoons!

She swallowed. Except for the day she'd stacked Trent's bike. Trent had been so good about that. She really liked him and now she'd never see him except with three hundred other people around at school. She was going to die of boredom out here.

As she walked up the steep dusty track towards the house she heard what sounded like a truck slow down on the road and turn into the drive. She kept walking with her head lowered, but the vehicle was noisily coming up the driveway behind her.

A rattly four-wheel drive utility pulled up and a cloud of dust enveloped her, swirling round her feet then rising until she was suffocating. This day just kept getting better.

She coughed and turned her head, and saw a blue-eyed jillaroo type leaning across to open the door. 'You must be Mia. I'm Soretta. Jump in.'

Soretta. The landlady. Not a lot she could do about the choice of getting in, then. So Mia opened the square door wider and climbed up into the dusty cabin of the vehicle.

'Hi,' she mumbled, clutching her school satchel and digging her fingers into the canvas material.

Soretta frowned. 'What's wrong with you?'

Embarrassed at being caught out feeling sorry for herself, her cheeks heated. 'Nothing.'

She glanced swiftly at the woman with her red hair pulled back from her sun-browned face and met the no-nonsense eyes. The jillaroo shrugged and revved the engine to start up the hill again, then changed gears. 'You'll get used to the bus.'

Well, she wasn't going to get used to it. 'I doubt it.'

Soretta shrugged again and Mia got the impression that she didn't care either way. Mia bunched the satchel under her fingers

harder. She was going to hate this place. The engine roared as they climbed the hill to the house.

Soretta must have thought the same. 'Do you even like animals?'

'I love animals.' That was true enough. 'Just never had a chance to have any.'

'Lucky, then. I'll show you how to feed the orphan lambs I've been keeping in the laundry shed. I usually get home later than this and they're starving by the time I arrive. It's not really working and I was going to have to put them back with the mob earlier than I wanted. It would help if you could start feeding them when you get off the bus in the afternoons.'

'I don't know how.'

Soretta looked at her. 'It's not rocket science. You'll only need to watch once.'

Mia wasn't sure if she should be offended or pleased that Soretta had already given her a job. But the idea of a lamb she could talk to and maybe even name was almost cool.

Soretta pulled up outside the steps of the house but didn't turn off the engine. 'Jump out. I'll put the ute away in the shed.'

'Oh. Okay. Thanks for the lift.' Mia climbed down and shut the door.

Soretta didn't answer, she just drove away.

Strange person, Mia thought a little wildly, and looked up at the sound of the door opening. Her mother came out of the screen door onto the big shaded verandah looking too stinking happy.

Billie spread her arms. 'Welcome home, Mia. Isn't it fabulous?'

Mia couldn't help herself. The words tumbled out with all the confusion of being seriously out of her comfort zone. 'No! I hate it. I hate the bus. I want to live in town.'

Her mother looked like she was going to snap back at her but didn't. Just closed her eyes and Mia bet she was counting to ten. Well, all the counting to ten in the world wasn't going to make her like this place. No siree.

She heard her mother sigh. She hated it when her mother did that. 'Come in when you can be civil and say hello to Daphne.'

Damn. She'd forgotten Daphne would be here, too. Daphne didn't deserve her bad temper. *Neither did her mother,* a tiny voice whispered, and she could feel the heat in her cheeks. She hadn't meant to let it all explode out of her like that, but she'd felt on the back foot all day knowing she had to get on a strange bus and then meeting Soretta hadn't helped, as she'd made her feel like a dumbo. Now she felt small and she hated that, too. 'Sorry,' she mumbled, and followed her mother inside.

Her mother stopped suddenly and Mia ran into the back of her.

It was something she hadn't done for years, but when she'd been younger it seemed to happen all the time and they'd both end up laughing at her clumsiness. For it to occur now so unexpectedly, after feeling blue for most of the day, made Mia giggle like the little girl she used to be.

Billie turned and leant forward to hug her daughter. 'Thank goodness for that. Give it a go,' she said quietly, 'I think this is going to work out fine.'

Ten minutes later Mia followed Soretta down the steps and across the yard to a leaning outbuilding that looked like it had been there for a hundred years. It probably had, though the house was pretty cool.

They passed a heavily pregnant brown kelpie and her mate, a black-and-tan fellow with pointy ears and a bouncing step. Mia loved dogs, had always wanted one, and she bent down to pat them both.

She looked up at Soretta, who was watching her. 'What are the dogs' names?'

'George and Gigi.'

Mia repeated the names in her mind so she would remember. Stood up again and marvelled at the swinging teats of the mother dog. 'When are the pups due?'

'Soon. I'm making her a safe place.'

When Soretta opened the shed door, Mia saw a big old child's playpen in the corner of the floor sitting on a tarpaulin and two eager creamy lambs butted against the bars.

Soretta said, 'I put them inside when I come home and we let them back into the lamb yard in the morning. There's a pack of wild dogs getting pretty cheeky at the moment.'

Mia shuddered and her attention was again fixed on the fluffy animals. They were like toys. She could feel her mouth curve as she fought to remain disinterested. She really hadn't wanted to come here. But it was too much for her.

'So what do you feed them?' Mia lounged against the door and tried not to laugh out loud as they gambolled and jumped with the excitement of approaching milk.

Soretta raised her eyebrows. Didn't say anything except, 'Pseudo Shepherd, two hundred and fifty mils twice a day.'

She watched Soretta walk towards a cracked slate benchtop beside a steel sink with those old brass laundry taps you saw in books. Then she watched her pick up a bottle she'd had soaking

and tip the water out of it. 'How many scoops in the bottle?'

'Are you interested in taking on the job?' Soretta said, her tone noncommittal.

Yes. But she didn't want to fall on her neck. 'I suppose so.'

Apparently that didn't wash. 'If you don't want to, that's fine. But there's no suppose about it, princess. They die if you forget.'

Mia could feel her cheeks warm. The boss lady was no push-over like her mother, but very strangely that was okay. She stood up away from the door and dropped her fake disinterest. 'Yes, please. How many scoops?'

Soretta pointed to the bag. 'Read it. I can tell you but if I'm not here and you forget how are you going to find out? You'll need to do it in the morning and at night. As they eat more solid food we wean them down to one feed before we let them out.'

When Mia learned the correct number of scoops, Soretta showed her how to make up the milk powder and put a teat on the end of each bottle. When they pushed the teats through the bars of the playpen, Mia laughed out loud at the eager way the lambs butted against the bottles. She glanced at Soretta shyly. 'Thanks for showing me.'

'One less job. Though we've got a few weeks of lambing to go so you'll probably end up with more before the season's over. My grandad reckons it's a waste of money when others are dying, but I need the comfort of them sometimes.'

Mia nodded. 'I can see how they'd make you smile.' Her face felt stretched in a grin so wide she thought it would split as tiny woolly heads bumped their wet noses against her knees through the playpen columns. And there would be puppies to come, too. Brand new puppies. She couldn't wait.

'In the morning drag the tarp out and hang it over the fence and bring it back in before you bring the lambs back for the night.' She gave Mia a penetrating stare. 'You right with that?'

'Sure.' She'd have to be. Soretta could be a scary woman. It was only later that she realised that while she was feeding the lambs she'd somehow forgotten about her own bad mood.

Three days later at the start of the new week, Billie paused beside Morgan's desk and waited until he looked up. 'Thanks for coming out on Friday, and helping with the furniture.'

She just might have caught the hint of a smile there in his face. 'You're welcome. It looks like an interesting set-up.'

Billie thought about the occasional territorial awkwardness that seemed to have all but disappeared by Sunday night. 'We had a great weekend.' She laughed. 'For a couple of single ladies looking for a home with a difference it's perfect. And Mia loves the animals.'

He raised his brows. 'Hope Lachlan finds it convivial when he comes home from the hospital. I'm afraid it's not my idea of fun living with that many women.'

Now why would he say that? And the fact that she was spending a little time worrying about the same thing made him even more annoying. *Grr.* 'I was thinking you seemed like a bit of a misogynist.'

She felt his scrutiny like a warm breeze, appreciative yet impersonal and sparing nothing. She wasn't sure how he did it but it couldn't be misconstrued as sexual, more analytical, because she felt like she came up short every time he did it. 'Oh, I like women all right. Just not en masse.'

She tossed her hair back and straightened. 'I like men. Just don't want to live with one.'

The words and a long look reverberated between them. Finally he said, 'I'll remember that.'

She stepped away as if she'd forgotten the conversation already but could feel his eyes on her back. Well, for goodness sake. She'd just said thank you, she hadn't asked for a discussion about whether she'd done the right thing moving out there. And why did she always feel like she was the loser in the conversation? She was out of her depth with him. Admit it. Face it. Get over it.

Four days later Mia found the brown kelpie, Gigi, panting under the tank stand. She'd been checking every morning before she went to school and as soon as she came home in the afternoon. All the angst about moving out of town was forgotten as the lambs and the dogs and the speed with which she was learning from Soretta had captivated her in a way she hadn't expected. She certainly wasn't going to tell her mother how much she was loving it all, but she had to admit that life was pretty darn good. They even had a four-wheel motorbike that Soretta said she'd teach her to drive.

But now, this moment, was the best. Because after a closer look, she could see that half a dozen squeaking puppies surrounded Gigi.

Mia gasped as she peered under the shade of the tank. The dog looked at her and then away at her rear end, and then, incredibly, another puppy squeezed out under Gigi's tail in its missile-shaped amniotic sack to plop onto the ground. The shiny tube of puppy gladwrap lay still on the warm leaf mulch and Mia didn't know what to do. Should she touch it, leave it alone, call for help?

Then Gigi stretched slowly, taking her time, before she licked gently at the sac, until she broke through to the still puppy inside and proceeded to stroke it firmly now with her tongue until the little head with its tightly shut eyes lifted up and whimpered. The unhurried pattern of resuscitation was the most incredible thing she'd ever seen and Mia's respect for the animal kingdom soared.

This was a moment in time that crystallised into a thought that had been growing inside her all week. She actually knew what she wanted to do with her life. Now she understood how her mother could say she'd always wanted to be a flying doctor. Mia got it, because, as of this moment she wanted to be a vet.

Gigi wagged her tail as if to say, Look what I've done. 'Hello there, Gigi, you clever thing,' Mia whispered, and waited to see if the dog was unhappy about her presence near her puppies, but Gigi just wagged her tail more. 'Okay. Then let's have a look and see how many you have.' Careful not to get too close, Mia counted the puppies. Four brown and three black with brown markings. 'Seven babies. You champion. Soooo cute.'

Eyes shut and squirming, the puppies wriggled and squeaked and Gigi pushed them around with her nose, upending each one to check its tummy and Mia could have watched for hours. But she wanted to share the news with someone.

Then another one arrived and it all began again. Instilled with faith at Gigi's natural capabilities, Mia knew it would be okay to leave her so that she could tell Daphne.

Easing away slowly, Mia stood and ran back up the stairs to Daphne, whom Mia felt had been a part of their lives for years, not weeks.

'The puppies are here,' she called. Daphne came out wiping her

hands on a tea towel and her face lit up. 'That's exciting. Show me.'

Together they crept back to look over the edge of the rockery to the small enclave Gigi had decided was much better than the nice bed Soretta had made for her in the shed.

'Why didn't she like the shed?' Daphne asked and Mia frowned.

'I thought about that. Maybe it just smelled too much like humans? I'll ask Soretta when she comes home. Do you think she'll let me keep one?'

Daphne tilted her head. 'Your mother?'

'No. I meant Soretta,' Mia said. 'Mum will because she's happy here and we won't end up in a flat this time. I hate flats.'

Mia looked around the nooks and crannies of the tank stand and worried about snakes. 'Should we move them to the shed?'

Daphne frowned. 'I've never had puppies but I don't think we can. Even if Gigi let us, I think she'd just bring them back here.'

Soretta agreed when she got home. 'I'll sort something tomorrow. At least she seems to have managed well and they all look healthy.'

Mia frowned. 'Does it always go well?'

'Usually. Dogs are instinctive and don't get strange ideas like humans do. Though sometimes dogs accidently lie on their puppies, which is why I thought she'd be better in the shed.' She looked searchingly at her. 'In all the excitement did you feed the lambs?'

Mia nodded, still thinking about the puppies. 'Yep. They look good, too. That biggest one is being a hog, though.'

'Lambs can't be pigs,' Soretta said straight-faced and Mia stared at her, her jaw almost dropping.

'Did you just make a joke?'

Soretta grinned. 'Cheeky bugger.'

EIGHT

Two weeks later Daphne had returned from a cardiac retrieval to Adelaide when she heard Billie take a call from Pallinup Station. She listened while she restocked the cupboard. The door was open so Daphne could hear the conversation clearly over the loudspeaker.

'Pallinup Station here. We need the flying doctor. The cook's cut his finger off and now he's fainted.'

Daphne bet she knew who that was. She saw Rex look up and shake his head. They grinned at each other, then Rex called out to Billie, 'Forty minutes till arrival time,' as he headed out the door to prepare the aircraft again.

Billie's voice was calm. 'He's fainted you say? Is his breathing okay?'

'Yep, and he's got a hard head.' The woman's voice was settling down in response to Billie's steadiness. 'I guess he'll come round in a minute.'

Daphne suppressed a smile as Billie said, 'Have you managed to control the bleeding from the stump?'

'My husband's holding a pressure bandage on it so it's probably good he's out. We're binding it while he's still too groggy and

can't complain. The bleeding seems to be slowing. Do we put a tourniquet on?'

Billie said, 'If you can manage, elevate it instead. If he's on the floor you could loosely support his wrist on a chair above his head. Tourniquet only if you can't stop major blood loss. It can interfere with reattaching the finger.'

'Okay.'

Billie said, 'Um, do you still have the finger?'

The voice sounded slightly fainter. 'Yes, but I can't stand looking at it.'

Poor Rita. Daphne knew the station manager's wife and she was a good egg but squeamish. Accidental Al was the last person you should have working for you if you were squeamish.

'Sorry.' Billie bit her lip and Daphne reckoned she was trying not to smile, too, even though it was an emergency. 'If you can, get someone to pick it up with a clean cloth and drop it into a plastic bag. Have you got any of those snap-lock plastic bags?'

'Yep, we use them for the meat when we butcher.' There was the sound of a small retch. Daphne finished her restocking and grabbed a couple of extra bandages for the trip and two ice packs that activated to cold when you squeezed them.

She saw Billie wince sympathetically. 'Okay. When it's in the bag, leave a bit of air in there to cushion it, then seal it. Pop a couple of ice cubes in a bowl with a lid, and some water, and float the bag in there to keep it cool. Don't let the finger touch the ice. The aircraft will be there in forty minutes. If he needs pain relief ring me back and I'll stand by for support when you give the injection.'

Rita made a funny strangled noise that was almost a laugh. 'I don't think he'll need that. He's scared of needles.'

Billie frowned. 'But not knives?'

'He should be,' Rita said with a sigh. 'Thank you. He's waking up now. We'll see how we go.'

'Phone back if you're worried.'

'Will do.'

Billie raised her voice towards Daphne. 'There's a cook out at Pallinup, he's amputated his finger. I'm guessing you and Rex are right to go?'

Daphne tried to keep the grin off her face. 'Yep.' A chuckle escaped and she saw the look Billie gave her and shook her head, pulling her mouth back under control. 'Sorry. It's Accidental Al.'

'Why does that ring a bell?' Then Billie also smiled. 'I remember now. The guy with the nail gun in the leg.'

'Yep.'

'Did you hear the conversation?'

'Got it all. Rex will be ready and we know where to go. This is our third trip out there in three months. The first time he got buried under a pile of hay bales trying to catch a rat and almost suffocated.'

'It's a wonder he's still got a job if he's that accident-prone.'

'Yeah, well, he drinks a bit, but the guy is an absolute champion, cooks like a dream, and has a heart as big as the desert. Hard to fire him, I guess.'

When Daphne and Rex arrived at the scene, Al was sitting sheepishly, and a little pale, in the front seat of the boss's utility waiting for the plane. He had a lidded ice-cream container on his lap. Daphne couldn't see through it but assumed it held the severed digit.

'Hi, Al,' Daphne said breezily. 'How's the pain?'

'Okay.' She wasn't surprised. She guessed that Al's incredibly high pain tolerance was nature's way of compensating for his attraction to disaster.

She took his pulse and blood pressure and they were remarkably normal. Typical Al. 'Going to pop a cannula in, Al, in case it starts to bleed in flight.' The young man tinged green and Daphne remembered his needle phobia. 'You know they'll have to put one in for theatre so at least it'll be already there.'

'You never hurt me, Daphne.' He shuddered. 'It's just the thought.'

'When did you last eat?'

'Just before I started cutting up the vegies for lunch.'

Daphne checked her watch. 'So eleven a.m.?'

'Yep.'

'Last drink?'

'You mean me last blinder?'

Daphne laughed. 'I'm guessing that was last night.' She hid the flash of the needle in the sunlight as she wiped his arm. Deftly, she inserted the cannula and Al didn't notice. There was a high-octane emission occurring every time Al breathed on her. 'I meant the last time today you had water or non-alcoholic fluids. So I can tell them for planning your surgery.'

'Just a mug of tea this morning.'

'Okay. So no more food or fluids till they've seen you. You know the routine.'

Al sighed. 'I should.' He looked at her with his big blue eyes, confused by the vagrancies of fate. 'Why do you reckon this happens to me, Daphne?'

Daphne smiled gently. 'Why do you reckon it happens after a blinder, Al?'

He shook his head sadly and sincerely. 'It's a bleedin' mystery. That's what it is.'

All was right in Daphne's world. She and Rex had left their patient in Adelaide, where he was on the way to surgery to reattach his finger, and they were on the home run with just the two of them in the aircraft.

Rex always invited her in to the cockpit when they had the chance and she loved it. It wasn't often, though, that they had no other passengers. The service actually encouraged the nurses to observe the habits of the pilots in case of pilot illness in an emergency, and Daphne had no problem observing Rex.

The cockpit smelt faintly of Rex's inexpensive, old-fashioned cologne, one that her ex-husband would never deign to use thankfully, and she decided again that she liked it very much.

They'd taken off in silence, Rex murmuring to the tower via his microphone, and she allowed her gaze to rest briefly on the hand holding the control. A strong, work-worn hand, with piano-player fingers, guiding the aircraft not just by science and technology, but with an inherent instinct she'd admired in dire times. She admired it now just for the pleasure of it.

He must have noticed her watching because he looked across and gave her one of his warm and toe-wriggling smiles that she hugged to herself and stored away for the nights she couldn't sleep.

'I love to fly.' He glanced around with that unobtrusive alertness he carried at all times, gesturing with one hand. 'Love my job.'

He looked so relaxed as he flew the aircraft home and yet she could feel her cheeks heating when all she wanted was to be calm and

collected . . . and attractive to him. She loved being here with him.

'You love it too, don't you, Daphne?'

For a moment there she thought he knew she fancied him and then she got the drift. 'Yes. Yes I do. I feel privileged to be able to share the importance of what we do.'

He nodded, looking happy. 'That's exactly how I feel.'

But at the moment she was thinking how much she enjoyed these quiet times with Rex. How he'd never look at her the way she dreamt he would but that it was okay. She was happy with this.

She breathed in deeply and basked in her surroundings. She never tired of the expanse of sky and land in front of her. It was magic looking out of the cabin windows down the back, but nothing beat the uninterrupted vista of the cockpit and the view ahead.

They flew on over brown land with darker snakes of dry creek beds and the occasional slag heap of an abandoned mine.

Rex broke the silence and interrupted her thoughts. 'The Silver City Cup is on back at Broken Hill next month. You ever been?'

'No. Never been,' she said. 'I didn't know you were a punter, Rex.'

'Not a punter. I'm just a mug. I do like the country race meets, though. Thought I might stay a couple of nights. I'd like your company if you want to come.'

Daphne froze and the view outside the window pixelated. She slowly turned her face towards him but he was looking straight out the windshield at the sky ahead. That was good because she knew her cheeks were an ugly red and getting redder. She turned back to the window and moistened her suddenly dry mouth. Tried to keep the nervousness out of her voice. *Be nonchalant*, she ordered silently. 'I'd like that.'

She turned back to see him grin at her and she stored that one away, too. 'Fine. We'll sort it out next week.'

That afternoon on the main verandah overlooking the paddocks the blue hills were splashed with the gold of sunset. Four wicker chairs and a couple of side tables had gravitated to where Daphne and Billie usually settled in for their half hour before tea. There was a lovely view over the blue bush and shiny outcrops of rocks and down to the road, while the actual heat of the sun was shaded by the big gum tree beside the house.

They'd started the ritual of an evening cup of tea so that they could all sit together, relax or just chat about their day or whatever was coming up, and even Soretta had begun to drift in to join them.

Daphne thought about the day. There was only her and Billie so far and they sat in companionable silence. She thought about Rex's offer, about how much she'd been hurt before because a man had believed she was more than she was, and how terrified she was that it could happen again.

She checked that Mia wasn't on the other side of the kitchen window before speaking in a low voice. 'Billie? Can I ask you a personal question?'

Billie looked up from the iPad she was skimming. Switched it off and sat up straighter, giving Daphne her full attention, and making her nervous once more. 'Sure, Daphne. We're friends aren't we?'

Warmth stole under her ribs and her nerves settled a little. 'I like to think so.'

Billie leaned over and topped up her cup with the teapot. 'We are. And I value your friendship. So spill.'

'Thank you. I value your friendship, too. I guess it's more advice that I'm after.'

Billie raised her eyebrows, giving her a slow smile. 'About a man? Because if it's about men I'm not so hot on that subject.' She shrugged.

Daphne laughed. 'Good. I won't feel so stupid then. Have you had boyfriends?'

'I've had dates,' Billie said cautiously.

Daphne could sense a thread of something darker in her new friend's voice.

Billie looked pensive before she said very quietly, 'And one short, very bad relationship that should never have happened, but that was a long time ago.'

Daphne checked that they were alone again and lowered her voice further. 'Mia's father?'

'Hmm. But what was your question?' Billie took a sip of her tea.

Fair enough. *Stop prying, Daphne*, she scolded herself. 'Rex asked me to go to the Silver City races at Broken Hill next month for a couple of nights.'

The smile on Billie's face as she turned to look at her made Daphne's cheeks heat for a second time. 'Just as a friend, of course.'

'Oh, of course.' Billie grinned. Then she said, 'You sure?'

Her cheeks burned. 'He said he'd booked two rooms for two nights.'

Billie shook her head, the smile still in her eyes. 'Well, he couldn't exactly book one, could he? That would be presumptuous.

I'm very pleased for you. If I'm not mistaken, you've actually noticed Rex's sterling qualities before. You were watching him pretty closely when he was moving furniture.'

'And you were watching Morgan,' Daphne remembered with delayed insight. But then, as if ready to say it out loud properly, she admitted, 'I do like Rex. A lot. But I didn't think he'd ask me out.' Daphne still marvelled at the unexpectedness of it. 'And to make it more stressful he's bought tickets for the race marquee. I used to be horribly shy at social events, which was tragic as far as my ex and my father were concerned. Thankfully, since I've been nursing it's helped me realise what's really important to me, so I'm not so bad now.' She shrugged. 'But I'm a little worried I'll pick the wrong things to wear. I don't know if I want to put myself through that.' There. It was out and now, she hoped, Billie would help her get a grip.

Billie smiled reassuringly and it sort of helped. 'But it's not like Rex doesn't know you better than a lot of other men. He probably wanted to spoil you with the marquee. It's not usually something men choose for themselves. You'll be fine with Rex. He's seen you in action, Daphne. The real you. You're a star.'

The heat rushed back into her cheeks. 'No, I'm not.'

Billie frowned. 'I can see I'll have to stand beside you at the bathroom mirror every morning and make you say it. Daphne is a star!'

They heard footsteps and Soretta crossed the yard just as Billie said the words and she smiled at them both as she leapt up the steps.

'You are, you know.' She turned to Billie. 'You should've seen her the day my grandad was hurt. The plane steps came down and

Daphne striding across with her kit was the best thing I've ever seen in my life.' Soretta's eyes glinted with the memories and she brushed the moisture away.

'You were incredible,' she said to Daphne. 'Like a machine saving his life.' She leant down and hugged her warmly, which was all the more surprising because Soretta didn't give away hugs liberally and Daphne thought her throat was going to close. 'I'll never forget you saving my grandad that day.'

Daphne swallowed. Her own eyes filled and her face felt hot. It was probably all blotchy with emotion. 'Stop it. I was doing my job.'

'You did everything better and faster than I'd seen it ever done before. And when I thanked Rex, he said you were the awesome one.'

Rex thought she was awesome? There was the problem. She was none of those things. And he'd see it when they were surrounded by beautifully dressed and assured women at the races, just like her ex had. Just like she'd always been a disappointment to her father despite her many step 'aunties' trying to make a 'silk glove out of a sow's ear', as one of them had said.

'Just say thank you.' Billie patted her arm. 'Funny how that's one of the hardest things we seem to have to do.'

Soretta nodded and agreed. 'I know. If someone says, you do a good job on the station, I wince. It feels undeserved. And I usually end up saying something stupid like, "not as good as I should", and then I think, hang on a minute. I'm doing a freaking fabulous job here.' She shrugged. 'Must be a woman thing.'

'I think so.' Daphne thought about Morgan or even Rex. 'Rex would never say he wasn't a good pilot if someone complimented him.'

'Let's make a new pact,' Billie said. 'About compliments and accepting them. We will practise.'

Oh, Lord.

'And if you want me to come shopping with you for a new frock, bag, shoes, whatever, just let me know.'

Billie's suggestion was tempting, but all Daphne could remember were the horrible times when she'd been dragged and pulled into clothes she hated. 'Thanks. I'll think about it.' With dread.

'Where's Mia?' Billie looked past Soretta towards the shed.

'She's in with the puppies. That girl can't get enough of them. Then she said she was going over to check on one of the lambs we weaned. She'll be fine.'

Daphne's gaze met Billie's in shared amusement. What Soretta meant was, 'She'd better not get into strife or else!'

The day dawned hot and dry like the hundred before and it'd just get hotter. Soretta glared accusingly at the cloudless sky. The dam had completely dried now, the first time that she could remember it happening, though grandad had seen it before, and she needed to check the far troughs because the sheep were getting desperate anytime the bore water slowed up.

Yesterday she'd seen two small kangaroos in there with the sheep trying to catch the water as it pumped from the bore. She'd checked the house tanks last night and they hadn't used as much water as she'd feared considering the influx of people and the extra drain on water resources. Her housemates were good people.

The phone rang, and she grinned to herself because she'd have to answer it. It was lunchtime and her house was empty for

a change. The phone had been one thing she hadn't had to deal with lately, though it had been ringing more than ever with all the women in the house.

Normally Mia was onto it like a shot, but she was still at school. 'Is that you, Soretta?'

She couldn't place the voice. 'Yes. Who's this?'

'Just the person I wanted. Lorna Lamerton. I came out a month ago with Daphne.'

The old doctor's wife. A sweetie and quite a card, Soretta thought. 'Yes, Mrs Lamerton. I remember. What can I do for you?'

The voice was hesitant and Soretta wiped the hallway table with her finger while she waited. No dust. And she hadn't done the hall yet. Daphne was encroaching on her cleaning duties, she could see. The voice strengthened and Soretta paid attention. 'I wondered if you still had any rooms to let. Or have you reached capacity?'

Soretta lifted her head and stared at the wall. Had she reached capacity? Could the house hold any more? It was working well now. Might another person create problems? She still had to settle her grandfather back into a world of women he wasn't used to when he came out of hospital, but he had his own room. And she was making headway with the bills so he had no excuse to rush into selling.

She stalled. 'Do you know someone who needs accommodation?' If it was a man maybe they could stay down at the quarters with Klaus. She needed an extra farmhand who wasn't a boarder.

'Just one. A single woman.'

She could probably take one more single. And a woman would be easier than a single man in the house considering the bathroom

situation. Another hundred dollars a week and that was decent income once a month until the rain came.

'Do they know it's a shared bathroom? My grandfather has his but the rest of us share.'

'It's for me, dear. Just for a couple of months as a wee break for my son and his wife. Just for a holiday with all you lovely ladies.'

Soretta tried to keep her face straight. It would be a wee break for Lorna away from her son's wife. Interesting times coming up. 'In that case I'm sure we could fit you in, Mrs Lamerton. When would you like to come?'

'I was thinking a taxi could bring me out tonight.'

'How about I pick you up after I visit my grandfather this afternoon. Around five?'

'That would be lovely.'

Billie put down the note Soretta had left and smiled at Daphne. 'You say she's eighty?'

'Turned eighty recently. She was an outback nurse fifty years ago and she's quicker on her feet than I am.'

Billie looked sceptical. 'Never.'

'Maybe not,' Daphne conceded, 'but tough as old leather and been the doctor's wife for almost that long. Nursed him through the last two years of terminal dementia at home. She's not a frail eighty.' Daphne's voice dropped to a softer note. 'She remembers your parents.'

An unexpected sadness buffeted Billie, like a willy-willy passing, leaving her disorientated and churning and covered in memories. But then she thought of the little house and the new family living

there. And of having a job she loved in the town her parents had loved. It was good to be back in Mica Ridge.

Last week she'd taken Mia past her old home on the way to school and talked about her memories of growing up there and in the town. Mia had listened quietly and even leaned across and kissed her before she'd got out.

After a minute Billie said, 'I've never known anyone except for my aunt who remembered my parents.'

'Lorna said you were young when they died.'

'Sixteen. The same as Mia is now.' Billie thought about that and shuddered. Who would look after her daughter if anything happened to her? She forced the words out in as light a tone as she could manage. 'There aren't any aunts left now, so I'd better stay healthy.'

'I'm sure you will.' She heard the hesitation in Daphne's voice. 'But remember, Mia is your daughter and she's had the best example of what rising above heartbreak and challenges means.'

There was actual comfort in those words. And the fact that Billie had set up a trust fund that ensured Mia would be housed and educated for as long as she needed.

Still, Billie looked at this woman she'd known for barely a month, and except for those first few years when Mia had been young and her aunt had been there, she'd never had a friend like Daphne before.

'How did you get to be so wise?'

'I'm not wise,' Daphne said. 'I'd better get back to the kitchen. Wise cooks don't let their cakes burn.'

'I can't imagine you doing that.' Billie called after her. 'I'll look forward to seeing if Lorna likes to cook. Maybe you'll have to fight for the kitchen.'

Daphne turned back, blinked, and then saw Billie was teasing her and started to laugh. 'Having to fight for cooking, that would be a change,' she teased.

They both knew Daphne revelled in it.

NINE

Lorna arrived with Soretta at ten past five in the afternoon. She'd packed two old polished leather suitcases, which must have been worth a lot of money in the days before weighing suitcases made leather carry-ons a niche market.

Soretta and Mia heaved the suitcases up the stairs with strain on their red faces, while Billie hid her smile and was glad the young ones were here to carry.

Lorna Lamerton had dressed for the occasion. Her purple hair had been recently permed and pouffed, her cream cashmere twin-set, while it had short sleeves, seemed too hot for the warmth of the afternoon, even though it did set off the beautiful crystal flower spray brooch she wore, accompanied by stockings and black buckled shoes that were definitely too hot.

Billie found herself saying, 'Welcome to the ranks of the Homestead Girls,' off the top of her head, and she had no idea where that came from but it amused her. Soretta laughed.

Daphne held the door for the straining porters and Mia followed Soretta, panting, trying not to drag the suitcase down the hallway to Lorna's new room that Daphne had polished to within an inch of its life.

Lorna inclined her head regally, but the twinkle in her eyes hinted at the mischief and glee bursting inside her at being here. Billie suspected Lorna was very much looking forward to diving into their world and remembered Daphne saying how lonely she'd been since her husband had passed away.

Billie held out her hand and shook the soft fingers of their new housemate and squeezed them. 'You are very welcome and I for one can't wait to hear about your days as a nurse in the outback.'

Lorna squeezed back. 'I remember your mother, dear. You have the look of her. She was a beautiful woman. I'm sure your parents would be very proud of you, young Williamina, back here as a flying doctor. I'm a big supporter of the service.'

'Thank you.' Williamina. Nobody had called her that for years. She stepped back, feeling like she'd just had an audience with the queen, and Daphne ushered the older lady in after her luggage.

Billie gazed after her and had the feeling that Lorna was going to be an interesting and amusing fifth housemate.

Lorna was soon ensconced in her room and Daphne encouraged her to consider the sitting room she used hers as well. Billie had no doubt that Daphne would enjoy the extra company.

She wondered how Mia would find living with an older lady. Her daughter had been very young when Billie's aunt had died and she'd never had the opportunity to interact with a grandmotherly figure.

Another benefit was there would be someone at the homestead practically all the time now, and perhaps Soretta's grandfather might be able to come home from the hospital a little earlier than he otherwise would have.

That would have two effects at least. Hopefully, Lachlan would be happier in his own house than the hospital, though now that it

was full of women it would be very different to what he remembered. And the other positive would be that Soretta would be able to cease her time-consuming trips to town to visit him and the costs involved in that.

The phone rang and Billie picked it up before Mia could swoop.

It was Morgan. Brief and to the point. 'Head into town, will you, we're on stand-by for a major incident. Bring Daphne.'

She didn't bother to ask why. Just popped her head into Lorna's room, where Daphne was helping her settle in.

'Morgan wants us in town on stand-by. You right to leave in five minutes?'

Daphne looked up at Billie, before turning to Lorna, who looked more excited than fazed by the fact that her hostesses were leaving her immediately.

'Shoo,' Lorna said with an expansive wave of the hands. 'I'll be fine. I lived with a man leaving at the drop of a hat for fifty years.'

'Silly me. Of course you will.' Daphne smiled. 'Coming, Billie.'

They arrived at the base within the fifteen minutes of Morgan's call, and while it all seemed calm there was a tense set to Morgan's mouth that Billie could see. She wondered if the others noticed. Rex was there, as were Hector and Michael, though Rex and Hector were on their way out the door to ready their aircraft.

'Unconfirmed multiple trauma near Belly Girth Bluff. Sounds like a school excursion bus from Sydney, so possibly up to twenty children and two teachers. We're waiting for the local cattle truck driver to arrive on site—he picked up the two-way call that no one else heard and called us. We'll have to assess the need to fly the critical direct to Adelaide and maybe get some help from Broken Hill.'

'Trauma kits and neck braces, then,' Daphne muttered and

hurried off to the storeroom. Michael followed her, which left Billie and Morgan alone. Morgan was on the computer zeroing in on the apparent site of the accident and Billie leaned over his shoulder. 'I hate these situations,' he said. 'The waiting for confirmation when you know you could be on your way and maybe get there before someone dies. But both teams will take off as soon as they can.'

She got that. 'Do you know exactly where it is?'

He shook his head. 'Nope. The call came through on a patchy cell. Somewhere near here.' He pointed to the screen. 'Our contact is taking a load of goats through the back way and is driving out to find the site. He's got a satellite phone.'

Just then the phone rang and Morgan picked it up with slow deliberation. Billie drew a breath and held it. Morgan switched on the loudspeaker.

'It's Tom, from Cart'n'go. Hello.'

'We hear you, Tom. Have you on loudspeaker. Have you found the site?'

'My word I've found it. Dog's breakfast is what it is. That bus won't drive again.'

'Can you give us a location?' Morgan was to the point.

Tom didn't seem to mind. 'Belly Girth Bluff junction. The sign says ninety-seven kilometres to the border and a hundred and fifty to Mica Ridge. He must've missed the turn.'

Billie frowned at the map. That was near Barbara Tomkins's place.

Morgan went on. 'Nearest station with landing strip?'

She heard Tom say, 'I'd reckon Golden Ridge. Nineteen kilometres, it says on the road sign here.' Billie nodded in satisfaction. She was getting the hang of this.

'Right. How many injured?'

'Just got here, mate, but I'll put you onto one of the teachers.' There was a brief offside conversation and then a woman's voice came on.

'Georgina Harvey. Teacher at St Fergus School. Who am I speaking to?'

'Morgan Fraser, at Mica Ridge Flying Doctor Base. Georgina, when you're ready can you give me an idea of the injured to the best of your knowledge please.'

They heard the big indrawn breath as the woman wrestled with composure and then in a remarkably steady voice she said, 'Bob, the bus driver, has had a heart attack I think. He slumped and the bus crashed. I managed with some of the boys to get him out of the bus and we performed cardiac massage.' She took a shuddering breath. 'It worked but he's in pain, sitting up and conscious.'

'Good job, Georgina. Sitting him up and keeping him quiet is all you can do now. Can you tell me how many people in total on the bus?'

'Twenty children aged from nine to eleven and two teachers.'

Morgan's voice was steady and calm. 'That's great. Are you hurt at all yourself?'

There was another shuddering breath. 'No. I bumped my head but I'm okay. The other teacher has a broken leg I think, and he hit his head, too. He's not making much sense, but he's trapped in the seat he fell into when the bus hit the boulder and when we tried to move him he said not to. So I can't do much there.'

She went on, the words coming faster now that she had someone to share them with. 'Luckily most of the children had their seatbelts on and the bus is generally intact. I have two ten-year-olds

who were knocked out when they hit the bar on the seat in front, but both are awake now and breathing fine.' She gave a shaky laugh. 'One girl is a notorious fainter, so I'm hoping hers was just shock, and several others are complaining of being unable to move their arms without it hurting.'

She stopped. As if the torrent of words had exhausted her. Her voice cracked. 'Sorry. Cuts and bruises and crying. I don't know where to start.'

'You've done a great job already. We'll be there as quickly as we can. We'll stay on the line to give you advice until then.'

'So what should I do now?'

'You started at the most important place. Get Tom to help you check everyone again. He'll help you find any major problems, but it sounds like you have it pretty much under control. Tom will have another first-aid kit. Have someone stay with the kids who were knocked out. You right with that?'

'Yes.' She sounded composed again and Billie felt her throat tighten in sympathy. People were amazing when they had to be.

Morgan was saying, 'We'll contact the owners of the nearest station. They'll come out to help until we get there. Two aircraft will take off in a few minutes with a doctor and two nurses.' He glanced at the map. 'They'll land on the road. So plan on trying to keep people calm and out of the sun until we get there. I'll organise another bus for the walking wounded. Keep everyone together and don't let them wander off.'

After a tense flight into the setting sun, Billie, Daphne, Michael, the two pilots and all their emergency gear were driven the hundred

metres to the crash site by Lionel, Barbara's husband, who shook Billie's, Rex's and Daphne's hands warmly, his big eyes crinkling with a flash of pleasure at seeing them.

'Prefer better circumstances to see you guys,' he drawled, his expression grave, as he drove speedily along the dirt track to the crash site. 'Barb and Gwyn are down there to help with the children.'

He slowed for an emu that dashed in front of the car. 'Was thinking we might be better moving the ones that are okay to the station and put them all up for the night instead of moving them on, but we didn't want to move anyone until you could sus them out.'

'Sounds like a plan,' Billie said. 'We'll check with Morgan, who's liaising with the school as well.'

They arrived quickly and from a distance the bus looked normal until they got closer and saw the mashed metal on the side wheel from its tangle with a boulder and two scrubby trees.

A few children were sitting in the shade of a tree with Gwyn and Barbara, who'd come as soon as Morgan had rung her, and was dishing out cool drinks and cake.

The teacher, Georgina, was much younger than she'd sounded on the phone, and she stood pale and trembling as she waited for them all to get out and take the responsibility from her shoulders.

Billie and Daphne shook her hand. 'You must be Georgina. What a day you've had.'

Georgina started to nod, brushed away sudden tears and Daphne stepped forward and enfolded her in a hug.

'There, there. You can relax now. We'll sort it out.' She looked around at the ordered chaos. 'You've done really well,' she said.

Billie agreed and the girl threw a grateful peep at Daphne when she stepped back.

'I'm just a wee bit fragile now you're here.' She sniffed.

Billie smiled sympathetically. 'Best time to be fragile is when help arrives. This would be daunting for anyone.' Let alone this slip of a girl in one of the most remote places in Australia.

'It got a lot better when Mrs Tomkins from the station arrived.'

'I'll bet.' Billie and Daphne followed her over to the bus and Michael and Hector veered off to check out the children, who all looked fairly unscathed from a distance.

A sheet was slung over the sunny side of the bus to shade the window of the teacher who couldn't move, and Billie, Daphne, Rex and Georgina headed for the driver.

The bus driver was sitting on the ground and looked in poor condition, though still conscious. He had a blue tinge to his lips and tongue and he was slumped up against the side of the bus. Billie decided he would be the first to leave and crouched down beside him as Daphne moved on to check the teacher trapped inside, taking Georgina with her.

Billie opened her kit and removed a tourniquet and two cannulas. 'Hello there. You must be Bob. I'm Dr Billie Green. I'm going to slip this oxygen mask onto your mouth while I pop a couple of needles in your arm. That okay with you?'

The man nodded grimly. 'Sorry for the mess,' he said faintly.

'Could've been a whole lot worse,' Billie said. 'You did well. Let's just get you fixed up enough to fly you out to Adelaide.' Michael appeared at her shoulder and she nodded towards her patient. 'I'm thinking you and Hector should take this guy to Adelaide.'

'Yep. No problem. Daphne has another to go, the teacher trapped in the bus. They're just trying to figure out how to get him out.'

He pointed to Lionel Tomkins, a no-nonsense ex-miner. 'Lionel thinks we could cut the side of the bus open pretty easily, so it's looking like we might be taking two in flight as soon as that's done. He's headed back to get the gear and reckons it'll be a fairly quick job.'

'As long as it is. My friend here isn't feeling too sprightly.' She attached ECG leads to his chest as she spoke. The erratic heart rate bounced up on the screen and they both studied the cardiac rhythm with concern.

'Hmm.' Billie didn't like the thought of Bob having another heart attack mid-flight. 'I'll see what's happening with the others and I might travel with him myself.'

She stood up and Michael crouched down next to Bob. 'Tag,' he said and smiled at Bob. 'I'm Michael, the flight nurse. She's the boss.' He adjusted the oxygen mask, which had started to slip. 'I'll do some more obs while we wait for her here, what do you reckon, mate?'

Billie smiled as she walked quickly towards the bus, thinking to herself how much she loved working with these guys, and climbed inside where Daphne was crouched down talking to a man with his leg wedged under the seat. His leg was at a very unattractive angle and she winced. *That's gotta hurt*, she thought, but smiled reassuringly. The man was sucking on the pain relief inhaler and his face began to relax as she watched.

Daphne said, 'We'll get his pain sorted, his observations are also settling, and he's stable until they can cut him out.'

Rex was beside Daphne. 'If there's nothing you can do until Lionel comes back with his equipment, I can stay with him if you want to check the rest.'

Daphne looked up at Billie who nodded, and they moved off together to discuss Daphne's triage of the children. She'd found lots of bruises and sprains but no obvious breaks, and the little boys were more interested in reliving the excitement of the crash while the little girls were fascinated by Gwyn.

The young teacher was sitting now with a young girl hugged into her as she wiped the blood from her elbow.

Tom, the cattle truck driver, poked his phone under Billie's nose. 'The guy wants to talk to you.'

She put the phone to her ear and spoke into it. 'Dr Green here.'

'Dr Fraser here.' Morgan's voice was crisp and she might have detected a hint of steel in the tone. 'If you have had time to assess the situation perhaps I could have an update.'

'Certainly.' What was up his nose? Though she guessed she should have touched base with Morgan as soon as she'd seen the two critical patients. 'One suspected myocardial infarct, with inverted T waves on ECG, unstable and critical.' There was no comment so she went on.

'One trapped forty-year-old male has obvious femur, tib and fib fracture and trauma to the right leg but haemodynamically stable. The plan is to cut out the side of the bus to extricate him. Both critical patients need to be transported to Adelaide for specialist care and it's my opinion they will need a medical officer to escort them.'

'Planned departure time?'

'Depends on extrication of trapped patient.'

'That could take quite a while. I think you should consider the option of taking the cardiac patient and go ASAP.'

She'd wondered about that herself but wasn't used to being ordered to change her plan of care. Then she reviewed what she could see from where she stood, allowed the desolation to sink in, the stretch of flat land in every direction, the red dust, the saltbush and loose rocks of an arid wasteland. There was a man standing beside her who was the sole inhabitant of the nearest town. Of course Morgan was right. She was in the middle of Australia in one of the remotest parts of the country, miles from a major centre. And her patient could deteriorate at any minute.

'Roger,' she told him, then turned to Daphne.

'Daphne. I'll take Bob the bus driver to Adelaide. Might see you there later.'

'Sounds good.' Daphne nodded. 'I'll talk to Morgan about the children while you get organised.'

Billie handed the phone over with relief. She'd thought she was doing well, but it was a first for her to be triaging a large incident so remotely.

This situation certainly raised her already high opinion of the whole team. The way the pilots were available for support, the way people like Barbara and her husband instantly helped, and the livestock carrier who used his phone and diverted his truck, then stayed to help. Every single one of them selflessly giving. It made her proud to be a part of this far-flung community.

TEN

By the time she'd flown to Adelaide and back, Billie's neck was stiff with tension and her shoulders ached. Her lower back twinged from the crouched position she'd spent so much time in and it was one of the rare times she wished she still lived at the flat and could soak in the bath.

Bob the bus driver had been very unstable during the trip and she wouldn't be surprised if he progressed straight to the operating theatre for more than one coronary artery bypass. Michael and Hector had flown the injured teacher to Adelaide as well, and because they had taken longer to get away they'd had to stay overnight.

Daphne stayed out at Golden Ridge with Barbara in case any complications arose through the night and one of the children needed urgent attention.

Morgan was there, waiting for her and Rex at the base, when she walked back in late in the evening for her bag. He looked tall and unruffled and, she could almost believe, pleased to see her! He probably could have gone home and seen her in the morning, but she acknowledged, to herself at least, that she was glad he was there. It had been a big day.

'How are you?' There was genuine concern in his voice. And definitely some warmth of pleasure at seeing her.

This was a nice surprise. 'I'm fine.'

He studied her and she must have looked acceptable despite the fact she felt like she could sleep for a week because he nodded, and then shrugged, as if explaining to himself why he was asking. 'It was your first triage in a major incident. You did well.'

It was her turn to study him. She felt a little of her tiredness fall away with the relief that he really thought so. She'd wondered, especially when he'd suggested she change her transfer plans.

'We were lucky. There weren't too many casualties and the young teacher, Georgina, did a great job. And Barbara and her husband were so good. And the truck driver. He was a card. You have to love the way everyone pulls together out here.' Her tongue was running away with her and she closed her mouth.

He nodded. 'The school got off lighter than they could have with the children. Having seatbelts in long-distance coaches is a blessing.'

They both thought about that soberly. Rex waved and left for home and Billie glanced around, acknowledging that most of the lights were off and Morgan had had a big day as well. 'I imagine it must be hard for you being at the other end of the phone. Do you wish you were out there with us?'

He shook his head. 'Wouldn't do me much good if I did wish that. Someone has to coordinate the services and be available to escalate. I'm glad it went well. Sorry to call you in on your days off.'

She thought about that and remembered Lorna. Mia would have spent time with her by now and she'd missed the introduction.

Mentally she shrugged. Soretta would have handled it all with her usual aplomb. 'Have you met Mrs Lamerton? She's been raising funds for the service for years.'

His eyebrows jerked. 'Lorna? Of course.'

'She moved in to Blue Hills today.'

He laughed and it was a good sound. They were actually having a normal conversation and despite her tiredness she didn't want it to end. 'What's Lachlan think about that?'

'I'm not sure he knows but I think, for us, she'll be fun. She took our quick departure in her stride, no problem. Said her husband had rushed off all their married life.'

'What a menagerie.'

'Excuse me?' Billie could almost be offended, but he laughed and steered her towards the door.

'Just stirring you. Off you go.' Then he frowned. 'Drive carefully. This is when I'm not sure living out of town is such a good idea.'

'I know the shift-working nurses at the hospital do it all the time. I'll be fine.'

'See that you are.'

He shut the door behind them and waited until she'd opened her car door and slid in before he went to his own vehicle. She started the car and drove away but she was thinking about the almost companionable conversation they'd had. She hadn't expected that. He'd waited to watch her go, too. She'd have thought he'd had enough waiting today.

By the time she got home things were getting fuzzy with tiredness. It had actually been helpful and quite invigorating talking it through with Morgan and she was too tired to worry about the

implications of that. But as she showered and prepared for bed she was glad she had the next day off, and sank into a dreamless sleep.

Mia was sitting with Lorna at the breakfast table. Daphne was at work and her mother had been called out. Something to do with cover for Morgan, who'd been summoned to Broken Hill for an emergency-department heads meeting and both wouldn't be back until teatime. That left her with Mrs Lamerton for hours.

'I have a little fundraiser next week. Every year at this time I run it,' Lorna said as she sipped her tea.

Mia decided the old lady was looking at her the way her mother did when she was planning on a spring clean of the flat. They hadn't spent much time together and now she wished she'd gone early with Soretta instead of opting for a later run out to the yards.

'That's nice,' she said unenthusiastically.

'It's for the Flying Doctor Service. I do a doorknock and ask for donations. Raise money for equipment.'

Mia's gaze began roaming around. Stinker. She wished someone else was here. Nobody did doorknocks anymore. How embarrassing. Imagine if Trent saw her walking down the street with Lorna knocking on doors.

Soretta had left with Klaus at six a.m. to start bringing in the mob from the furthest paddocks to separate another mob of now grown lambs. She wasn't coming back until well after lunchtime. Mia was supposed to slice the corned beef and take it down to the pens at lunch so she was stuck here for a couple of hours at least.

She came back to the doorknock thing. 'Why don't you just

email them for donations? Make up a flier and send it out on the internet?'

Lorna smiled. 'Young people. Such good ideas. I know you have a computer, dear. But I really don't understand the internet. And tell me about email, I never quite got the hang of that.'

An hour later, even Mia was amazed by Lorna's quick grasp of the concepts of wi-fi communication. The elderly woman's shrewd questions had her revising her 'mad old lady' label and together they decided that a webpage for their area would be a help, with historical photos and that it, along with a combined monthly newsletter of current events, could be the answer to avoiding the doorknock event.

The idea of that certainly made Mia feel more comfortable because there was no way she was knocking on some stranger's door with Lorna and she didn't trust her mother not to put her in for it.

While Mia pulled a template from the internet for a website they both liked, Lorna dug into one of her leather cases and pulled out a bound folio of ancient photographs of some of the early air-craft and transport methods the flying doctors from the past had used and all of a sudden it began to take shape. Lorna even found some black-and-white pictures of her own adventures as a nurse.

'Is that you on a camel?' Mia's peel of laughter had Lorna's crinkled face creasing in an indulgent smile.

'Yes, it is, you scallywag, and I'll have some respect for my skirt, if you please.'

Mia valiantly swallowed back another giggle. 'I can't believe you wore a skirt to ride a camel.'

Lorna shrugged. 'It was worse riding the horse in my uniform.'

'So you actually rode a horse all this way when Soretta's dad was born?'

Lorna lifted her head and gazed out the window as if seeing a different time. After a few moments she mused, 'I did. And rode back into town again, of course.'

'It's bad enough on the bus.' Mia thought about the horror bus trip. Although, admittedly, it had improved. And one of Trent's friends had lounged in the seat opposite her and teased her a bit lately. Yesterday's ride home had been almost fun.

'Is the bus that terrible?' There was no judgement in the question, just interest and, instead of firing up, Mia had to admit the truth of it.

'Maybe it's not so bad.'

'I think living out here is far nicer than in town. Much quieter.'

'Too quiet.'

Lorna looked at her. 'Have you had time to be bored? I've noticed you've been pretty busy helping Soretta. And the puppies.' Again there was no judgement.

Mia had to smile. 'Okay. I'm not bored. And I do love the animals, though I wish we didn't have to put the lambs back with the mob when they grow up.'

Lorna snorted at that. 'I can imagine a small herd of house-trained sheep waiting for Soretta's grandfather when he comes home on Sunday.'

Mia screwed up her nose as she enlarged a copy of a photograph she'd emailed to herself from her phone. Just snapping pics of Lorna's old photos seemed to work okay for insertion on the web page. 'That's going to be weird. Having a man in the house.'

She heard Lorna sigh. 'It's something I've really missed.'

Of course. Lorna was a widow. Had a whole life and husband and family before she was the purple-haired old lady sitting beside her. A bit of a wake-up call, really. Mia said quietly, 'I'm sorry your husband died.'

Lorna's fingers reached across and touched her arm. 'Thank you, dear. I was blessed for a long time.' Her smile looked almost normal. 'And now I have your lovely mother and you and Daphne and Soretta to talk to on my little holiday out here. I'd say I was very blessed again.'

Mia's thoughts came back to herself. And the changes that were about to happen. 'Still, it'll be weird to have a man in the house,' she said again. And one who owned it, and wasn't very well so he wouldn't be going out onto the station for a while. So he'd be home. All day.

She changed the subject because she didn't like the squirming in her belly when she thought about it. 'I never met my father. He's dead. It's always been me and Mum, except for when Mum's aunt was alive, but I was young when she died and don't remember her much.'

'Your mother must have been very busy balancing a medical career and a young child.'

Her mother was always busy, Mia thought, and stifled the disloyal words. She knew her mother tried to be there for her but she just didn't understand Mia at all. 'I spent a lot of time in child care. Then after-school care. Later on we had a lady come in three times a week, when Mum worked, to clean the flat and cook a meal for dinner until Mum came home.'

Lorna smiled. 'My husband was a doctor. He had me to do that. And I was the one who helped my son with all his maths

exams. He's an engineer, you know. Your mother's been so busy she really needed a wife.'

Mia rolled her eyes. 'You're funny.'

Lorna ignored that and peered at the web page. 'Oh my. How many people will see me like that?'

Mia grinned. 'Hopefully millions. When we launch it I'll put a link on Facebook and Pinterest and tweet it. So all my friends from my old school will "Like" it. Then their friends will see it and then their friends. It has to be fun and make people want to show others.'

Lorna looked doubtful. 'But will they donate to the cause or will they just laugh and go and look at something else?'

'We need a prize. For donating. Or an online auction. Like a signed picture of a superstar. Do you know any superstars?' she asked.

'No, dear. No young ones, anyway.'

Mia was on a roll. 'Maybe we could auction off signed pictures of the staff at the Flying Doctor Base. That boss of Mum and Daphne's looks pretty good, if you like old men.'

Lorna's eyes twinkled. 'I promise I won't tell Morgan Fraser he looks old.'

Billie cornered Morgan before he knew what she was about. 'Lorna wants me to take a photograph for you to sign so she can auction it off on their new website to raise money for the Mica Ridge Base.'

'A photograph of what?'

'You, the boss. Apparently, you are sufficiently attractive to invite donations to our new website.'

He frowned darkly. 'I cannot believe Lorna managed permission

from the powers that be for that site. Your daughter's fault.'

Billie shrugged. She wasn't all that comfortable herself, but Lorna and Mia were so enthusiastic she couldn't face a fight.

'It amuses them and maybe it will do more than we expect. You'll be happy if you end up with a wad of money to buy new equipment with, won't you?'

He laughed. 'True. So I guess I'd better sign the dreaded picture.'

'Not so fast. I haven't taken it yet. I'm told we have to go outside for you to lean nonchalantly against one of the aircraft, looking sexy. I have to take it with my phone and email it to my daughter.'

He rolled his eyes and shuddered. 'You think this is hilarious.' He pointed his finger at her face, which she was struggling to keep straight.

'I think it's a scream.'

Two minutes later they were outside in the hot sun and Morgan was standing uncomfortably beside the Mica Ridge Base insignia on the aircraft fuselage. Billie couldn't believe how amusing it was to see the super assured Morgan looking so uncomfortable. 'Come on, big boy. Strut your stuff.'

'Be careful.'

Billie giggled. A sound she was not known for. Seriously, this was the funniest thing she'd done in a while. She took her time. 'Smile.'

'Get it over with,' Morgan said through gritted teeth.

'Now put your hand on the aircraft.'

'What? And burn myself? The metal's a hundred degrees.'

Fair enough. 'You could pretend to. Would still look like it.'

As she looked at the photograph she saw a genuine smile crease Morgan's face. 'That's better. You're loosening up.'

'Pop over there next to him, Billie.' The voice behind her made her jump and she spun around to see Daphne holding her own camera. 'Come on. A lovely shot with the two of you.'

'They don't want me.'

'Just for fun. Not for the site.'

'And I'm melting here so get a move on,' said Morgan, the voice of authority.

Billie moved reluctantly to stand beside Morgan.

'Closer,' Daphne directed, not moving her head from behind the camera.

Billie leaned a fraction closer and now not all the heat was coming off the plane. Some of it was building in the tiny space between them and she could feel her face start to burn.

Later that day, when Daphne sent through the photo of her and Morgan, Billie couldn't help the little glow of satisfaction to see herself standing beside her boss. They both looked pretty darn good.

Three days later Billie felt Lorna's gaze drift over her at breakfast and she wasn't sure she liked her calculating expression. 'I noticed you got home late last night.' There was a definite sparkle to the statement.

Billie shook her head. 'I worked late, thank you very much. Doing Flying Doctor stuff.'

Lorna sat back. 'Oh. I hope everyone is all right.'

'Everyone's okay in the end. They'll all feel better this morning.'

'Here I was thinking you were finally spending time with a bit of male company.'

Billie tried hard not to let her face show how close to home that remark had fallen. She'd been thinking the same thing herself lately. Had actually woken this morning with some very vivid dreams. That was a first. She didn't even want to think about hot thoughts like that. Certainly not in front of Lorna. Instead she said, 'And here's me thinking you were a nice, genteel lady.'

Lorna snorted again. 'Well look at you.' Lorna nodded her head. 'Young, beautiful, and a doctor. How come some man hasn't snaffled you up?'

She lifted her chin. 'Plenty have tried.' They grinned at each other. 'But seriously, I'm waiting until Mia's finished school.'

Lorna shook her head. 'What sort of crack-brained idea is that? Life is far too short for that nonsense.' There was a bite to the last word. It seemed Lorna wasn't having a bar of that excuse.

Billie sighed and decided maybe she was beginning to agree with Lorna. Maybe it was crack-brained to wait any longer to live life to the full. But she said the right thing. 'My first responsibility is to my daughter. We don't want to end up with a psycho for a step-dad.' She heard the flatness in that statement and chewed her lip. It was too much to hope Lorna wouldn't notice.

'That sounds like prior experience.' Lorna was peering at her through her new snazzy red glasses, which they'd encouraged her to buy when they'd all gone shopping with Daphne yesterday. She looked a little like Dame Edna. 'Was Mia's father a bad man?'

'He started off nicely enough. I was still fragile from the loss of my parents and he said he was from a small town, too. He was flattering and funny and seemed larger than life. Big drinker. Big

cars. Big laugh. My aunt hated him.'

'Your aunt probably had more life experience to draw from.'

'Well I was swept along by him until it started to go sour. He wasn't nice—especially at the end. He threatened me when I said I was leaving him.' She'd never told anyone that in seventeen years. And before then she'd only told her student advisory mentor about the threats when she'd changed universities to get away from him. And she had escaped. Then found out she was pregnant. And maybe it had made her too wary of men ever since.

'A bad man.' Lorna repeated and for a moment there she thought Lorna was actually going to spit the way her mouth pursed. 'Does Mia know that?'

'No.' Billie shrugged away the dilemma that had haunted her all these years. 'How could I tell my daughter her father was a creep?' She lowered her voice. 'I said he was dead.'

Lorna raised her brows. 'And you're not worried he'll turn up one day? And bite you on the bottom?'

Bite her on the bottom. She almost smiled at that. He probably would. But it was a strange relief to actually talk about it after all this time with someone she trusted. Billie wasn't sure how she'd come to trust Daphne and Lorna as much as she did, but there was no doubting that she had complete faith in both of them.

'Yep. Guess I've worried about it for a while now. One day he'll turn up. She'll find out. And I'll wear it.'

Lorna's eyes softened. 'You could just tell her. Now.'

Billie could see that Lorna wasn't blaming her. She believed in loyalty and was genuinely worried about her. 'That must take a toll, dear. On your own for so long. You *need* a man.' Lorna nodded decisively. 'A great big muscly one.'

Billie laughed. 'I'm not that keen on snuggling up to a world champion wrestler, but a normal guy would be nice.'

Not to solve her problems, she assured herself. But there was a voice inside that whispered that she was getting sick of being responsible for everything. That was weak. 'I'd *like* a man friend.' Lover would be good too, but she didn't say it. She qualified, 'I'd like one but I don't *need* one.'

Lorna smiled as well. 'You young things. So feisty. But there are good men out there. Some closer than you think.'

Billie shrugged, ignoring the obvious answer. 'Maybe soon I'll have time to look. Mia will be finished school in a year.'

'Another year!' Lorna squeaked. And a shadow seemed to pass over the older lady's face. 'Wasting time.' Then Lorna outed the great big muscly elephant in the room. 'So you're not looking at our Dr Morgan?'

No. She wasn't looking at Morgan. Or not much.

There had been a couple of quite companionable coffees together lately after the 'photo shoot' when the rest of the staff had gone out on flights. Some laughs. But there was nothing between her and Morgan. 'No matchmaking, Lorna.'

'Only if I think there's a need.' She sat back and crossed her arms as if to signify her mind wasn't being swayed on that topic.

'Soretta looks happy. This has been a good move for us all, I think,' Billie said, trying to change the subject.

Lorna sighed, apparently brought back to the transience of her stay. 'I'm certainly having fun on my holiday.'

The roar of a mangled gear change on the driveway made them both look in its direction.

Mia, with her learner's plate firmly attached to the front of the

farm utility, ground up the hill. It had come to Billie's attention that Mia listened to Soretta more than she listened to her own mother, and when help had been offered with the driving lessons Billie had jumped at the chance.

The amusing part was that when Soretta took her, Mia had to drive the diesel farm vehicle because as far as Soretta was concerned anyone could drive an automatic car. The truck pulled up beside the house, Soretta got out, and Mia jerked away into the shed.

Soretta was scowling as she climbed the stairs. 'She nearly dropped the gearbox on the driveway. She'll be beating herself up all day.'

Billie schooled her face into a sympathetic look. 'Sorry.'

'She hadn't missed a beat all morning and I think she gets nervous when she knows you're both looking.'

'I really appreciate you taking her,' Billie said.

'It's fine. Grandad taught me and it wasn't so long ago that I don't remember how hard it is to drive the car, keep an eye on the road and watch for roos all at once.'

Billie laughed. In her experience it was the other cars you had to watch out for. 'Have you driven in Sydney or Adelaide?'

'Nope. Never want to. Gives me claustrophobia with all those people. I did some competitive hockey before I left boarding school, so I've been to most of the capital cities with the team.'

Billie was impressed. 'Must have been some team.'

'Country schoolgirls.'

Billie clapped. 'You're my hero. I always wanted to be good at hockey.'

Soretta cocked an eyebrow. 'Says the doctor who still managed

to raise a daughter single-handedly.'

'Nothing wrong with a bit of mutual appreciation,' Lorna agreed.

They both turned to Lorna and Soretta said, 'You're no slouch. Riding ten kilometres on a horse to deliver a baby.'

Soretta grinned at Lorna and Billie felt her chest tighten with emotion at the genuine warmth for this elderly lady. They were so blessed with the growing sense of family, which had only increased since Lorna's arrival. It was almost too good for something that couldn't last forever.

ELEVEN

A week later, Billie thought again about Lorna's observations, especially on a day when Morgan had been behaving in a particularly unusual manner. It had all started when she'd mentioned that Soretta had taken Mia out of school a day early to drive the long distance to a riding gymkhana and was staying away for two nights. And she'd added that Lorna was having tea with her son in town.

She'd watched him slap Rex on the back when he'd offered to drive Daphne out to Barbara Tomkins's station to mind Gwyn while Barbara and her husband had rushed off to visit a terminal relative. He'd been joking with everyone and complimenting them on their work, so much so she'd felt like asking where the real Morgan was and what had he done with him.

Then at the end of the day he'd walked companionably out with her to her car and stopped beside her as she prepared to put the keys in the lock.

'Would you like to come to my place for dinner? You said you'd be alone at the station tonight.'

No planning. On her side anyway. Now this offer. That persistent ember of attraction she'd had simmering underneath her

professional exterior flickered into life again, no doubt buttered up by the congenial man today. But he was her boss. One didn't socialise with the boss. Not a good idea.

'Um, thank you. That's kind of you but I'll be fine.'

Morgan laughed. 'I wasn't being kind.'

She turned to look at him and he was waiting patiently. Very patiently, for him, and she could feel the difference in the air between them. Suddenly she was back to being Alice in Wonderland and Morgan looking big and sexy. Right there on the footpath beside her.

'I was asking you to dinner. But you don't have to come if you don't want to.' He shrugged a little self-consciously and he had her. Right then. Morgan self-conscious? 'I've been angling towards it all day.'

Was that why he'd been strange? The idea made her want to fan her face. 'Oh. Um. Always happy for someone else to cook. Sure, thank you.'

He laughed again and now that she really looked at him he did seem suddenly very relaxed and happy. 'Wow. I'm flattered you'll at least eat my food.'

She played back what she'd said and laughed herself. 'Don't want you to get a big head.'

'Not much hope of that with you around,' he said cryptically.

Because he lived within five minutes of work, she didn't have much time to think before Morgan was holding his front door open for her. Billie wasn't quite sure how she'd arrived at this moment.

His home, the top floor of an office building, with views to the craggy Mica Ridge above them, was right in front of her and

there was nothing else she could do but go in. After work. Alone with Morgan. So she went in, and he followed her, closing the door behind them.

His voice startled her out of her tumbling thoughts. 'Can I get you a drink?'

She jumped. 'I have to drive home later.'

'Then a soft drink?' He crossed the room, opened a small bar fridge and removed a can of lemon squash without asking her more. He then popped the lid and poured it into a glass. 'Here.'

She took the glass and shivered as his fingers brushed over hers. Felt the heat in her cheeks and looked away in embarrassment. Damn. She must be coming down with a virus. Man flu.

'I won't be long.' His drawl promised more in her ears than he probably intended as he walked away. In the last few weeks she'd stopped hearing the undercurrents, the subtle sexiness, but this afternoon it was as if every word was draped in he-man suggestive-ness. Was he playing a game or was she being fanciful?

She took a cooling sip of her drink, casting her eye over the room. Probably the latter. Morgan wasn't the type to play games. She hoped. She'd been burned once and it was a pretty big turn-around for her that she was here to begin with.

She wasn't sure what she'd imagined his house would be like, maybe sparse and barren, but it wasn't. There were plenty of points of interest—gumtrees in oils on the walls, two divine water-colours of native birds, and an old colonial writing desk with a silver-framed photograph on it. She wandered over for a closer look. A dark-eyed woman stared back at her.

'Come through to the kitchen.' She heard him say. 'It's what I like to do.'

Talk to people in the kitchen? Her brain started working again. 'Cook?' A man who actually liked to cook? He just got better and better.

'Yep.'

She'd have thought he'd be a take-away and paper plates kind of guy. Or maybe that was because that had always been her fantasy. Funny how the idea of Morgan and fantasy sat so well together. She allowed him to usher her in front and direct her onto the stool he pulled out for her at the island bench.

The kitchen was really impressive. If you liked kitchens. She was happier to be the observer in this situation. 'I see you take your workspace seriously.'

His brows climbed. 'This is the first time you noticed?'

She thought of the organised space on his desk at the base and shook her head. 'You're right. I shouldn't be surprised considering what you're like at work.'

He nodded, giving her a lazy smile that sent a wave of heat from the top of her head to the tips of her toes, then he began to melt the butter, tossing in some shallots.

'Where did you learn to cook?'

He shrugged. 'My mother was a chef. My father was a lawyer who worked the hours my mother didn't. She encouraged me to try experimental recipes out on him when she couldn't be home. Not all of them were successes and that amused her. But it was something I actually enjoyed so I was glad for the opportunity.'

'It sounds fun.' Though she wasn't quite sure if it had been for him.

Morgan smiled. 'Sometimes it was.' He juggled some more ingredients then shrugged. 'Until they divorced. I doubt they even

noticed they weren't married any more because they so rarely saw each other.' He glanced away from the pan and through to the sitting room as if talking to someone else. 'I promised I wouldn't have that sort of marriage.'

'They got together at least once and produced something special,' Billie said softly. 'And it smells like you're still a good cook.'

He grinned at her. 'And we'll leave that topic there. Tonight I'm making porcini mushrooms, chicken and pasta in cream. Okay?'

She moistened her dry mouth, trying to pretend nonchalance. 'That sounds delicious.' Maybe she needed a wine after all.

'If you change your mind about wine, I've got a very nice Italian-style Prosecco, which has a low alcohol content.'

'Just one, then.' Or else she'd be unable to go home. For several reasons.

'Of course. But you'll have to stay more than an hour.' He smiled, went to the fridge and poured a glass from an already opened bottle.

'I could probably manage that.' She took the proffered glass and watched him sear, dice, and scatter herbs and spices, his big hands deft and elegant in their joyful dance over the food.

She finished her squash first because her mouth was going dry watching him. 'You really do love to cook.'

His hands stilled and he looked up at her. Smiled again. 'I do.' Big shoulders shrugged under the loose open-necked shirt he'd changed into. She wished she'd been able to change. Her own collar felt a little tight and she was warming up way too much. 'Even more so if I'm cooking for someone else.'

Which was exactly the right lead-in for her to ask him about his relationship history. She couldn't help but be curious. 'So why

don't you have a someone else here all the time?'

He paused. 'I'm between guests.'

She almost choked on her first sip of wine. 'Lucky me.'

He nodded. 'Extremely.'

She laughed. 'I'm happy to eat but I'm not looking for a relationship.'

'No problem. I'm not either.' And suddenly there it was—out on the kitchen bench between the mushrooms and the cream pot— the fact that neither of them was looking for a relationship but that the attraction was mutual.

He fancied her. No strings. And she fancied him. No strings.

He said, 'I've been thinking about what you said on Monday. Your "I like men but I don't want to live with a man" comment.'

She couldn't believe she'd actually voiced that.

He went on. 'I wondered if occasionally we could spend some after-work hours together? Platonic if you like – to begin with.' The air seemed to shimmer as the temperature in the room went up another ten degrees.

His gaze locked onto hers. Billie had the weird feeling the clock on the wall had braked, pausing the passage of time for a moment. He rinsed his hands under the tap on the island bench, then proceeded to wipe them dry with a towel, keeping their intimate connection throughout.

Then, still pinning her from a distance, he came around the bench and took both her hands, stood her up until she was in front of him, and she had to look away then, by focusing on her hands. She could feel him waiting for her to lift her face.

Eventually she did.

Up close, his eyes were brown, not black. The faint edgy scent

of male and herbs and the light beer he'd poured himself melded into an aromatic aphrodisiac and she didn't know how to deal with it all.

'What do you think?'

What did she think? It was impossible to make her brain function. Her mouth felt like the desert. Her wrist pulsated where it was held between his fingers and she was a touch mesmerised as she looked at his strong jaw. 'Out of work hours. It's an idea. It might work,' she finally managed.

Then his head came down and his full, chiselled lips grazed one side of her mouth before they moved to the other and she sucked in a breath.

Now another subtle whiff of his expensive men's aftershave clouded her already foggy brain, but his lips were on hers and the room disappeared into strong arms, a rock-hard chest and a mouth that teased and tasted and tempted her to lose the little control she was hanging onto by the barest thread. She nearly lost it.

Only she didn't. She pulled back and he let her. Smiled and said, 'I knew you'd taste good.'

'Lemon squash.'

'Billie squash.'

She wished he'd squash her again but the whole thing was very close to getting out of hand. 'Hmm. A tad explosive at first brush.'

She widened the distance between them. 'I'm suddenly not sure this is a smart thing to do when we work together.'

'Me either.' He helped her sit down again as if nothing had happened. Maybe not for him, but for her the world had tilted into a whole new confusing place. He returned to his cooking.

His voice calm he said, 'I meant it when I said I didn't want

a relationship. But I'm up for some mutually beneficial company with no strings.'

His voice was even, reassuring. Like the one he used when people phoned in with an emergency. Billie felt like she was having an emergency.

'I have a teenage daughter. I can't be seen slipping off to my boss's for a bit of bump in the night.'

'I can see that could be a problem.' He sighed and then wriggled his brows suggestively. 'How about a one-night stand?'

She smiled and shook her head. 'Too much on the downside. I'd have to work with you,' she added with a little flurry of bravery, 'imagining you naked.' She shrugged. 'Too hard.'

He smiled and she was relieved to see there were no hard feelings. Not that kind of hard feeling anyway.

'You have a point there,' he said. 'Which I knew myself.' Then he glanced wickedly at her chest and to her embarrassment she actually had two points sticking through the fabric of her shirt. He didn't comment on that. 'It was worth asking, though.'

She laughed. This conversation was funny and crazy and out of her comfort zone. 'Very forward. Will dinner be long?'

'Fifteen minutes. And you have fifty minutes before you're allowed to drive.' He gestured to the cutlery piled at the side of the bench. 'Perhaps you'd like to set the table. Or put on some music?'

The idea of getting out of the heat of the kitchen sounded excellent. 'I'd like that.' She gathered up the knives and forks in one hand and her half full glass in the other and threw him a wary smile before she scuttled away. She'd like to think she sauntered out but scuttle was probably more accurate.

Billie put the cutlery and glass down on the table in the corner

of the open-plan lounge room and fanned her face with her fingers. Hooley dooley, that man could kiss. It had been a short one. Thankfully. Their first. She wasn't very experienced in kissing. She'd been out with a couple of men over the last fifteen years, but she'd never found the concept of casual sex interesting enough to progress to the next level. Until now?

The only man she had slept with had left her with scars she didn't want to resurrect. But what if she did want to sleep with someone? What if she wanted to sleep with Morgan? Or stay awake with him?

What if she never found someone she wanted to sleep with as much as she might want to sleep with Morgan? Hooley dooley, all right. She shook her head, trying to perish the thought. But common sense was the thing that was wilting, not the vision of being masterfully captured in those strong arms.

Damn Morgan Blake. But in fairness it wasn't his fault some guy had tricked her into a toxic relationship a long time ago and had left her with hang-ups.

Then her gaze was caught by a small black spider crouched in the corner of the room like an omen. She shivered. On his bad days Mia's father had been like that. Crouched. Waiting. He'd stalked her when she'd tried to get away.

She was still staring at the small black house spider when Morgan came back into the room and vaguely she heard him put down the dishes. Then she felt him come over to her, and stand close to investigate what she was looking at. Decisively, he picked up a newspaper and thwacked the intruder, making her jump in surprise. Then he casually pulled a tissue from a box and squashed the dead body into it. Crushed it in his hand.

'Arachnophobia?'

'Something like that.'

'I usually just put them outside. But I don't like the black ones that look like crabs.'

She shivered. 'Me either.'

He dropped a kiss on her forehead. 'Sit.' He gestured with the hand that held the tissue. 'I'll be back in a sec.'

Billie blinked. She was being stupid. But she had the horrible feeling that the night was ruined.

They never quite got the rapport going well after that, though the dinner was amazing, and as soon as the hour was up after her half glass of wine, Billie went home.

On Monday, when Billie went into work, it wasn't as awkward as she'd thought it would be.

'Thanks for dinner on Friday,' she said to Morgan.

His eyes were kind. 'No problem. I enjoyed it.'

Her cheeks heated. 'Thanks for lying.'

He shook his head. 'I'd like to try again another night.'

She wasn't sure she could survive another attempt. 'I know what you'd like to try.'

He gave her a long, slow smile that made the tips of her ears warm. 'Only if it suits you, too.'

'Maybe if the stars align again.' She met his eyes determinedly. She was a grown-up, and she was tempted. 'I have commitments.'

'I see that,' he said.

'And my boss works me very hard,' she added, tongue in cheek.

'As he should.' Apparently, she'd crossed the line because he changed into that very person.

'I have meetings for most of the day so you're in charge. Michael and Hector will be back soon so they're your main team. You right with that?'

'Of course.'

He narrowed his eyes as he looked at her. 'Text me if you have problems and I'll get back to you.'

'I don't have problems. I have moments of unusual interest.'

'Good to hear. But if you need help—text me!'

By the end of the day, Billie was feeling good about her ability to manage the control room in Morgan's absence. She hadn't needed to text him. He'd seemed impressed when he'd returned and she felt as if she was beginning to grasp most of the intricacies of the job. She loved all of it as much as she'd thought she would.

Driving back towards Blue Hills Station, she found herself thinking about Morgan as she sang a Mary Coughlan song. Something about wanting to be seduced. She compressed her lips to contain the grin that was threatening to break out. And she knew exactly who she wanted to be seduced by. Lucky she wouldn't have the chance to act on that because the whole sleeping-with-the-boss thing was a very dumb idea. She should be thinking about her daughter who'd been away.

She turned into the driveway and as she rattled up the drive she was looking forward to seeing Mia and hearing about how she'd gone with Soretta on their weekend stay in the gooseneck of the horse float.

Billie still couldn't believe how easily Mia had attached herself to the other girl's brusque and barely tolerant friendship. Not that Soretta was mean, just so busy and bossy with her workload that Mia had to learn on the trot, or be corrected without kid gloves.

When she entered the house the aroma of a delicious slow roast prickled her nose. God bless Lorna, who must have put it on because Daphne was away. Living with Daphne, Soretta, and Lorna, was like a utopian fantasy. Her daughter stood up and crossed to hug her to welcome her home and her world was complete.

The next day Mia floated happily across the road, enjoying the fact that Trent had fallen back through the crowd to talk to her even though he'd been chatting with his friend at the time.

It was nine a.m. and another group of high-school children flowed off a bus and followed them across a pedestrian crossing in front of a waiting line of cars. They were laughing and carrying towels to the local swimming pool, and judging by the four main colours, anyone could've guessed that it was a school swimming carnival.

Mia glanced at the nearest car, one of those American muscle cars you saw in the movies, that was waiting for them to pass. Her eyes met those of a dark-haired older man, good-looking in a flashy sort of way, who stared at her with a startled expression on his face. She moved instinctively closer to Trent as she looked away, but her neck prickled.

That afternoon she noticed the same car driving out of Blue Hills Gate just before the school bus pulled up to let her off. Dust still swirled from the homestead driveway. The car accelerated away before she got out, but that didn't stop her staring after it with a frown on her face.

*

It was the following Friday and Morgan had returned from being called away again to Broken Hill.

'Thanks for that, Billie. Great job.' Morgan took back the pager from her and Billie ignored the ridiculous thrill such minor praise gave her. It was beginning to feel like hormone flushes when he approved her work!

'No problem.' She avoided catching his eye and moved towards the door. 'I'll head home then. Lorna's had Mia under her feet all day. Too many pupil-free days around here.'

'Got a minute?'

She stopped and turned around to face him again. 'Of course. Did you want me for something?' She saw him smile at that and she felt her face heat. What was with that? She was far too old for this sort of embarrassment, but the way she'd run away last time came back to haunt her. He probably thought she'd acted like a child.

'Yeah, well, I'm at work so I won't answer that one.'

She blushed but didn't say anything.

'A date. Tomorrow night. Nothing to do with work. Six o'clock, dinner, and I'll pick you up from Blue Hills.'

A date? With the man who doesn't do relationships? 'Dinner? Is anything open after six p.m.?'

He tilted his chin as if offended. 'I know a place.'

Yeah right. 'It wouldn't be your place?'

He wagged his finger. 'I said a proper date.'

So she nodded. 'A no-strings, proper date.' She pretended to consider. 'I'll have to see if Mia has anything planned.' It was a weak excuse, but she couldn't get her head around the idea of a real date, let alone a planned date with her boss. 'I'll let you know.'

He inclined his head and was the boss once again. 'By lunch tomorrow, then.'

'I'll text you.'

'Only if you're coming. Talk to me if you're not.'

Darn.

'Sure.'

TWELVE

Six o'clock Saturday arrived before Billie was ready. She'd been helping Daphne and Lorna spring-clean the kitchen and main lounge room in preparation for Soretta's grandad coming home the next day.

Mia, in unusually good spirits, had popped in from the sheep yards when she'd first arrived home, said a night out for her mother was a great idea, picked up some more lemonade Daphne had made and left again soon after. She and Soretta still weren't back.

Billie suspected her daughter enjoyed driving to and fro on the quad bike and stifled her misgivings. She consoled herself that Mia was too scared of Soretta's wrath to risk an accident on the farm equipment. Hopefully, Mia kept that fear at the front of her mind as she puttered around.

And Mia's last maths exam results had been her best yet. It seemed Lorna had been swotting with her. This place just kept getting better and better.

She heard the dogs bark as a vehicle slowed on the road at the bottom of the hill, then they barked louder as a car turned into the driveway. Her hand wobbled at the wrong moment with the mascara. Damn it. She dabbed at the black streak, took several

deep breaths and reapplied it, until finally she heard the car pull up outside.

Her stomach seemed to twist into a knot and she gritted her teeth. Why was she going out with this man when she was so scared of intimacy? One look at Morgan and any woman knew he wasn't the sort to want a platonic relationship—in as much as he didn't want a relationship at all—and he wouldn't want to talk about the weather all night. What was happening with the weather? Maybe she should quickly check the forecast for the week. She was going mad!

Still, she couldn't deny she wanted to go out with him. To be treated like a woman, not a mother, for at least one night was incredibly attractive. Maybe she'd be fine. It was a restaurant for goodness sake. She'd been to plenty of those with a few men in the past. And afterwards? Nothing would happen afterwards. He'd bring her home.

Or not.

If it all went well and she wanted to go home with him then maybe she wouldn't freeze and humiliate them both, or worse, have a panic attack.

An hour later in a very ambient restaurant with a candle on their table, Morgan smiled lazily. 'You seem a bit tense.'

'Do I?' A dumb comment. Of course she did. She'd dropped the fork she was playing with twice while waiting for the entree.

Billie was over herself and the stress of it all. She should just ask him to take her to his flat, make love to her so she could get it over with, and then she could enjoy her dinner. Her lips twitched

at the idea so she kept her head down, but the tension eased from her shoulders a bit. Maybe that's exactly what she needed to jump-start a normal adult life.

'You do that a lot,' he said.

She glanced at the fork. 'What?'

'Smile secretly at something. It drives me wild when I don't know what it is.' He added softly, 'In a good way.'

The warmth in her belly expanded. She lifted her eyes to his and blurted out, 'I was thinking I should sleep with you first to get over my nerves and then I might be able to enjoy my dinner.'

What the heck? She forced her gaze to stay where it was. Registered his sudden blink, the brown-black of his eyes hiding the dilation of his pupils, the corner of his mouth lifting. 'Your wish is my command.' He pushed out his chair.

She lifted her hand, stifled a laugh, and looked around at the other diners. 'No. It's fine. I feel better just getting that out.'

'Glad someone does.' He hesitated, then waggled his eyebrows as if to say, 'We could go now?' When she didn't stand up he dragged his chair back in. 'Damn.'

She laughed and suddenly everything was okay. The awkward tension had somehow seeped away and there was extra warmth in Morgan's eyes that wasn't all about sex.

The entree arrived. Great timing. 'Prawn cocktail seems ridiculous in the middle of Australia.' At least she'd said something.

'They're frozen, of course,' he ate one, 'but it tastes great.'

That conversation carried them through until the empty plates went away and the main course, wagyu beef, came a little too quickly after that. It was so expensive she couldn't bear to leave any so she ate it slowly.

Finally, the conversation began to flow and she realised she was having fun. He asked about Mia settling into the farm, asked about her work at the doctor's surgery back in Sydney and she told him about the little girl who poked things in her ears and nose.

He told her a funny story about Lorna's fundraising last year when they'd auctioned off Rex, and how the woman who'd bought him had just wanted someone to hang a heap of picture hooks in her house and wash her car. Rex had been relieved because he'd been worried about an improper proposal.

'Tell me more.'

He was looking at her and smiling and she smiled back as he said, 'Daphne's dying to attend her first annual Christmas pudding week.'

She had her chin on her hands, watching him intently. 'I think she mentioned that. What is it?'

'It's a fundraiser for the Flying Doctor Service, where mothers and grandmothers and great-grandmothers of the auxiliary make hundreds of secret recipe Christmas puddings that sell out in days.'

'Women from town make them?'

'And women from distant stations and those who'd moved to town from distant stations. They all come in for a hectic week of making puddings, made in the same way since the 1950s.'

She could see it clearly. Like the Country Women's Association on steroids. 'That's wonderful. Sounds like it's right up Daphne's alley.'

'Lorna is one of the original organisers. The ages of the women range from young to early nineties. Daphne's requested a week's holiday so she could join them.'

Typical. 'Daphne's a treasure.'

THE HOMESTEAD GIRLS

He was serious. 'Daphne epitomises the spirit of the service. That much goodness has to rub off on the rest of us mere mortals.'

Billie nodded. 'She cares about everyone.'

He signalled for coffee. 'She needs to realise people care about her, too.' The waiter came over and they ordered coffee.

While they waited he said, 'There's something I've been meaning to ask that puzzles me. We moved her stuff out to Blue Hills, a whole trailer load, but there was nothing of yours. Do you have a storage unit somewhere with all your furniture?'

It had to happen eventually. The delve into her past. Her weird ways and unusual lifestyle. That's how it started and it was about now that she ordinarily pulled back and never went out with that man again.

She shrugged. 'I don't do "stuff".' She shook her head. 'Mia and I have two suitcases each, a box of kitchen staple supplies and a vacuum cleaner. It all fits in my car. I've always rented a furnished flat or apartment. No upkeep like a house. No removalist when you go.'

She saw his brows draw together as he thought about that. Well, let him think! It suited her.

He'd sat back to watch her. 'You moved that often?'

She shrugged. 'Sometimes places didn't work out.' He'd read her resume, so he would've seen how many short-term appointments there were, but she'd explained it away as gathering different experiences for the future. She'd been assembling skills instead of possessions. Experience that would help her with this job.

'So you never want to buy knick-knacks? Say a painting or a vase or something to cherish in your home?'

'Maybe one day. But up until now I wanted to be able to move

169

easily, learn something new, and that's worked for us. Mia can buy what she likes as long as she's happy to give it away when we move. I always donate a load of odd bits and pieces to the local Vinnies. She'll probably be a hoarder when she gets her own house, just for the fun of it.'

She didn't want to think about the time an instrument rep had made a sales appointment to see the doctor and he'd turned out to be Mia's father. Before she'd bundled him out, he'd almost seen the photograph of Mia and her on the desk.

Billie took a discreet breath and let it out. Refused to let the past spoil a lovely evening. Again!

She leant her cheek into her hand and looked at him, determined to move past this. She'd heard nothing about him. 'What's your story, Morgan Fraser?'

'There's no story.'

'Who's the lady in the silver frame in your flat?'

His eyes narrowed and he studied her thoughtfully. All humour was now gone from his face. Lord, she hoped his wife hadn't died three months ago with unborn twins or something. Why couldn't she have kept her mouth shut?

'The woman I was going to spend my life with. I leave her there to remind me to stay focused.'

She nearly asked if she was dead, but she somehow managed to stop herself at the last second. 'She's beautiful.'

'She left me standing in the church. Not one of my happiest moments.'

Oh, that was just horrible. 'Did you get to speak to her before . . . ?'

'Nope.' He said it flatly as if he'd drained as much emotion out

of it as he could. 'I found out why later, but it was stuff she should have told me earlier. Would you like to comfort me? Maybe give me a hug?'

'What, here?' She gestured dramatically to the other diners. 'Do you think they'd mind?'

She saw his shoulders relax now that he'd put it out there. He gave a little shake of his head and his mouth formed a tiny smile. 'I wasn't going to do this again, you know.'

She tilted her head. 'You hug women in restaurants all the time?'

'No.'

'Then you're not going to do what again?'

'Build rapport. Become intrigued.' He sat forward, his face almost touching hers as she also moved close to hear. He whispered, 'I was thinking maybe we could just have sex.' He eased back and she did the same. But the buzzing had started in her stomach and she couldn't keep the smile off her face.

In a more normal voice he said, 'But now I'm thinking you're right.'

'In what way?'

He'd sat well back in his chair now. Physically creating distance between them. 'I'm beginning to think this is a bad idea.'

Damn. 'No problem. I quite understand.'

'I'll take you home.'

Double damn.

Soretta helped her grandfather from the car on Sunday morning, her heart twisting in her chest as she watched him pull himself carefully up the stairs. The doctors said he would eventually regain

his strength. His abdominal wounds had been extensive, infected post surgery, and they were going to be slow to heal. But at least he was alive.

There had been a tiny gift of rain three nights ago, so there was a film of greenish tinge to the ground cover for the first time in months, as if welcoming him home with a promise.

Soretta lifted her head. It *was* a promise. Everything would be fine. It had to be.

The others had gone into town for a Sunday market day, but Soretta suspected they'd planned to give her a chance to ease her grandfather back into his home without them there. She was finding that these new women in her life were incredibly thoughtful.

She followed him inside with his bag in her hand, thinking a cup of tea in the kitchen would be nice. But he bypassed the homey kitchen, and headed straight down the polished-floorboard hall to his room, head lowered. Sorretta wondered how much the drive, in fact the whole debilitating experience, had taken out of him. Two months was a long time to be in hospital.

'That room there is Daphne's, Lorna next to her. On the other side Billie and then Mia. They seem very happy here.'

Lachlan paused. He'd been kept up to date with the comings and goings in his house. But he barely glanced at the open doors. Though he did pause and look at his granddaughter, and his face softened. 'You've done well. Can't say it won't be strange, though, seeing other women in your grandmother's house.'

'Gran would've loved them all. I love them all.' And suddenly she realised that she did. In such a short time those women had become a part of her life. Even the annoying Mia who wasn't so annoying anymore.

And the rent money had stopped the downhill slope of creeping debt and the feminine company had lifted her spirits so much her feet no longer felt like lead as she completed her daily tasks.

Her grandfather straightened, winced and then his old smile drew the corners of his mouth up. 'I'm pleased, then. You're a good girl. The house looks good. The whole place looks good. I'll be able to help soon.'

'I know you will. But in the meantime, get over the trip out here. The others will be home soon and the place will get noisier.'

Lachlan nodded. 'Hospitals are noisy, too,' he said, and started walking again until he made the length of the corridor and his own room. 'I'll have a rest and meet them all later.'

'Okay.' Soretta scooted past him and put his bag down on the lid of the long camphorwood chest at the bottom of his bed. She checked to make sure everything was perfect and then looked back at the face she'd thought she'd never see here again. 'It's good to have you home, Grandad.'

He kissed her brow tenderly. 'I'm sorry.'

'What for?'

'Making you hold the fort. Frightening you.' He grimaced. 'Missing your birthday. You didn't even have a cake.'

She shook her head, remembering, before smiling a bit tearily. 'That's not true. Daphne brought me some cake and a candle the first night at the hospital.'

He grimaced again. 'More I have to thank her for.'

'Daphne would hate it if you thanked her. Don't worry about anything for the moment.' She said again, 'It's good to have you home.' She allowed herself the comfort of holding him close for a moment, before straightening her shoulders and stepping away.

Then she quietly closed the door and left him to rest.

When the others came home that afternoon they brought a couple of cooked chickens, gourmet bread rolls, lettuce and tomatoes, and homemade ice-cream wrapped in layers of newspaper and pulled from the esky. While Lachlan was sorting himself to meet the boarders, they made a low-key spread on the verandah, pushing small tables together and arranging chairs. Soon there was plenty of finger food to enjoy in the shade and celebrate.

Soretta thought it a brilliant idea. Whether it was avoiding the formality of them all sitting down at the table or Billie and Daphne's ease at helping people relax, Lachlan's worried frown disappeared before the first roll was eaten. With Lorna sitting beside him and Soretta herself jumping up at his every want, he had to hold up his hand and ask them all to stop fussing.

'I like the company. I like seeing my Soretta surrounded by women. Welcome.'

Soretta felt the tears prickle behind her eyes because she'd wanted him to be fine with this so badly. And so far so good.

The next Tuesday, Soretta made her way slowly back to the house on the quad bike, her eyes scanning the paddocks for fault in the fences or sickly animals. A part of her mind was still on her recent conversation with Klaus about the new man.

Joseph Porter had started today and looked fine on his resume, over-qualified but apparently desperate for work. His references checked out. He seemed to communicate well with Klaus, which was sometimes a struggle for the best of them, and he did his work for board and lodging and the meagre pay they could afford. But

the dogs didn't like him and she suspected he kicked at them when she wasn't looking.

But not all people were animal people and two men were better than one as they came up to the busy time, and the yards needed renovating before the mob had to go through fast.

She'd always been hopeless at carpentry, and after the last belt on the finger with the hammer she'd decided her loss of production from injury just wasn't worth it. Her grandfather had said thank goodness there was something she couldn't do. She still smiled at that.

But a broken run, or chute, or gate, courted disaster and could cost them hours of lost production at a time when she had extra staff. So it was good he was here. Maybe she was imagining her misgivings. She'd have a word to her grandad and see what he said. He seemed to be stronger since his arrival almost a week ago and Lorna had made him laugh yesterday, though she suspected it had hurt his stomach.

She saw the bus pull up at the gate and turned towards the slope down to the road with the dogs following her. There was no doubt Mia had taken some of the load off her. Soretta suspected she was also hitting her studies harder now after the discussion they'd had about the town needing a new vet in the future, and apparently Lorna was an unexpected genius with homework. She was glad. It wasn't Soretta's strong point and so she hadn't offered.

Mia was ridiculously good with animals though, seemed to understand their minds on a different level to Soretta, and they'd both been surprised by how easily the girl had taken to animal husbandry considering this was her first exposure. She'd been impressed with how much Gigi had trusted Mia with her pups.

Soretta stopped beside her when she came in the gate. The dogs rushed to greet her as soon as she crossed the invisible line onto the station. 'Take the bike up. I want to walk along this fence line.'

Mia finished roughing up the dogs who loved her attention. 'Sure. You don't want me to come?'

'Nope. Sort the lambs and I'll be up soon. And make Gigi stay, she's left the pups again.'

'Okay. They all still fine?'

'Yes, stop worrying.' They swapped and Mia revved the engine.

Soretta raised her eyebrows. 'Not over twenty or you're dead.' Mia flashed her a cheeky smile but she did drive off sedately. Soretta knew Billie was nervous about Mia being on the bike, but you could mollycoddle too much. Mia had a reckless streak but she also had a brain.

An hour later Soretta caught up with Mia as she was sorting the lambs. She inclined her head towards the homestead. 'What's happening up at the house?'

'Your grandfather and Lorna are squabbling.' Mia grinned at her. 'He looks much better.'

Soretta smiled back. 'I was worried.' She hesitated but she had the feeling Mia might understand. 'I was terrified he wouldn't be able to ever come home. That he'd sell the station, or worse, that something would happen and he'd die in the hospital.'

Mia nodded. 'He was in there a long time.'

'It's good to have him home.' She shook off the past, then looked at Mia. 'You seem to be getting along with your mum better now?'

Mia shrugged shyly. 'I think I've grown up a bit. I was mostly bored when she wasn't home, and got up to a bit of mischief, so it

was probably my fault that she didn't trust me.'

Soretta could understand that. 'You're doing great here. I appreciate your help.'

Mia blushed.' I love it.' They both looked at the playpen with the last of the lambs almost ready to go back to the mob.

'I'll miss them when they're gone,' Mia said.

Soretta shrugged. 'There's always something to look after. Puppies. Injured birds. Anyway, if you can finish here I'll go up to the house and have a shower. It was hot walking along the fence line.'

Mia grinned. 'Bet it was. I had a nice ride up to the house on the quad.'

THIRTEEN

Lorna Lamerton stood with her feet apart and poked her finger at Lachlan. 'I can shoot a tin can off the fence with a .22 at fifty paces.'

'I don't believe you, Lorna.' Lachlan clutched his stomach.

Billie hoped he managed to control himself because if he didn't it was going to hurt. She was grinning herself.

Lachlan had offended their octogenarian guest with his disbelief and now Lorna was telling him to get the rifle.

Lachlan was shaking his head. 'I'm sorry. I can't allow someone without a gun licence to handle a firearm.'

'Excuse me, Mr Byrnes, I carried a gun on my horse for ten years when I was a young woman. I've had my gun licence since I was asked to get one in 1996 and I've shot more rifles than you've had breakfasts. If I have to I can hold the biggest double-barrel shotgun you can find and blow a snake to smithereens.'

'In that case I believe you.'

Slightly mollified that Lachlan did seem to have come around, Lorna was calming down. 'So you should.' She fixed him with a gimlet stare. 'Now get that rifle.'

Lachlan stood up. 'I know I shouldn't do this.'

Billie watched them go. She wished she could share the moment with Daphne, who was late home today, because it would have had them both rolling around in stitches, and she was getting used to sharing her thoughts now. The little conversations about anything and everything, about the way you could put mustard in mayonnaise if you had to make a sauce, or the latest on a station family that highlighted a medical need. Or a type of bird that flew over the homestead roof and their friendly rivalry over identifying new ones.

The really fun stuff was the quick eye contact when Mia or Lorna did something amusing, or the bond they shared over protecting Soretta from some of her massive workload when they could.

For the first time ever she had a good friend, almost a sister. Working and living with Daphne had made her consider other people and how she might possibly think of letting them into her life. It was a big shift from when she'd first arrived.

She even toyed with the idea of letting Morgan in. Maybe stop the way the two of them were backing away like timid children from a game that might be dangerous.

Maybe she needed to talk to Daphne about her relationship with Morgan. Or her non-relationship with Morgan. She wanted to tell her how he hadn't kissed her goodnight after their first real date. How he'd escorted her home, and even though he'd come around to her side of the car when they arrived and held her door open, he hadn't followed her to the steps. He hadn't leaned in for a kiss, he'd just closed the door after her and, because she'd been waiting for him to make his move, she'd been surprised to hear him walking away.

Who knew why? She didn't. She may as well get over it. But perhaps she should start looking at the idea of male companionship. Put some feelers out. Heaven forbid, maybe even consider an internet dating site? Did they have those in Mica Ridge?

The idea didn't sit well and Billie went back to her paper until Soretta returned to the house.

When Soretta arrived her grandfather and Lorna were still shooting tin cans off the orchard fence and the discussion of .22 calibres over .222 rifles drifted towards the house.

Billie's feet were resting on the verandah rail as she flicked through the ads.

Soretta watched the two in the distance. 'Apart from the subdued crack of the rifles it's very peaceful here.'

Billie grinned. 'And your grandfather actually had to hold his stomach to laugh, but he's looking stronger every day and the person he's enjoying the most seems to be Lorna.'

'Then that's a good thing.'

'She's taking him gold prospecting tomorrow. Apparently, her son dropped around the metal detectors she and her husband used to use when they went camping.'

Soretta glanced around to make sure Lorna was out of earshot. 'Her son had afternoon tea with us yesterday. When Lorna went into the kitchen he was apologetic about Lorna being here, but I assured him we loved having her. Poor guy. His world has improved now the two women in his life have a bit of distance between them. He loves Lorna, but his wife was making life hell before Lorna left.'

Soretta grinned. 'Sometimes I can't quite imagine Lorna doing all the things I know she's done and then at other times I think of

course she would. I can't imagine anything fazing her.' She thought about that. 'Except maybe feeling like a third wheel.'

'So it's good she's here. She's pretty tough. I want to grow older like her. Speaking of growing older . . .' Billie looked around for her daughter. 'Where's Mia?'

'She's taken one of the lambs back to the mob. Thankfully in the other direction to our marksmen. The lamb was getting too big for its boots and stealing the milk from the smaller ones.'

'She's enjoying the animals.'

'Very much. And doing a good job helping around the station.'

Billie examined Soretta's face and it showed nothing but sincerity. But then when had Soretta ever said something she hadn't meant? Now that Billie thought about it, Soretta seemed less drawn, calmer, more at peace. Maybe because her grandad was home and becoming stronger every day. Perhaps the steady income had lightened the load as well. She hoped it was both of those things.

All Billie knew was that Soretta had become a role model Mia looked up to. If she hadn't been so pleased to see the improvement in her daughter's studies and attitude she might have been sick of the constant stream of 'Soretta said': 'Soretta said the sheep are looking better since even that drop of rain.' 'Soretta said the drought might ease if the clouds look like that for the next three days.' 'Soretta said . . .'

Billie smiled. 'Mia thinks the sun shines out of you.'

Soretta lifted her chin, and looked Billie in the eye. 'She's a help. All of you are a help, so thank you.'

'We love being here. Your grandad seems to be getting over the shock of a posse of women in his house.'

Soretta agreed. 'It's doing him good. I haven't seen him so amused since before my gran was sick.'

'I'm glad.'

'By the way, I just wanted to mention there's a new station hand arriving today. You might see his black car come and go. I doubt he'll come near the house but his name is Joseph.'

Billie winced. She'd thought for a moment Soretta had been going to say Jock. She shook off the past because there was movement at the steps. She and Soretta looked up as the two gun-toting cowboys arrived back on the verandah looking very pleased with themselves.

'I hope you didn't do any damage to your wound with the jolting of that rifle,' Soretta said to her grandfather.

'If Lorna can lean on a post then I can, too. So no harm done.'

'And who won?'

The shooters looked at each other. 'We were evenly matched,' Lorna said primly as she handed her weapon back to Lachlan to return to the gun safe.

He took it and waggled his head at her. 'Come on. I'll show you where the key is. Now I know I can trust you, there's a nice little four-ten shotgun I use for snakes around the house. Soretta doesn't like guns. And there're some shells there with rock salt that I use for scaring birds.'

Two days later Mia was over at the sheep pen checking how Tucker the sheep was settling down.

'Afternoon.'

The man had appeared to her left out of the setting sun as Mia

had been crouched down watching the sheep nose his way around the mob. She nearly lost her balance, so she straightened awkwardly to stand as he approached.

He was an older man, very good-looking in an old movie-star way, with dark hair like hers. He had sunglasses on, which seemed odd as she was used to Klaus and Lachlan not wearing them under their hats.

She had the feeling she'd seen him somewhere before. Then she remembered the crossing, and the car, the same one she'd seen leaving the station yesterday. Must be the new man Soretta told her about.

She said, 'Hello. Where'd you come from?'

He pointed towards the bunkhouse. 'Klaus asked me to check the gate was shut for this paddock because he could see the movement of the mob.'

'You're the new farm worker?'

'Joseph.' He held out his hand and reluctantly she took it. His fingers were softer than she expected, as if he was new to hard work. She dropped his hand fairly quickly.

'I'd better get back. Soretta told me to be fast.'

'She's a doer, that one. Young for a boss lady.'

'She's a star.' Unconsciously, Mia wiped her hands on her jeans. 'See ya.'

'What's your name?'

'Mia. Bye.' She turned and hurried over to the bike, but before she started it he said, 'How old are you?'

She didn't want to answer but she made the mistake of looking at him. Maybe she should have just pretended she didn't hear and turned on the ignition. But birthdays were hard not to mention,

even to people who made you feel uncomfortable. 'Seventeen next month.'

He smiled at her and she smiled back awkwardly. He looked as though she'd done something to please him, which was really odd. She started the quad. Gave a wave without looking at him and drove away.

Back at the house Mia passed Soretta picking lemons off the tree. They were having fish tonight. 'Who's the guy with Klaus?' Mia asked as she began to help her fill the small basket.

'Joseph Porter. Casual farm hand.'

'There's something familiar about him.'

'Not to me. I've never seen him around before. Apparently he came across from South Australia looking for work. Where'd you see him?'

'Klaus sent him over to see why the mob was shifting when I was checking on Tucker being back with them.'

'Klaus's doing well. Not sure if this bloke is going to turn out as good, but we get lots of transients.'

'Seems a bit flash for a farm worker,' Mia said.

'He does.' They'd filled the basket and turned towards the house together. 'Stay away from him.'

Mia turned to her mentor in mild surprise. 'Why?'

'Don't know.' Soretta looked thoughtfully over her shoulder. 'As soon as they fix the pens I'll ask him to leave.'

'Because I said he was flash?'

'My business.' And that was the end of that.

'Okay.' Mia shrugged and then went on, checking the house to make sure no one could hear her. 'Speaking of strange behaviour, did you notice Lorna looks a bit vague this afternoon?'

Soretta looked up, and thought about it before nodding. 'She said a couple of odd things. Maybe she isn't well. I'll mention it to Billie.'

At the Flying Doctor Base, Billie and Daphne were flying back to Boorenji. Daphne had asked if she could swap her shift so she could go on this particular run. They were delivering a special person back home.

Half an hour later a huddle of waiting passengers stood beside the plane. Belle looked anxiously at the aircraft and chewed her lip. Aunty May stoically avoided any glances towards the thing that was going to carry her so high across the orange-and-red plains. While baby Anthony, oblivious in his aunty's safe arms, made the snoring noise that most prem babies, even when they had grown up a little, seemed to make when they slept.

Daphne looked forward to a good catch-up with Barbara Tomkins—they hadn't had much of a chance at the bus accident—so she could find out how everything was going when she brought Gwyn in for a check-up, and she knew Billie felt the same. This was the community stuff she loved to bits and she knew it was becoming important to Billie, too.

She'd packed another bag of mandarins because the day promised to be a scorcher despite the thunderstorm last night. The tiny drops of rain they'd had were already evaporating off the hard ground.

'All aboard,' Rex said cheerfully and sent Daphne a smile that made her own mouth stretch wide instinctively.

She couldn't quite believe Rex was interested, but the days were counting down to Broken Hill Races, and though she'd bought a

lot of clothes with Billie's help—too blinking many—she needed to sort out what she was going to wear. Lorna had booked her into her hairdresser's for a style cut with an English girl after work today, and she was nervous about that, too.

Rex had mentioned he'd booked the rooms a couple of months ago before the best ones were taken. In spite of a severe talking to with herself, she couldn't help being incredibly curious about who he'd planned to take and why they'd cancelled.

'You coming, Daphne?' Billie's amused voice whispered in her ear and she blinked and returned to the real world. She was being silly, and distracted, and that wasn't like her, she admonished herself as she marched up the steps to help settle their passengers as comfortably as she could in the small space.

Anthony slept through the whole flight. Belle had her eyes closed but they were so tightly squeezed together that, along with the way her nails dug into the seatbelt, nobody considered her asleep. Aunty May had initially started the flight peering cautiously out of the window but after the first ten minutes had her nose pressed against the glass as she tried to see all there was to see from the vantage point of an eagle.

When they arrived the old container was still sitting there under its roof and the air-conditioner had been turned on so it was cool inside the consulting rooms. Aunty May, carrying Anthony, who had slept the entire flight, nodded her thanks, and ushered Belle towards a huddle of waiting women standing back from the main centre, and they were swallowed up in the group.

There was Barbara Tomkins and a happy looking Gwyn. Daphne hurried towards them with a smile and Billie was right behind her.

FOURTEEN

The next morning Lorna woke to golden rays of sunlight peeping through the curtains and stared at the ceiling. Her eyes blinked fuzzily only to stiffen in alarm moments later.

Was that a bat up there in the corner?

The light shifted and twisted into another bizarre shape, this time a rat, and she moaned, and then it, too, disappeared. She backed up against the bedhead, clutching the sheet to her thin chest. She stared at the painted pressed metal of the ceiling and saw a pattern she didn't recognise. In fact, she didn't recognise the room.

A cold trickle of fear slid down her neck and she glanced quickly to the left and the right. She was alone. She didn't understand.

The first big rays of sun came into the room and that wasn't right either. Her hand rose and clutched at her throat and her heart felt like a landed fish flopping in her chest. Nothing looked right. Not the ceiling, not the curtain-framed window, not the cast-iron bed she was lying in.

She could hear voices outside her bedroom door. Murmuring words she couldn't distinguish, but they struck cold daggers of

terror deep into her chest. Who were they? Where was she? She desperately needed to go to the toilet, but she didn't know where it was or even if the people who were outside would let her leave this strange room to find it.

The ball of fear rose up from her stomach, choking her, and she shivered in the warm air while she frantically searched the room for Wallace. Then she caught sight of his watch, the one she'd worn since he'd . . . ? Died! The thought crashed into her as she examined the timepiece lying peacefully on the side table that wasn't hers, and a lone tear slid from the corner of her eye.

Slowly, very slowly, most of it came back.

Blue Hills Station. Daphne. Soretta and Lachlan. Billie and Mia. She'd lived here for a month—how could she forget?

Then an even more frightening thought seeped insidiously into her suddenly freezing bones. Is that how it had started for dear Wallace? Maybe her daughter-in-law was right and she was going mad. Alzheimer's. Dementia. Crackers.

Deep, lonely sadness swamped her. And a grim determination to not be a burden on anyone. She'd have to leave her new friends after finding the first place she'd been happy in since Wallace had died.

Her galloping heart finally quietened and she climbed unsteadily out of bed. She listened at the door but the voices had gone. Lorna pulled on her dressing gown and shuffled to the bathroom with her head down.

Daphne dusted the blusher over her new matt foundation and decided it wasn't too bad. She hadn't worn much makeup since her divorce—the heat out here would probably melt it off anyway—but

Billie had been very patient with her instructions.

The new brand was subtle and she did feel it made her skin more even-toned. While she finished her makeup, Billie was at the bed helping her pack a soft carry-on bag for the weekend at the races with Rex.

No one had done that for her in the last twenty years. And not just packed, the outfits had been mapped out, colour coordinated and accessorised with military precision. There was even a chart taped to the lid in case Daphne couldn't remember.

That had been Billie's suggestion when Daphne had lamented she'd forget what went with what. So nothing was left to chance. Daphne's lack of confidence had been dealt with. Years of uncertainty with fashion were at an end. It felt pretty darn good to not have to stress. All she'd needed was a stylist like Billie. Or a mother. As if on cue a butterfly flew in and out of the open verandah door.

Funny how she could remember so clearly. Her mother's breathing ragged against the peach-coloured sheets—she could remember the exact colour of those, too—and a butterfly had flown out at the same time as her mother's last breath had ended on a sigh.

Twenty years ago she'd stared after that butterfly, refused to look towards the bed, to believe it had finally happened and the one person who loved her had gone, until one of the nurses had taken her hand and cried with her.

'You okay, Daphne?' Billie's voice broke through Daphne's memories.

She shook herself. 'Sure. Of course. Did you see the butterfly?'

'No.' Billie turned to look but it was gone.

Daphne sighed and lifted her head. 'There was one like that the

day my mum died. I always thought she floated out the window after it.' She couldn't believe she'd blurted that out. How embarrassing.

Billie's eyes softened and that made her feel like howling. Nobody had looked at her like that for a long time, either. She was acting like a child. *Get a grip.* Her nerves for this upcoming weekend were almost too much and she wasn't sure this was all worth it. She wasn't that unhappy on her own. Especially now that she had friends.

Billie looked across. 'Did you travel much as a child? Your dad being a politician?'

'No,' she said. 'When Mum was alive she preferred to stay at home. With me.'

And her father had always said business was no place for a child.

At home with Mum had been the best times she could remember. The times when she'd felt special and truly connected because her mother had seemed to understand her daughter was shy and hated the limelight. Her mother had been the only person to love her as she was, with all her faults.

She watched Billie fold the grey crinkley dress that seemed to float over the hips and bring out her best points. Billie had great taste in clothes, and shopping had been fun for the first time ever.

'Your mum was young when she died, you said?'

Daphne took her eyes from the dress. 'Yep. Lymphoma. Then multiple strokes at thirty-four. She kept having them, there was nothing the doctors could do, though I remember the drip and the fact that she seemed to just fade away. I was ten and she never spoke again after the first stroke, but she knew me when she looked at me.'

Billie shook her head. 'Terrible for a child to watch.'

Yep. Her voice dropped. 'It was like watching the most beautiful ice sculpture in the world melt in front of my eyes.'

And because Billie didn't say anything to pull her back, Daphne remembered the time when she'd watched her mother waste away more every day. 'The nurses my father hired to care for her were remarkable. And that's probably why I wanted to become a nurse.' They had included her where busier women would have finished their task more quickly without the awkward help of a young daughter. At least her father had done something right.

'What about your father?'

'He wasn't there much. He was busy, and disappointed in his life, disappointed in his wife who had succumbed to a lingering illness just as his career star had begun to shine.' And disappointed in his daughter, who'd bumbled along, shaming him.

She saw the frown on Billie's face and winced. She wasn't looking for sympathy. She had sympathy for her father. A better daughter would have been a hostess for him. Been what her mother had been before the illness. Oh, she'd tried. And failed. Like that time at Melbourne Cup when she'd organised a table for her father and husband and it had been a disaster.

So it didn't make sense that he'd encouraged her to marry a man very like himself, when she'd allowed herself to be primped and presented in clothes she hated, but she'd thought she'd done something right. She'd thought they'd be able to have a baby and she couldn't wait for that. But that had been the most foolish thing of all.

It hadn't taken long for Quinton to realise his mistake in marrying her and she'd easily recognised the disappointment in his eyes. She'd managed to alienate the two men in her life she had most

wanted to please. So no baby, and eventually no marriage, which was a good thing because Quinton's lack of respect for her had only made her worse.

When he'd left she'd done something crazy, taking herself to uni and becoming a registered nurse. And in doing so, had found a strength she didn't know she possessed. After reading a memoir of someone very much like Lorna must have been, she'd decided the Flying Doctor Service was where she wanted to be.

And she'd never looked back.

She straightened her shoulders and tried to drop the guilt. She bet Quinton hadn't given her another thought. Why hadn't that penny dropped before? 'I was stupid and married a man my father suggested. Stupid . . .'

There was no judgement in Billie's voice. 'Sometimes we make poor choices. Then we have to get out.'

'You're a widow, aren't you?'

'That's a story for another time,' Billie said, as she folded the new soft nightgown.

Billie looked sad. Daphne frowned and forced her mind back to clothes. Forced her mind back to happy things. Things that made her smile. Things that made Billie smile. It was a lovely nightgown. Extravagant. It was the result of her being urged on by Billie to splash out on herself for a change—and she had with a vengeance. The soft collar was still fairly high-necked with ribbons and made her feel feminine. The nicest thing about that little outfit was she felt like she belonged in it—she wasn't trying to climb into something that made her feel awkward.

'Woohoo.' Billie swung a bra around on her finger. 'I do love the frillies.'

Billie looked happy again as the subject shifted and Daphne watched the bundle of underwear settle into the case. The panties were incredibly soft and lacy, with a matching bra and, although they were admittedly waist-high and comfortable, they were also so . . . pretty. The result of more pushing from Billie to buy. It had been fun. And they were things she really liked.

Her mood lifted. 'Not that I'm showing them to anyone.'

Billie raised her eyebrows suggestively. 'You never know. Rex might be more of a devil than you expect.'

Daphne laughed. 'Two rooms. But it's a nice thought.'

They both looked at the no-crush, pale pink silk racing dress with the heart-shaped lace insert and shared a conspiratorial glance. 'You'll knock his socks off.'

'Hope so.' Imagine if he did fancy her in that. It was designed to fall from her breasts, not squash them, and it floated over her waist and then stopped at her knees to show off her legs. Billie was right. She did have nice legs, short but shapely, and Billie had dragged her for a pedicure and to the spray-tan salon, where she'd almost died standing in front of that girl with only a paper bra and bikini on. But, for the first time in her life, she was proud of her legs and feet, and the medium heels that were actually comfortable and gave her more height.

She watched Billie close the lid of the case. She couldn't believe everything was in there and it wouldn't crush. Even the grey-and-pink fascinator that matched the dress was crush resistant.

Billie must have read her mind. 'The hat makes the outfit. It matches everything. It looks great.'

She'd try to wear it.

'What time is Rex picking you up?'

'In an hour.'

'Then you'd better get dressed.'

Billie watched them drive away with a contented feeling.

'They'd call that a dirty weekend in my day,' Lorna observed with a strained twinkle in her faded blue eyes as she waved.

'I hope so.' Billie carried the teapot and put it on the wicker table and Lorna followed with the milk jug. Lorna was quiet this morning. In fact, Lorna didn't look herself at all. And Soretta had mentioned she thought Lorna was not on her game.

Billie tried to cheer her up. 'I love the way Lachlan enjoys your company. You're the one I see him laugh with.'

Lorna brushed that away. 'It's easy to talk to a man at my age. I know I have nothing to worry about.'

Billie laughed and winked. 'You never know. Handsome widower like that. It could be a romance,' Billie teased.

Lorna gave one of her trademark snorts. 'What do they call older ladies that go chasing younger men? Cougars. I'd be a cougar.'

'There's not that much difference in your ages.' Billie tried to hold back the grin. She couldn't think of anyone less like a cougar than Lorna and it was good to see the older lady had brightened slightly. 'You're a card. You know we love having you here.'

'All things come to an end. I won't be here forever.'

'Well, you can't possibly leave until you're sick of us. We won't have it.'

'We'll see,' said Lorna. 'It looks very dry,' she changed the subject, and pointed out the dryness of the paddock.

Billie accepted the diversion and took it all in. Despite the

dusty barrenness she enjoyed the vista of grey-green saltbush over red-and-orange rocks. The occasional glint of mica catching the sunlight. Once again she marvelled that cattle and sheep could find sustenance in such an arid landscape and remembered school excursions in her youth out to the old mines and stations that ringed the town.

She looked down at the tablecloth Lorna insisted they put down at morning teatime. Soretta's grandmother's china shone and clinked. It was all so homey, Billie thought. Morning tea on the verandah for anyone present around ten had become an institution. Like the evening drinks.

Lachlan had started to join them when he was in, but today he'd ventured to drive the utility across to the pens to assess the sheep. He'd be back in time for he and Lorna to spend the afternoon together at their new Saturday pastime. A bit of a flutter, Lorna called it. A couple of beers and an afternoon of fifty cents on the nags, Lachlan agreed, was a very reasonable thing.

There'd been a spring in his step this morning and Billie suspected Lachlan was at least halfway back to his former strength.

Lorna sighed. 'I hope what's-his-name sweeps her off her pretty little feet. That girl needs a good loving.'

'Rex,' Billie offered.

'I knew his name just wouldn't sit on my tongue. Nothing will today.'

Then she sighed and deflated like a puffer fish losing its air. Her shoulders sagged and her hands came down to rest despondently in her lap. 'I'll be sad when my holiday is up.'

Billie frowned. She thought about Blue Hills Station without Lorna's brand of common sense and wicked humour and the huge

gap she would leave. 'Do you have to go, Lorna? We love your company.'

To her distress Lorna's eyes filled with tears. 'That's very sweet of you, dear.' Lorna reached over and patted her hand. 'Lately I seem to be losing the plot and my memory isn't what it was.' She drew a shaky breath. 'Can I tell you something, Billie?'

'Of course.'

'It even took me a few minutes to remember where I was this morning when I woke up. It was the most horrible feeling.' A tear slipped down her cheek and Billie felt her heart squeeze. 'You don't want to be living with a mad woman,' she said, dabbing her eyes with a tissue.

Billie thought back to Lorna's arrival at the breakfast table. She and Daphne had been discussing the clothes she would take on her weekend away and she remembered thinking that Lorna had been quiet. Distracted. Remembered again Soretta's concern.

'Perhaps you've been doing more than usual?'

'I don't think so. Less probably. My daughter-in-law might be right. Maybe I need to think about relocating to the retirement village.'

Billie studied her more closely. Apart from her slightly hectic cheeks her face looked pale. Her fingers shook now that Billie was looking properly. 'Do you feel well?'

Lorna sighed. 'As well as I can be for an old woman.'

Now that didn't sound like Lorna, and Billie leant forward to study her further. She listened properly to the thread of panic in the usually calm and no-nonsense voice.

The older lady went on. 'I'm tired, getting confused, and I can't be a nuisance to you lovely ladies forever.'

Billie considered her. And started there. 'You are not a nuisance' Her brows rose as a thought crashed in. 'Maybe you need to see a doctor?' she said. 'I'm a doctor. Maybe you just need a check-up. Some blood tests? A urine check? Urinary infections can cause even full-blown confusion in older ladies that goes away when the antibiotics kick in.' Delirium or dementia?

Lorna looked up and frowned. She straightened in her chair and her trembling lip made Billie's eyes sting. 'Can I make an appointment?'

Billie reached across and took Lorna's thin, veined wrist in hers and felt her pulse. It was bounding. 'I'm pretty sure I can fit you in now. Then I'll take the blood and specimens and drop them into the hospital pathology. I want to pick something up from town this morning anyway.'

'Do the tests here, you mean?' Lorna gave her a watery smile. 'Seven day service. Just like when my husband was alive.'

'And I have a starter pack of antibiotics while we wait for a result. The more I think about it the more I do think something else is going on.' She took her fingers from Lorna's wrist and patted her hand.

'And no more of this talk of us wanting you to go. You leave when you've had enough of us. Look how much Mia's schoolwork has improved since you took to sitting with her in the evenings. She'd never let me do that. We'll sort it out.' She stood up. 'Stay here. I'll just get my doctor's bag. I haven't used it since I moved up here.'

FIFTEEN

Daphne had never been in an aircraft smaller than the King Air B200 but she wasn't worried. She knew the pilot.

'What are you smiling about?' Rex asked as they pulled up at the private end of the airfield, where the authentic Auster, a small four-seater fabric aircraft that Rex had lovingly restored, was waiting for them. His crinkled eyes held a tenderness she hadn't seen directed at her before and it sat in her chest like a freshly heated wheat bag. Warm, radiant and heavy with promise.

'Just thinking how much faith I had in the pilot.'

'Had?'

She had to laugh at that. 'Have.'

He gave her a wink. 'That's lucky,' he said, pointing at the sky. 'Though the weather promises to be smooth with good visibility.'

His eyes were alight and he wasn't quite rubbing his hands as he looked at his ancient plane, but she could tell he was excited. It added to the happy feeling in her chest to see him so animated. 'I'll take a level trip. Have you always been a fan of flying?'

'Yep,' he said. 'Used to lie on my back in the paddock and watch the eagles wheel in the sky. Vowed I'd do that someday.'

'I'm glad you feel that way. It's nice.'

'You're nice.' He smiled at her and she saw a hint of promise as they pulled their overnight cases from the boot. Before his words even sank in, as if he knew she'd be stuck in a confusion of embarrassment because he'd complimented her, he went on. 'Have you been to the races anywhere up here?'

'No.' Thank goodness for a change of subject. She resisted the urge to fan her face with her hand.

'I've been to a couple of meets,' he said, closing the boot. 'I do enjoy a country race day.'

She hurried into speech, almost falling over her words in case he thought she wasn't talking enough. 'Lorna bets every Saturday. Mia showed her the secrets of internet punting, though how a sixteen-year-old girl would know that is baffling.'

She shook her head with wonder. Mia had many hidden talents. 'Now Lorna backs every Sydney race on the card and she's started Lachlan on it. They make a day of Saturdays. Everyone else laughs.'

Rex raised his brows. 'Her son might be worried about that.'

'I doubt it. They only bet fifty cents a race and she seems to come out ahead every week. Unlike Lachlan, who seems to do his seven dollars fifty for the day. One week she almost got the quadrella with a fifty-cent bet and the pay-out was about ten thousand!'

He took her case, sent her a look when she tried to pick it up, and she put up her hands. *Okay. You can carry my bag. Sheesh.* He'd opened the door for her when they'd left this morning, too. She loved it.

'Funny set-up you girls have out there. How's Lachlan coping with all the women?'

'He's quiet. Though Soretta says he's almost boisterous compared to what he was before the accident. But he seems to be fine with the invasion.'

Rex put the cases down beside the aircraft, and scratched the back of his head. 'I don't know how I'd go with that many women living in my house.'

'He gets on well with Lorna, or he can go to the other end of the house or out on the farm when he wants to get away.'

She'd wondered about the man next to her. She should probably wait for later but the conversation was so easy now and there'd be no talking once they were up in the air. 'Have you ever lived with a woman, Rex?'

'Once, a long time ago. I was married. But it only lasted a year. I was working in Nigeria, flying for an oil company and we were saving to buy our own home.'

He shrugged and began to walk around the plane. Checking rudders and wind speed instruments. The wings, the tail. The wooden propeller.

She could watch him all day, except her eyes were drawn back to his face as he dropped the news she'd had no idea about after six months of working together.

His voice was matter-of-fact. 'She found someone else while I was away and I guess I was lucky that I didn't miss the signs and continue in ignorant bliss for years. She seemed to think I was making a big deal of it and was shocked when I asked for a divorce.'

She licked her lips. May as well get it all out there before they took off. 'My husband preferred more sophisticated women and that wasn't me. He only married me for my father's patronage. Neither of them were patient men.'

Rex shot her a look and his eyes were kind. 'Seems unfair that we pay for their lack of foresight, I always thought. But at least we can move on and they're stuck with themselves.'

Daphne blinked in surprise, and from somewhere deep inside herself she started to relax. To smile. And finally to laugh.

'I'll try to look at it that way from now on.'

Rex paused, holding her eyes with his level gaze. 'He was a fool, Daphne. You're the real deal.'

He opened the passenger door for her but before she could move past him he put his hand gently on her arm. 'I've watched you the last six months and you're one of the most sincere people I've ever met. You don't always get that with sophistication.'

Her face flamed. The blotches would be ugly but there was nothing she could do about it. She wished she could start accepting that, too.

Billie's gentle reminder rang in her ears: *Take compliments graciously.* 'Thank you, Rex. I enjoy working with you, too.' Phew. That hadn't been too hard.

'Good. Jump in. We'll get going on this weekend shall we?' he said as he winked at her. 'Now for the exciting part.'

There were more exciting things to come? She thought of her new clothes. Little did he know!

The small red-and-yellow aircraft shone in the sunlight. Rex stowed the gear behind the seats with care. Daphne decided she'd buy herself two smaller soft-sided bags for next time. Next time?

'Lucky you travel light.'

'And you,' she said, allowing herself to revel in the pleasure of being here. On a weekend away. With a man. With Rex! Except for her not-so-memorable honeymoon, she'd never done this before

with a man, and the only other times had been when she'd attended those two-day midwifery conferences in Sydney, which had always been on her own.

He pointed to the black line on the wing where she had to put her foot, then nodded in appreciation that she had the flat slip-on pumps Billie had suggested she buy for climbing in and out of the aircraft. It had been a good choice. She couldn't imagine scratching Rex's little plane with nasty heels.

Then her leg was through and she sank down into one of the two side-by-side cockpit seats. Both sides had hand and feet controls and she stayed well away from the U-shaped rudder.

Rex leaned in to help her with her seatbelt. His hands were quick and confident—and impersonal. 'This used to be a Flying Doctor plane down in Tasmania when they flew around without radios in the early sixties. That's why I fell in love with it. I heard a story of them taking out the back window in a plane like this and feeding a bloke in through that way on a spine board.'

They looked at each other, sharing a mutual admiration for the logistics of the pioneers of the service and their larrikin ingenuity. 'We've got it easy.'

'Easier,' he agreed.

She shrugged, and looked admiringly at the plane again. It was a no-nonsense little ripper. 'Were there many models of Auster or just this one?'

'A few. This is a J5 Autocar. Took me two years to have it pass the regulation requirements because it had run out of flying hours. I've got a licensed engineer friend in Broken Hill who helped me rebuild it from scratch, and it's got nearly a thousand hours on it to go. It'll see me out for all the recreational flying I do.'

He handed her a gloriously old-fashioned leather helmet that strapped under the chin. 'I won two of these off a guy with a Tiger Moth. I have the windows open a lot of the time and wear mine. Would you put it on? I've always wanted to see a woman wear one in my plane.'

'I'd love to.' His eyes twinkled at her as she pulled on the helmet and now she felt like Amelia Earhart. This was very cool.

Rex checked the integrity of her seatbelt buckle again and stepped back. 'You're set.' He jumped down. 'I'll just do the walk around again and then swing the prop.'

During the next ten minutes Daphne adjusted her helmet and put on the headphones Rex had pointed out. They were decades older than the ones she was used to, but it was all part of the fun and the leather helmet kept them in place. She studied the instruments in front of her and the two half-steering wheels for the two front seats. The whole aircraft was just so immaculately maintained.

Then Rex called out to the empty tarmac, 'All clear!' He sent her a look that warmed her all the way down to her flat shoes, then swung the wooden propeller.

The engine started first go, which was always reassuring, she thought with an inward smile, pleased she wasn't at all nervous. Just exhilarated at the noise and air rushing at her from the propeller because Rex had all the front sliding widows open to let out the heat.

She twisted her head to see him come around the rear of the aircraft to the opposite door and climb in. Rex. Gorgeous Rex, who she'd admired from afar, was sharing his love of flying with her.

His eyes twinkled as he pulled on his own leather helmet and earphones, and she heard him speak to the tower, then he put his

thumbs up and revved the engine. She felt like the female lead in an adventure movie and her mouth was so widely stretched with the joy of it all she thought her face might split.

They took off with the sun behind them, and she glanced out at the view she'd seen so many times before: the airport shrinking in their wake, the rows of houses and the main street with its big and small roofs and gardens. Further out there was the quick transition from green to brown flat land, with rocky outcrops punching through the earth like dinosaur backs. And to the left were the darker wriggling lines of dried creek beds. Even the empty dam below the homestead at Blue Hills Station looked wonderful.

Rex tapped her on the shoulder and pointed down and she leant to peer below again. She could see the sheep yards, and a vehicle beside them, and someone on a quad bike, probably Soretta. She sat back as they fell behind and looked out the front into the clear skies ahead with a sense of everything being right in the world.

Their plane bore noisily onwards. Even through the headphones, the wind rushed into her face as the cabin cooled, until finally Rex gestured for her to shut her sliding window. The noise died down marginally and Rex crackled in her ear.

'She's different to the King Air.'

She nodded at him and pressed her reply button. 'Much more fun.'

He gave her the thumbs up and they angled away towards Broken Hill and a wicked weekend. She hoped.

The house seemed empty without Daphne. Billie hadn't realised how much she'd become accustomed to her friend's company. And

it wasn't just the cooking. It was the debriefing of the day from their systems at night or a worry that could be shared.

Like Lorna being sick. She was ready to run into town, but she was waiting for Mia or Lachlan to come in before she could leave.

Mia bounced in. 'Hey, Mum, whatcha doin'?'

'Is that hey, or hay, Miss Farmgirl?'

'Wish we had hay, to give to the ewes dropping late lambs.'

'Who are you? Where's my daughter?'

Mia gave her a hug. 'I'm here. Maybe I've just grown up a bit.'

'You've grown up a lot and I couldn't be more proud of you. Has Soretta got anything planned for you this weekend?'

'There's a gymkhana on Sunday over at Menindee. I was going to ask if we could go tonight instead of tomorrow morning. She's going to show me more of what's involved. Trent's sister's in it, too.' She looked at her mother thoughtfully. 'Will you be okay if I go? With Daphne away?'

Billie felt the rush of love for this girl-woman, who she would lay down her life for. 'Why thank you. It's very kind of you to be concerned but I might just take Lorna and go on an adventure.' Or Lorna might take her on an adventure neither of them wanted to go on. 'Watch Lorna for me, will you? Just until Lachlan comes back. She's not well and I'm running into town to get her some more medication.'

Billie saw the concern on her daughter's face as she replied, 'Of course.'

'She's fragile,' Billie added and Mia nodded her understanding.

Half an hour later Billie drove into town to the hospital pathology department with a frown between her eyes and dropped off

Lorna's samples. She hadn't thought about the pharmacy closing for lunch, but this was the country not the city and they had only one pharmacist.

'Billie?' An unexpected relief coursed through her at the sound of Morgan's voice.

Excellent. This could be a wonderful chance to talk to Morgan about her worry for Lorna. 'Morgan. It's so good to see you.'

He took her arm and steered her across to an alcove. 'You too.' He leaned close and looked searchingly into her face. 'You okay?'

'Oh. Yes. I guess I am.' She almost blurted it out there and then. Something happened this morning! But she didn't know where to start.

'Would you like a coffee?'

She checked her watch. The hand had only moved five minutes and she had twenty-five to go until the pharmacy opened.

'Sure. Thanks. Why are you at the hospital?'

'Just checking on Jack Fortescue. He came off his quad bike and broke his hip.' He steered her as he spoke and within seconds she found herself sitting at a corner table that afforded a tad more privacy than you normally found in a hospital cafeteria.

'Poor guy.'

'Yep.' He said, piercing her with this dark eyes. 'What's up?'

She grimaced ruefully. 'Is it that obvious?'

'To me it is.' The words were flat and didn't invite comment, as if he wasn't comfortable with his own perception.

'It's Lorna. She woke confused this morning. Didn't know where she was.'

He frowned. 'She's all right now?'

'Seems to be. I think she's quite shaken by the thought that she

might be heading to dementia.'

'I imagine so. Something everyone jokes about but only because they're terrified.' He grimaced. 'They reckon it's the number one concern for anyone over fifty. It ranks higher than worries about financial security.' He shook his head. 'But is this the first sign she'd noticed? It's a bit too soon for that conclusion, isn't it?'

'That's what I said.' The waitress arrived and they ordered their coffees, declining food. Billie picked up a paper napkin and began to smooth it out.

His hand came over and stilled hers momentarily, before he took it away again. 'It was bad, then.' His touch broke into her thoughts.

'She said her daughter-in-law mentioned she might need place-ment if her memory got worse. I think she'd brushed that off until now and suddenly it seems real. But she woke disorientated and I guess she's thinking of her husband's illness.'

She folded the napkin again and looked at him. 'She's just been so happy, and settled, and we all love having her. It's a horrible thought and I want to dismiss the idea that Lorna could have early signs of Alzheimer's.'

'There could be other causes.'

She nodded. 'I know. I told her sometimes it was an infection that could send people off. So I took some bloods and a urine sam-ple and I've just dropped them in.'

'That's good. Sensible.' His voice softened and his hand came across and patted hers. 'Did you offer the five-minute test for dementia?'

'Yes. I sat her down, explained about the Mini Mental Status Examination, and we talked through it.' She frowned as she told

him the result. 'Lorna scored really high considering her level of education. But I think there's a marked deterioration from her previous clarity of thinking.'

He squeezed her hand as his eyes stared at a point on her collar. She could tell he was running through his own knowledge of mental deterioration in the elderly for something that would help her. It felt good to know that he cared. It felt even better to know he was a fabulous resource she could rely on. The need to hug him was sudden and fierce in its intensity.

Finally he said, 'Then something is going on there.' She didn't think he noticed her pink cheeks from her uncomfortable thoughts. 'But you're right. It could be as simple as an infection. We brought a drover in with the same thing last year. Turned out he'd been brewing a huge ingrown-toe infection and hadn't told anyone until he went silly and started getting lost on the way between the bunkhouse and the homestead. Totally confused. Initially they thought he was drunk.'

He sat back and sighed, and with the movement his hand slid away. She instantly missed his warmth and sympathy, which was silly.

She talked to cover the loss. 'We'll do proper testing later, but in the meantime I've started Lorna on antibiotics. I'm just waiting for pharmacy to come back from lunch to get the full script filled.'

Her fingers drifted back to the serviette. 'I'm praying that's the reason Lorna is muddled. It's unbearable to think of someone so vibrant and caring being lost to confusion and, even more heartbreaking, I think she's terrified.'

Morgan voiced her own thoughts 'Dementia is such a mongrel disease. But this is sudden and I think you're jumping too quickly to the dark answers.'

She nodded. 'I keep telling myself that.' She sat back, feeling measurably calmer. And remembered something she should have thought about earlier. 'We had a sad case, too, now I think about it. A high-profile philanthropist at my last medical practice. She wasn't one of my patients but I knew her well. A lovely woman in her early seventies, very prim and proper and perfectly mannered at all times. They found her walking up the street naked and brought her into the surgery.' Billie shuddered at the memory.

'It was lunchtime on a market day and kids took photos on their mobile phones. It was splashed all over the internet. Her husband, another high-profile individual, had her admitted to a mental health care facility, where the first thing they did as a routine ward admission was a micro-urine test.

'When her UTI was corrected they discovered that her dementia had resolved as well, but her marriage crumbled. It was dreadful. Her embarrassment at being admitted to a mental institution and her behaviour took her months to overcome.'

They looked at each other and winced. Morgan sighed. 'A tough thing to recover from. Especially for a woman.'

She put her hand over her face. 'My worst nightmare!'

He grinned. 'So if you did strip off here and now you'd mind if I took a picture?'

She smiled at his teasing, some of her black mood shifting. 'I might forgive you if you didn't put it on the internet.'

'So I could arrange a private viewing?' he asked wickedly.

She shook her head. She appreciated his attempts to lift her mood, but enough was enough. 'Maybe another time.'

'That's better than nothing.' He smiled fully into her eyes and she forgot to breathe there for a moment. 'Tell me.' His voice

softened. 'Was there a good ending to your lady's experience?'

Billie nodded. 'The other doctor in our surgery asked me to speak to her and finally we suggested she tell her story publicly. Give an interview to help others. She was so brave. The subsequent newspaper article resulted in a flood of support and congratulations on her courage in going public. She and her husband were friends, at least the last time I heard.'

'It gives you the shudders to think of the outcome in the old days. Must've been asylums full of sane people driven mad by their circumstances.' He took her hand again. 'That's not going to happen to Lorna.'

Billie felt an enormous weight lift off her. She cared about Lorna and Morgan was showing he cared, too. 'Thanks for being here. I was wilting under the burden without Daphne. Though I had a word with Lachlan and he said he'd keep an eye on her in case she became confused again. They get on well, but I don't like being away too long.'

'Where's Daphne?'

'It's her and Rex's weekend at the races.'

He raised his brows. 'I'd forgotten about that.' He stared out the window and then nodded. 'Rex has fancied her for a while.'

'Has he? I never noticed,' she said, tongue in cheek.

'Women aren't the only ones who notice these things,' he said smugly. 'He's got good weather for it.'

'Good weather for what?'

Innocently he shrugged. 'The races, of course.'

They smiled at each other. Then, unexpectedly, he said, 'Invite me out for the afternoon. I could come with you back to the station. Spend the day out there. Be in the background. A second opinion.'

The instant clutching of the life line felt disproportional to the offer. Either Lorna's confusion had distressed her more than she'd realised, or she wanted Morgan's company more than she realised. Maybe both. Definitely both. 'I'd like that. Thank you.'

When they arrived at the station Lachlan and Lorna were listening to the races. Lachlan had a crease of worry on his brow and he seemed to be hovering beside Lorna's chair as if he was afraid she'd run away.

'Billie. Morgan. Good to see you both.' His relief was obvious and Billie felt her heart sink. So Lorna was getting worse.

Lorna squinted in their direction, as if she didn't know them. 'We have visitors, Wallace.'

'Hello, Lorna, I'm back.' Billie crossed the verandah and sat in the chair vacated by Lachlan. Lorna clearly didn't know who she was so she prompted, 'It's Billie. I've brought you some medicine for your tummy.' She indicated Morgan. 'You remember Morgan?'

'Of course,' Lorna said, displaying some of her trademark spunk. 'I'm not senile you know!'

Billie smiled but her chest was tight. She stood up again and motioned for Morgan to take her place. 'I'll just get you some water for your next tablet.'

Lachlan followed her inside to the kitchen and all the way over to the sink, where he leant towards her and lowered his voice before the words poured out. 'She's been totally off with the fairies,' he said sadly. 'Calling me Wallace. Can't remember which race or what horse.'

Billie put her hand on his arm. 'I'm so sorry. I shouldn't have

left you, but I wanted to get her more antibiotics. It's come on very suddenly, which makes it even more likely she'll be right as rain when the tablets kick in, but we won't leave you again.'

'I'm not worried about me.' Lachlan was offended. 'I'm worried about her. She'd hate to think she was losing her marbles. Like Tootles, in *Peter Pan*.'

It was such a funny thing to say that Billie laughed. Lachlan continued to surprise her. 'I'd forgotten about Tootles. And *Peter Pan*. But give us twelve hours and we'll see how she goes.'

Lachlan shook his head. 'I'm no doctor, but can't you stick it in her vein or something? Make it work quicker?'

Billie had thought of that, but it meant transferring her to hospital for a full work-up. 'I could, but she'd need to go into hospital and the unfamiliar place might make her worse before it makes her better. She could really go off in there and she'd hate that. I can't justify that without a thorough work-up. And I think it would upset her. Disorientate her more. I'm waiting for an early report on her pathology, which will give us a better idea of how to treat her.'

Lachlan nodded resignedly. 'I shouldn't be trying to tell you how to do your job.'

Billie patted his hand. 'Hey. I'm always happy for suggestions. You care. We all care.' She filled the glass and took another tablet from the pack on the windowsill to give to Lorna. She'd started her with a double dose. 'We'll take it slow today. Hopefully everything will get better.'

When they returned to the verandah, Morgan appeared relaxed and even Lorna looked more settled.

She took the pills. 'Thank you, Billie.' She glanced around. 'I think I'm a little off today.'

'The antibiotics should help. And it's Saturday. We all have the day off and can relax. Morgan's come to spend the day with us. '

'So how does that work if both the doctors are here?' Lachlan scratched his head.

Morgan answered. 'One of the locum doctors flies in to cover from Friday night to Monday morning. And Billie and I cover the rest. I'm still on call twenty-four hours a day, five days a week, but now Billie takes some of the workload off me.'

Lachlan shook his head. 'You all work too hard,' he suggested with a knowing look. 'You should take him up to the ridge later when Lorna has her rest. It's a great place to watch the sun go down across the Barrier Ranges.'

SIXTEEN

They did have a leisurely day. Lachlan won a couple of races and even Billie chose one with a name she liked. Lorna was muddled but not upset and everyone began to relax somewhat.

Later that afternoon, when Lorna had lain down for a nap, Morgan and Billie took that drive up to the ridge on the quad bike. It was bumpy and slow, but Billie decided the beauty of the landscape was best appreciated that way anyway, and they had a bit of time.

Who was she kidding? It was hard to concentrate on the scenery when her breasts were squashed up against Morgan's powerful back and her hands were clutched around his waist. She tightened her grip as they hit another small rock on the roughly graded track.

Morgan had been up to the ridge before and they had their phones with them in case Lachlan needed them.

She spoke into his ear. 'Soretta has been meaning to take Daphne and I up here, but we never seemed to find the time.'

He slowed and turned his head to answer. 'You'll only need to be shown once. It's a good spot. The road is rough but well-marked.'

The track led between two hills and across a wide, dry creek

bed that was achingly beautiful, even in its waterless state. They stopped just to drink in the sight even if they couldn't splash in any water. Billie was pleased to see that Morgan seemed to absorb as much pleasure as she did from the landscape. Stately white gums, some of their trunks arched back like dancers exposing their bellies to the leafy canopy above, while others reached up with long white fingers to the sky.

The deep orange soil of the parched creek was cracked into diamonds and squares of dried mud that had split apart and curled at the edges to look like panes in old-fashioned window frames. The grey-green leaves shimmered above and the occasional leaf and twig drifted down in eddies onto the diamonds as the noisy cockatoos settled into the branches for the late afternoon.

Morgan pointed to the clump of Sturt's desert pea tucked in a corner behind a rock. The runners of the ground-dwelling branches were covered with downy hairs and the long blood-red flowers rose in clusters on their upright stalks with the black centres like tiny featureless faces midway up the bloom. The pointy greenish ground cover filled the spaces between the red splashes of colour.

Billie had always loved the desert pea flowers. Could remember picnics with her parents at riverbeds just like this and searching for the clumps of red flowers after lunch. 'I tried to grow those in Sydney but they always died.' She'd thought of her parents more in the last months than she had for years. It was poignant but maybe time to remember the good times she'd blocked out in the past. She'd been too worried about Mia and Mia's father to dwell on the loving and wonderful childhood she'd had.

Morgan was still absorbed in the prolific flowers. 'They manage the dry.'

She looked around. 'I've missed this. Missed even the harshness of the place, the ebb and flow of drought and flood, and the vibrant colours. The sky so blue it dazzles and makes everything else look clearer and brighter. I wanted Mia to appreciate the outback, but she was always busy and keen to stay beach-side. I think now she's here it's growing on her pretty fast.'

'She seems to have settled in well,' he said with a smile in his voice. 'You may not be able to move her soon.'

She nodded. 'Soretta says she's never seen anyone as good with animals and she doesn't hand out compliments freely. And Mia's finally digging in at school. Her grades are great. Wants to be a vet and Lorna's been helping with her extra homework.'

They both sobered at the thought of Lorna.

'Homework help is not a pastime for someone with dementia,' he reassured her.

'I keep telling myself that.'

'Come on. We'd better get on or we'll miss the light, and when we can't describe it Lachlan will think we've been doing something else.'

She raised her brows. 'I can't imagine what you're talking about.'

He looked at her with a tinge of scepticism. 'I can almost believe that.' She laughed and climbed on behind him and gave his waist a squeeze. 'Oh, you mean . . . that?'

He started the engine. 'Yes. That.' She grinned into his back. This was nice. More than nice. Exciting. Fun. Not something she'd had a whole lot of in her life and she was actually in no rush to progress to emotional angst. But he did feel wonderful to hang onto. She imagined briefly what it would be like to wake up in the morning with Morgan's strong body next to hers. A great way to start the day. Imagine!

He turned his head briefly. 'You okay?'

She stared at his strong neck and shoulders right in front of her nose. 'Just enjoying the view,' she said into his ear.

They were climbing up the last part of the track and she could see it wouldn't be much further to the flat spot on top of the range.

Someone had dragged a rusted 1940s utility as a burial-ground feature against the sparse scenery. It added a surreal quality with the wheel-less chassis resting on the ground and a tumble of larger granite rocks piled around it.

The golden ball of the sun was almost to the distant skyline, and the undulating ranges behind them were dusted red-gold with the reflection. Long shadows stretched from rocks and stunted trees and side of the rusted vehicle cabin, and she leant against it to watch the shadows lengthen.

Morgan opened the creaking door and gestured her in. 'Where would you like to go?'

She declined. 'I like a few springs on my seat when I travel.'

He laughed. 'There's no pleasing some women.' Then he shut the door on the empty cab so she could rest against it and they both turned to the view.

'This is really beautiful.'

Morgan shifted up next to her and touched his hip to hers. 'Scenery's good, too.'

She turned her face towards him and he surprised her by taking her hand. His warm fingers stroked hers and he seemed to be waiting for a reaction.

She stared down at their entwined fingers. How long had it been since a man had caressed her like this? Since she'd let one? The gentleness was so beautiful she just allowed herself the luxury

of receiving it without comment or movement.

But that wasn't a good enough response for Morgan, apparently. 'Dead fish,' he said and shook her wrist, and she laughed though she felt like a shy schoolgirl on her first date.

'I was waiting to see your moves,' she quipped. It was his turn to laugh.

'Oh. I've got moves.' He kissed her lightly on the tip of her nose. 'Just want to make sure you're alive first.'

She blinked and then she stared at his mouth as it hovered. 'Try again,' she said.

So he did, gently kissed her lips and the sensation flew through her like a rush of warmth. 'Oh, I'm alive all right.' The touch of his mouth rocked her like a shudder had shifted the whole range under her foot. She hoped he didn't realise how much power he really had.

'As a move, four out of ten,' she whispered.

'That wasn't a move. That was sussing you out.' He looked deeply into her eyes. 'Four? That's a bit harsh.'

She lifted her gaze to his, her mouth curving, loving the promise of humour between them, something she hadn't seen in the beginning, and the promise of being swept away by someone she could grow to trust. 'Maybe a six.'

He laughed and pulled her around so she was leaning on him in the circle of his arms. 'You lie,' he said with conviction. His back was solid against the truck and she pressed her whole weight on him. He was like a rock. Even that aura of immovable power was worth a ten.

Then he lowered his head and with darkening eyes he brushed his mouth against hers gently, and then with more pressure, until

he took possession and kept it, enticing her until the concept of scoring was blown out of her shrinking mind.

Her legs gave way and he held her, easily, clasping the back of her head as if he couldn't bear the thought of her moving away and she quite agreed with him. The moment stretched into a hundred moments, some short, some infinitely long, none of them enough. Kissing Morgan properly was like a whole smorgasbord in itself and she didn't want to stop.

When he put her gently from him, the sun had slipped away unnoticed and she seriously didn't mind that she'd missed seeing it set. She drew a ragged breath and concentrated on feeling her feet on the ground.

He was looking smug. She tilted her head at him. 'Where did you learn to kiss?'

He shrugged. 'I may have been a gigolo in a past life.'

She touched her mouth wonderingly. 'I believe you.'

He laughed. 'You do not.' He sobered. 'In all seriousness I think my kissing definitely improves when I kiss you.'

She couldn't help the pleased smile she could feel on her face. 'I think that's a compliment.'

'It's a concern.' He seemed to study the deep red of the sunless sky. There was a crease against his forehead and his light mood had evaporated. *Darn it.* Why couldn't anything be smooth! It wasn't her fault he'd kissed her and they'd imploded.

'We'd better get back. I don't fancy the track in the dark.' And with those words he changed, became more serious. She knew this guy, too, and she wasn't sure what his problem was.

It was just a kiss. But the voice inside her head laughed at her. That was *not* just a kiss.

*

They made it back to the homestead as the last of the twilight faded. It sat serene and solid like welcoming arms and a promise of solace for the confusion she could feel bubbling inside her. She'd spent most of the trip with her cheek against his back just soaking in the smell of him. The verandah lights glowed as they drove the quad bike into the shed.

Lachlan was sitting at the kitchen table with his chequebook and bills spread over Lorna's favourite linen. He watched them approaching and gestured to the invoices in answer to their silent question. 'I'm taking my mind off poor Lorna's troubles. Soretta's done a stellar job while I've been gone managing the finances. Better than it should be.'

That was great for all of them and she hoped he passed that onto his granddaughter. 'How is Lorna?' Billie asked quietly and then held her breath.

'Still asleep. I just checked her. She looks peaceful.'

Billie let out a sigh. That was a relief. 'Sleep should help her recover. I'll wake her later for the next dose of antibiotics.' She wasn't looking forward to that if Lorna didn't recognise her.

Lachlan was looking way more relaxed and now he was smiling at them with a twinkle. 'How was the sunset?'

'Beautiful.' She tried not to blush. 'Is there a story to that old car up on the ridge?'

He nodded, diverted from teasing. 'My parents went on their honeymoon in that car. It's a 1942 Ford Jailbar. When it died my dad took it up there as a joke. So whenever my mum mentioned a holiday he'd take her up there and put her bag in the cab.'

'You men all have the same sense of humour.'

Lachlan and Morgan exchanged amused glances and she walked over to the slow cooker where Daphne had left a meatloaf cooking early this morning before she left. Aromatic tendrils drifted up when she lifted the lid and seduced her nose. Or was she feeling a little immersed in her senses at the moment? She sighed blissfully. 'That smells divine.'

'I put the potatoes on. And there's enough for you, too,' he said to Morgan. 'No offence, Billie, but occasionally male company doesn't go astray.'

'Too late. I'm offended.' She wasn't. Lachlan did well with all of them and it was nice that Morgan might stay. She was about to ask him if he would when he put down his keys. And that's when she realised he had been about to leave. So he had been going to run; it seemed their kiss really had rattled him.

He straightened. 'Of course I'll stay. It smells great. Thanks.'

Lachlan waggled his shaggy brows. 'We could tell him we made it.'

Billie shrugged. 'He wouldn't believe us.'

Morgan chuckled, finally looking more at ease. 'Let me guess. Daphne did?'

'Yep.' Billie thought about Daphne and Rex away. 'I hope they're having a great time.'

'So do I.' Morgan's expression was serious again. 'Last thing we need is broken hearts all over the base.'

Was that directed at her? The thought sent a cold trickle down her back. She hoped it wasn't about them. 'Spoken like the boss. I'm going to get a cardigan for that chill you just brought in. Then I'll be back to set the table.'

'I can start that,' Morgan said.

Was that an apology? Maybe, maybe not. Who knew with him? Mr Hot-Again-Cold-Again. 'Thanks.' But she didn't look at him as she left the room. Just thought about that scorching kiss on the ridge and the fact that now he was all bitter and twisted and running scared again. Like she was the expert here. Well, she wasn't.

When Daphne and Rex landed at Broken Hill airport, Daphne found herself much more aware of the physical aspects of landing in a 1950s aircraft: the bumping around, the roaring wind, and the incredibly loud noise even through the headphones. It was all very invigorating. She slid open the side window and more noise rushed in with the hot air.

She'd landed here so many times for work it seemed strange not to taxi up to the Flying Doctor part of the apron. Instead they turned right, with the big wooden propeller spinning in front of them. They passed the passenger terminal, the parked jet with its row of windows waiting for its next load off to Sydney. Finally, they drew to a halt outside the civil aviation hangar.

She stayed strapped in and waited patiently, just enjoying the fact there was no anxious patient to worry about, nothing to worry about it seemed, as Rex had everything under control. It felt good. More than good. It felt wonderful to take a metaphorical back seat.

The engine stopped, as did the propeller, and the noise died down so that she was able to pull off her ear muffs. Then, reluctantly, she removed her helmet and stroked the soft leather. This really was one fab helmet.

Rex helped her out and he took both their bags and ushered her

across the heating tarmac to the shed. A pencil-thin guy in shorts and a singlet handed over a set of car keys. He gestured to a rental, a comfortable AWD vehicle, and handed Rex a map.

When they opened the door the heat billowed out even though the car had been thoughtfully parked under a tree. 'We'll wait a minute,' Rex said.

Daphne's gaze travelled the airport surrounds. 'It looks different from this angle.'

'We're tourists.' He smiled and she smiled back.

While they waited for it to cool, Rex asked, 'Do you know Broken Hill well?'

She shook her head. 'I came for my interview, and we did a week's orientation here and in Brisbane.' Daphne thought about the blur that had been her first few weeks in the air. 'I got so tired in the early days on the flights I'd just go home to sleep.'

Rex nodded. 'They do twelve-hour shifts here, too, don't they? Until you get acclimatised the decreased oxygen in flight is enough to make you tired.'

He started the car and ran the aircon, and after a few minutes it was pleasantly cool. 'Okay. Hop in. We'll head over to the pub where we're staying and get unpacked, maybe do some sightseeing and take a run out to Silverton. I haven't been there either.'

Once they were buckled in, he pulled out into the sparse traffic.

'And we're going to do touristy things,' he commanded, his eyes crinkling. She loved it when they did that. They looked so soft and blue, like the sky he prized so much. He was an adorable man from any angle. Too adorable for her.

'You look sad. You okay?'

She straightened her obviously sagging face. *How embarrassing.*

'No. I'm fine. Having a wonderful time.' She straightened her shoulders higher and lifted her chin. 'I really appreciate you bringing me.'

He frowned, then did a quick check in the rear-vision mirror, before flicking on the indicator. Slowing down, he pulled over to the side of the road under a shady gum tree. Before she realised what he was doing, he'd stopped and turned off the car, unclicked his seatbelt and turned to face her. His face was serious.

'Tell me, Daphne. Why do you think I invited you to come with me?'

She forced herself to meet his gaze. Reminded herself that this was Rex, that she knew Rex and had always admired him. Only she wished she hadn't come now because if she said something stupid this could impact on their working relationship. 'For company. Because you'd booked two rooms.'

'And why did I book two rooms?'

She looked away. 'Um. For company.'

She felt his finger on her chin and he used it to turn her face back towards him. 'For you.'

'Well, yes, I understand the other room is for me, now.'

He nodded to himself. As if something had been confirmed. Had she said something stupid? She was so stupid.

He studied her intently. 'Stop.'

She jumped. 'What?'

'It was always for you. I booked that room for you. Took my time, made sure you would have time off, because I wanted you to come. I wanted to spend time with you outside work.'

'Me?' Had she squeaked? She settled her breathing and tried again, but all the words seemed stuck. 'Oh,' she said finally. 'Thank·

you.' And then she smiled because a tiny bubble of anticipation had slipped under her guard and made its way to her mouth. She grinned at him. 'So there wasn't anyone else who let you down and I'm the fill-in?'

He shook his head. 'Who else could there be?'

'Oh my.' Oops, she'd said that out loud.

'Oh my indeed.'

'In that case, let's go have fun.'

He nodded, before leaning over and kissing her cheek deliberately. Like he really meant it. He then turned on the engine and steered back onto the road.

Rex had kissed her. Because he wanted to kiss her cheek. Maybe Rex had wanted to do more. She resisted the urge to lift her hand and stroke the spot she could feel glowing. Apparently, Rex had moved on from his disastrous marriage and now it was time for her to do that, too.

In a normal voice, as if he didn't know he had just tilted Daphne's world into a whole new dimension, Rex said, 'So you've never been to the races?'

'Just the Melbourne Cup.' Her brain wasn't really working yet.

'Just.' He laughed. 'Well this isn't the Melbourne Cup.'

'Excellent. Flemington on race day terrified me.'

He frowned at her in confusion. 'How could a horse race terrify you?'

'Not the races, the women.' She really hadn't meant to say that. 'Not really the women, just the fashions and the fear of falling on my face.' In front of my husband. Or father. 'You know. Of dropping sauce down my dress.' She'd done both at the one Melbourne Cup she'd attended. And she hadn't had a drink like the newspaper

had suggested. Her husband had been furious. 'I have this dread of social disasters. I was pretty young then.'

Rex went on. 'This is a country race meeting. It's as laidback as we want so you can relax, enjoy yourself. Nobody cares.'

Enjoy herself. Daphne vowed to try to achieve that goal. She thought about the Melbourne Cup experience and mentally tossed it out of the window. 'Let's do that.'

They stayed at the Palace Hotel, which was on the main street of Broken Hill and famous for the scenes from the Australian cult movie *Priscilla Queen of the Desert*. The magnificent murals lined the entry hall, the towering ceiling, and above and beneath the stairs that led to their rooms. Daphne could feel the smile tugging on her lips as she climbed the stairs. The hand-painted murals just kept getting more extravagant.

'This is different,' she puffed, as Rex carried their two bags beside her. He wasn't even breathing heavily on the steep stairs, but she consoled herself with the fact that his legs were longer.

He grinned at her. 'I know. Can't help picturing the guy who painted the ceiling lying on his back painting Venus. He's no Botticelli, but he's definitely got the touch for grandeur.'

She examined the brochure in her hand. 'Seeing as how I'm not carrying any luggage, I've got a free hand to look at the descriptions,' she said cheekily. 'It says his name was Mario but the rest was painted by an Indigenous artist called Gordon Whey. Only took Gordon eight hours to paint the first one in the bar.'

'Just a little something he whipped up. We might have to sit out on the steps with a drink later and just soak them in.'

Ooh, she'd love that. Loved the idea that Rex had the mental space to devote time to just admiring something that appealed to him. It appealed to her, too. She could easily imagine sitting on an old wooden step surrounded by hand-painted extravagant oil murals, with Rex sipping a glass of beer. Maybe he'd put his arm around her shoulders, and they'd smile and imagine what the artist had been thinking while he painted. Truth be told, it sounded better than the races.

Rex stopped at the top. 'So this is yours, m'lady.' The sign read 'Priscilla Suite'.

'A suite to myself?'

His eyes twinkled. 'So it seems.' He nodded at the room next door. 'And that's me.'

She checked the sign on the door and then the brochure in her hand. 'So I have the room with the murals?' She could feel the heat in her cheeks as she realised he'd wanted to please her. Make her smile. That he cared enough to give her the best room.

'It's an old hotel. We're doing fun not grand.'

She pushed open the door and gasped. An oil-painted stream cascaded across the wall flanked by gum trees. 'Truly magnificent.' She took a peek at him. 'How long ago did you say you booked this room?'

He shrugged. 'There was a cancellation.'

He was very sweet. 'Thank you. I love it.'

He put down her bag and looked mightily pleased with himself. 'I'm glad. We're here for two days. Maybe you'd like to unpack and I'll knock on your door in ten minutes.'

She almost saluted. But he was gone and that was more Billie's style anyway. She thought of the girls at home and how much

she would astonish Billie and Lorna with Rex's thoughtfulness. Describing it would be like reliving this adventure all over again. She hadn't had that many adventures she'd wanted to relive.

She reminded herself to enjoy the present moment. The now. Scanning the room, she marvelled again at the huge mural on her wall and allowed the pleasure to soak in. It was dated and delightful. Bless Rex.

They met ten minutes later, decided on a drive, and Rex steered them out past the long line of load from the silver mine that dominated the skyline and out into the undulating sparseness of saltbush and dirt. That part was like home.

Rex pulled over at the Menindee Lookout and she climbed out before she realised he'd intended to open her door. Damn, she'd have to practise that waiting thing.

They stood at the side of the drop-off and stared over the brown land with the green-grey patches of desert foliage and outcrops of rock. She'd seen this so many times from the air but it was just as glorious to see it up close in the three-dimensional reality.

Rex slipped his arm around her waist and edged her back from the steep slope. 'Daredevil,' he said mildly and kept his arm there. She guessed it was so she wouldn't fall, but it didn't matter why he did it because it felt nice and started a gentle thrum in her knees.

She twisted her neck to peer at his face. He was gazing over the expanse and she could see his strong throat and the faint beginnings of the light-coloured regrowth on his chin. There was something attractive about a man's regrowth and she'd always had a sneaking admiration of Rex with stubble.

He squeezed her waist as their eyes met. 'Ready to move on?'

Was there a hidden meaning in that? And if he had put a different layer of question in there . . . Was she ready?

She took a breath. 'Absolutely. I'm loving this, Rex.' Two could put a double meaning in a comment.

He squeezed her waist again and steered her towards the car, and this time she waited until he opened her door.

They had a late lunch at Silverton in the original pub that had been christened with more than a dozen names, its walls plastered with newspaper clippings and old signed photographs of movie stars, commercials and photo shoots, all of which were made in the almost deserted mining town. Then they drove back towards Broken Hill and veered into the Living Desert Reserve before the tourist buses arrived at sunset.

This time, when Rex opened her door, he took her hand and kept it cradled in his own as they climbed the path to the top of the hill. She could feel the strength of his fingers, the extra ten beats of her heart, and the heat in her cheeks.

She tried to concentrate on the sculptures that soared from their footings on the red soil and read the plaques explaining each artist's concept of his creation.

There was a window of time between the people ahead of them leaving and the next arriving, and Rex guided her into a shady spot and stopped.

'I'd like to kiss you.'

She blinked. Could feel herself heat up and start to panic. No. She wasn't going to ruin this.

She nodded, but then decided that wasn't enough. 'I'd like that,' she said a touch primly, but the important thing was that

she'd said it and she saw him lean closer before she closed her eyes. She should have kept them open a while longer because she waited and nothing happened. When she opened her eyes he was smiling at her.

'You looked so worried I wasn't sure I should. How about you kiss me?'

She glared at him and he must have known he'd done the wrong thing because he laughed and pulled her to him and kissed her with a toe-curling thoroughness that made her forget her awkwardness. She slid her hands up and around his neck and pulled him closer. The tang of his aftershave mixed with the warm fresh smell of Rex and the whole gamut was intoxicating.

He was the one who heard the footsteps coming up the path, she certainly didn't, because he set her away from him with gentle firmness and took her hand again.

'I knew that would would be worth waiting for,' he murmured, and drew her along to a wooden seat that looked over the hectares of reserve protecting the natural fauna and flora, and winding between the outcrops. They could see the long walking path they'd missed by driving to the summit.

But her eyes were too full of stars to care much about the view. My Lord, he was good at that kissing business. Who would have thought it?

The hidden talents of a bush pilot.

SEVENTEEN

More people arrived at the sculptures and the first of the buses hissed with the doors opening as the afternoon drew closer to sunset.

Rex leant across and spoke quietly into her ear. 'Would you like to wait for the sunset?'

No siree. The idea of people setting up picnics around them wasn't really what she had in mind. What she wanted was to find somewhere quiet and be kissed by Rex again. 'Not really, unless you want to.'

'Let's go then,' he said and pulled her to her feet, keeping her hand, making her feel relaxed and comfortable and incredibly safe. She could get used to this.

They drove back into town with the long shadows from the afternoon sun behind them. Back at the Palace Hotel Rex suggested they change for dinner, not to hurry, and he'd meet her on the verandah outside their rooms to watch the sunset.

Daphne could feel the trickle of sweat down her back and she'd rubbed off most of her makeup. The idea of standing under a stream of cool water and emerging refreshed was too tempting, so she set out the floaty silver dress and the strappy heels that went with it, and dived into the shower.

Twenty minutes later when she stepped onto the verandah, lightly made up and faintly perfumed, Rex was waiting. He'd changed into light-coloured jeans and an open-necked blue shirt that matched his eyes. Eyes that appreciated her warmly. He looked strong and casual and very relaxed. She wished she had half his composure.

'You look beautiful,' he said.

She froze like a rabbit in headlights until she remembered Billie. Sucking in a breath, she forced out a, 'Thank you, kind sir,' with as much nonchalance as she could muster. It felt stilted but she'd done it. Accepted a compliment and it hadn't killed her.

He pulled out the chair at the little wrought-iron table between their rooms, leant into her hair as she sat down and murmured, 'You smell good, too.'

She sat down with more of a bump than a graceful settle, but he didn't seem to notice because he was paying attention to the wine. Rex the connoisseur. Hidden talents? She stifled a nervous giggle.

He'd acquired an ice bucket and bottle of expensive sparkling white and she looked longingly at it. That's what she needed. A settling sip of alcohol.

She raised her brows at the glass he poured for himself. 'Now that's a first. I wondered if you even drank,' she teased.

He shrugged. 'Not often. My dad was a drover who settled in Mica Ridge and he liked a bender. He was a happy drunk but if I drink – it's not much. It's over twenty-four hours until I fly again,' he said seriously, 'and this is a special occasion.' She hugged that comment to herself and stored away a little bit of family history that you never heard from Rex.

He lifted his glass. 'To us and a good day at the races.' He grinned at her. 'But you can have most of it.'

No thanks. Who knew what she'd say if she drank too much? 'Are you trying to get me sloshed, Rex?'

'I have an idea that could be entertaining, but no. We're going to have a good day tomorrow at the races and I don't want you there with a hangover.'

Lord, she seconded that, and reminded herself to have two glasses, max. That was the thing. With their job they rarely drank because they were so frequently on call. So more than a glass of wine tended to hit her like a hammer.

She looked across the varnished verandah boards to the wrought-iron balcony. The sun had almost disappeared behind the buildings opposite, everything lay bathed in a golden-red glow, and patterns were appearing from the black metal lace on the roof. 'This is gorgeous.'

'They said it was a good place in the afternoons.' He topped up her glass of the effervescent wine and it threatened to foam over the top. 'Out of practice,' he murmured.

She felt herself warm at his habit of talking to himself. She hadn't noticed that before, it wasn't something he did when flying, but apparently he did so when he was with her. It endeared him to her. So maybe he wasn't as sure of himself as he seemed and that made her way more relaxed.

They raised the wine and it caught the sun with a suitably romantic sparkle until the tiny non-resonant clunk from cheap glasses made them smile. 'I've had a lovely day, Rex.'

'Me too.' He took a sip and put the glass down. Reached across and stroked her cheek with his finger. 'You looking forward to

tomorrow?' He sat back and studied her with leisure.

She could feel the awareness run down her neck and into her belly. And lower. Looking forward to tomorrow. And perhaps tonight as well. She licked suddenly dry lips. 'Very much.'

'So am I.' He slid a folded newspaper across the table and she picked it up. 'The form guide.' He pointed to a race. 'The Silver City Cup. I'm going for She Flies High.'

Daphne studied the list of names. 'I think I fancy In With A Chance.' It had a good ring to it, she thought vaguely.

'I was hoping you'd go for that one.' Rex laughed out loud.

Daphne realised what she'd said, took a quick sip from her glass to cover her confusion, and inhaled her wine. The coughing fit lasted for a couple of minutes. By the time she'd recovered Rex had her standing up, leaning her head on his chest, and was patting her back.

'Does that mean I'm not in with a chance?'

She wiped her streaming eyes. 'You set me up.'

'You took the bait beautifully, but I really didn't want to see you choke.'

'Of course you did,' she said. Then she thought of another time with Rex. A tense and desperate flight full of last-minute anxiety. 'Remember the time I thought that patient was going to choke to death and you got me down on the ground so fast we managed to get a tube in between us just in time.'

He nodded. His face suddenly serious. 'I remember.' His voice lowered to a murmer. 'I've lost count of the times I've shaken my head and wondered how you managed to get them to the destination without them dying. You're incredible, Daphne.'

She tried to drop her chin but he wouldn't let her. He lifted her

face with his finger again, refusing to take no for an answer. 'You are incredible, Daphne.'

Like a child she recited, 'Thank you, Rex.'

'Better,' he said and kissed her nose. Then her eyelids. Her cheeks. Finally her mouth.

He started slowly with a gentle sweep of her lips, his hand cupping the back of her head, and then he applied more pressure against her mouth. She could feel herself melt against him. Melting felt so damn good. Why had she never known about this, she wondered, but then the thought was gone as he teased her lips apart and a whole new dimension opened. She lost all power of thought as the world narrowed to the taste and delicious tangle of their tongues in the age-old dance of seduction.

She was lost for a long time, and the shadows were all gone when finally Rex pulled back. Even she could see his reluctance, and she loosened her death grip on his shoulders and allowed herself to be put away from him. He looked a little dangerous and she found herself smiling up at him. She liked the look and she was feeling a little dangerous herself.

He set his jaw. 'Where would you like to go for dinner?' She touched the tension at the side of his mouth. Her turn to tease.

'Do we have to?'

He blinked. 'I've no idea.'

She raised her brows. 'Did I show you the mural in my room?'

His eyes darkened again. 'Briefly.'

She took him by the hand and drew him towards her door. 'Come and have a better look.'

*

The next morning Daphne woke with her head on Rex's chest. He had much more hair on his chest than she expected, but she decided if she counted them then it would come out at the perfect number. She sighed happily and felt his hand stroking her shoulder.

'Hello, beautiful,' he said.

She grinned. 'Damn, I was just going to say that.'

His chest shook under her and then he shifted and suddenly she was beneath him, her cheeks cradled in his hands, his strong body suspended over her. 'Good morning.'

'It seems it is.' She smiled shyly up at him and he lowered his head towards her. That was all she thought about for a while.

Several hours later Daphne studied herself in the mirror. She didn't look any different. Well, actually, she glowed.

It wasn't just the makeup, and the lovely pink crinkle dress, or even the tiny grey fascinator, which she'd pinned with more ease than she expected onto her hair. Her lips were pretty pink with the smudge-free lipstick that Billie had assured her she wouldn't get on her teeth or Rex's shirt. She laughed at the fact there was a reasonable chance of that, but maybe Billie had been doubly right.

She looked again. It was her eyes. They seemed brighter, even wicked, definitely more confident and able to meet coiffed women with aplomb. Maybe she had slain that ghost of shyness.

These were not the eyes of a woman who couldn't hold her own, she assured herself.

She thought about last night, this morning, even playing footsies at breakfast. Life was pretty darn good and she had the sneaking suspicion she was in love, as opposed to in lust, with Rex.

Though it would be reasonable to say she was in lust with him, too. Excitement fizzed in her belly and she couldn't remember ever being this happy.

One more tweak of her hat and she picked up her matching bag and sailed out the door.

Her new lover's eyes lit up and then darkened when he saw her, and she could feel the blush heating her cheeks. She refused to be embarrassed and twirled in front of him. He slid his hand into hers and pulled her against him gently so he could kiss her. Then stepped back. 'Maybe I shouldn't muck up your lipstick?'

'Billie assures me it's non-smudge.'

'God bless Billie, then,' he said and kissed her thoroughly. Afterwards she stood back and surveyed him, then wiped the tiniest hint of colour off his lips.

Rex looked very dapper with his white RM shirt and fawn trousers, even the riding boots were polished and looked perfect. Lord, she was lucky. She couldn't wait to see him with the black akubra he carried in one hand.

'You are a stylish man when you decide to dress up.'

'Aw shucks.' It seemed Rex didn't have any problems taking a compliment. To her delight he added a snippet of personal history. Something she'd heard more of in this one trip than in all of the last six months.

'My mother used to sew all the time when my father was away. She'd make clothes for people. School uniforms for kids and me, of course. I was an only child. I guess I think of her when I buy a new shirt because I tend to choose the ones that would make her smile.

'Well, you both have good taste.'

'I'll take you to meet her. She doesn't get around as well as she did and she lives in a unit in the retirement village. But she still sews.'

'I'd like to meet her, Rex.'

'It's on the list,' he said cryptically. Then he glanced at his watch and took her arm. 'Let's go to the races.'

Fifteen minutes later when they arrived at the track, the picnic tables under shade sails beside the track were filling fast. The throng had the full spectrum of fashion, from jeans, shorts and thongs on feet, summer shifts vying with designer outfits and Sunday best, as people streamed in the gate. Hats were everywhere.

She nudged Rex and pointed out a face they both knew. The big man had a beer in his hand already and it was barely eleven o'clock. Daphne couldn't see how his reattached finger looked from here, but he seemed to have five.

Rex leaned down. 'We'll stay away from Accidental Al.' They turned the other way. No work today.

Designated-driver buses spilled their cargo of happy racegoers and Daphne looked around with unexpected enjoyment.

'Great isn't it?' Rex was watching her face.

'It is,' she answered, admiring a young woman in a bright-yellow sundress and purple accessories. It was the smile and joy in life that shone from her happy face that completed the picture. 'She'll win.'

'Fashion in the field?'

'Perfect.'

'You look perfect. You should go in it.'

Daphne raised her brows. 'I would rather have all my teeth removed without anaesthetic.'

Rex laughed. 'Okay then.' He chuckled again. 'I won't ask again.'

'You should go in it. Now that I would enjoy.'

'Give me the chair at the dentist next to you,' he said fervently and took her hand and squeezed it.

After four races, and the crowning of Daphne's pick for Fashions on the Field, the mood on the course had risen to new heights as the runners in the cup surged into the mounting yard. Brightly coloured jockeys bounced and leaned to their horses' heads and the crowd drifted to the rails to admire their chosen contenders.

It was slightly tricky on the uneven dusty ground for those in high heels, but the men were up to the task of steadying their ladies. Rex's arm was solidly around Daphne.

Rex's horse stamped her feet and Daphne's bet seemed to have a smile in his equine eyes that resonated with Daphne's own feeling of euphoria.

Then the horses were out on the track trotting towards the starting post and anticipation raised the swell of voices from the crowd again. The racegoers drifted back towards the trackside viewpoints and the tension increased as the race caller's voice announced the field was almost ready. There was a small hold-up at the starting gates, and people became more desperate to see over the heads of others.

Groups of young men were clustered, some with the serious faces of those who had plunged too heavily on this heady but precarious way of making money, and others were climbing onto low walls to see.

Daphne soaked in the thrill, lost Rex's arm for a moment as he bent down to pick up a hat that had blown off a woman's head

and returned it to her, and heard a tinkle of breaking glass from behind her just as the gate bell clanged.

They were off. The horses bounded from their starting gates, but Daphne turned in the opposite direction to the rest of the crowd in time to see a young man, late teens, standing by himself at the back of the wall, the remains of his beer glass falling at his feet.

He was holding his wrist in a useless attempt to stop the blood that was spurting through his clutching fingers and crumpled in a faint just as Daphne reached his side.

She put out her arms, not silly enough to take all his weight, but to slow his descent to the ground. Unfortunately, the arc of crimson blood sprayed her face and neck, and she wiped her cheek with her arm as she reached over and clamped her fingers around the jagged tear in the flesh of his wrist.

She had to blink through the film of blood that dripped off her forehead and hoped he hadn't given her any bloodborne diseases. The blood was still pumping out. This was serious.

She was just about to call Rex when she realised he was already by her side, his face creased in concern.

'I can't let go. Take his tie off. I need a tourniquet,' she said, as the blood welled and splattered beneath her hand, and she wondered just how much more blood the boy would lose before they could contain it.

Rex slid the tie up the young man's arm above the elbow and tightened it. The flow of blood lessened and Daphne allowed her death grip on his arm to loosen. She wadded the handkerchief poking out of the jacket under her fingers across the wound and checked her watch. 'Tourniquet on at three thirty-six.'

A woman screamed and pointed. Not at the white-faced young man on the ground, but at the blood-spattered spectre of a woman beside him. Her.

Bloody hell.

People began to crowd around. She heard a whir as a camera clicked. She ignored the blush of colour heating her face, ignored the mumble of horrified onlookers. She could imagine the gore and the gossip. She simply waited, with her hands pressing down on the wound to stem the flow, and shut the thought of how she must look away for later when no doubt she would wallow in it miserably. The people staring at her didn't matter.

'I'll call an ambulance? He'll need surgery.'

She nodded thankfully at Rex, and he pulled out his mobile phone just as the course paramedic arrived.

The next ten minutes passed quickly and Daphne was handed a damp towel by a course official, who thanked her profusely for saving the boy's life but couldn't help his look of revulsion at the mess she was in.

Rex took the towel from her and wiped her face and neck, then produced a light raincoat from somewhere that covered the rest of her and she could have kissed him.

He helped her to her feet, took her across to a tap and washed some of the blood off her hands and dried them. She felt like a baby, but for some strange reason her mind wasn't functioning at that moment. Luckily Rex's was.

He ushered her towards the car past curious onlookers and she watched the ground in front as she was led away.

She'd done it again. Been a magnet for drama and mess and social awkwardness and all in front of Rex. He was stuck with a

blood-soaked robot when he should have been enjoying himself. Though, now she thought about it, thank goodness it had happened in front of Rex.

'Thanks, Rex. For being there,' she said, her voice a faint whisper.

'I think that young man should thank you for being there. I'd say he would've died if that lot had been responsible for saving him.'

A few minutes later they pulled up at the pub and she leaned with post-adrenaline weariness back in the seat until he opened her door.

'Come on, Florence Nightingale. Upstairs and into the shower.' He took her arm gently and even prised her key from her shaking, bloodied fingers and opened her door.

He urged her in, turned back and closed the door to the corridor, then led her past the huge mural on the wall of her room through to the bathroom and turned on the shower. There he helped her strip off until her lovely dress was a ruined heap on the shower floor and tenderly pushed her in.

The blood ran from her hair and her arms in a crimson whirlpool that splashed against the white tiles before it twirled down the drain. It had even soaked through into her bra. She unclipped it and dropped the messy lace confection into the swirl of bloody water on the floor of the shower stall.

Rex coughed. How had she forgotten Rex? Her head jerked up and then Rex whistled. She had to grin sheepishly at that. She slid another peek at him and suddenly realised it was okay. This was Rex. His eyes were filled with caring and pride, and a suggestion he was trying to be good and not look at her in a predatory way.

That made the beginnings of a smile lift her lips. She looked down then at her saturated lacy underwear and back at Rex.

Then timid, demure Daphne slid her hands over her hips and made a show of removing her panties burlesque-style, and that was too much for him.

She started to laugh as he removed his own blood-splattered clothes and stepped in.

EIGHTEEN

A new Daphne returned on Sunday after lunch and Billie grinned at the sight of her. She couldn't help feeling a little envious of her friend's obvious glow of happiness, but it was so good to see Daphne, head held high and happy, and Rex handing her out of the car like she was a fragile china doll.

Fragile! Daphne, who could throw herself headlong into the most traumatic and tense situation, and take control of disaster with aplomb.

'You look fabulous, Daphne,' Billie said.

Daphne rolled her eyes at her companion. 'How do you think Rex looks?'

'Pretty damn good.'

Rex laughed. 'I have to go before I start blushing.' He kissed Daphne's lips softly but passionately. Billie's eyebrows rose and she looked away. It seemed all had gone well and she couldn't wait to hear Daphne's side of it. Finally Rex reluctantly climbed back into his car and Daphne was waving.

Billie waved too, and they stood together and watched his dust go down the driveway. 'So it's like that, is it?'

'Oh yes. Oh my goodness, yes.' Daphne turned a dreamy face to

Billie and sighed. 'He's wonderful.' Then her brows drew together. 'What's been happening here?'

'Wow.' How could Daphne tell anything was wrong? Especially when she'd just been floating on cloud nine. 'Let's enjoy your story first.'

'Mine can wait. It has a good ending.' Daphne looked Billie up and down. 'Something's worrying you.'

So she told her about Lorna, about Morgan's assessment agreeing with her own, about Lachlan's concern, and the slight improvement they could all see today.

'So it looks like it was a urinary tract infection that set her off. But Lorna's taking it hard. She says she doesn't want to be a burden. That she'll go quietly into an aged-care facility before she does something silly. I can't seem to change her mind.'

Billie felt better even though Daphne said, 'I can't see an answer we can act on right now except allowing her some time. Maybe we take it day by day. It's Mia's birthday tea tomorrow night. Lorna can't go before that. And we're working all week.'

Billie nodded. 'Day by day sounds at least like a plan. I guess we could all just refuse to take her anywhere and she'd have to stay here.' A path of subtle resistance.

If they worked together, between the four of them, with all that women power, they could work it out. 'It's good to have you back, Daphne.' Billie hugged her impulsively. 'And now, I'm dying to hear about your weekend.'

Yesterday had been Mia's seventeenth birthday. It fell on the Monday and had been the best one yet. No stinking bus trip home

because her mother had finished work early to take her for her driver's test.

Soretta had told her not to be stupid and just concentrate when the assessor asked her to drive places. Lorna had kissed her on the cheek, and wished her well. Daphne had bought her a new wallet to hold the licence when she got it. And her mum had a surprise for afterwards.

Even a day later Mia couldn't forget that feeling of walking away from the Motor Registry, after the harrowing experience of the test, with her photograph on her new provisional drivers licence. It had to be one of the most exhilarating moments of her life.

Then her mother had taken her to the one used-car yard and she still couldn't believe she was sitting behind the wheel of her own sporty red utility with the music she wanted to play blasting out of the iPod dock driving home from school on a Tuesday.

Her little red baby had a few dings and a couple of rattles, but it was streets better than the 'cute' yellow compact sedan her mother had fancied for her.

Mia patted the dash with proprietary pleasure. This pint-sized workhorse with its useful tray in the back, towing bar, and bucket seats in the front, had caught her eye. She loved the shiny silver roo bar and the big spotty headlights and the fact that she could go off road if she wanted to.

She felt like she could conquer the world in this.

She grinned at herself in the mirror. And hadn't Trent been impressed when she'd driven it to school this morning. Her chest tightened with pleasure. This beat riding in the bus hands down and she still couldn't believe her mother had let her have her wings.

Trent was coming out on the weekend and they'd do some off-road driving over the property and check fences for Soretta.

She glanced at the speedometer and made sure she was below the speed limit. She was not going to do anything to jeopardise this freedom.

Then she saw the old American muscle car that belonged to the farmworker, Joseph. He was standing beside the road with the bonnet up on his car, and he looked like he needed help.

She hesitated. Soretta had said to stay away from him, and she would be very happy to do so, but she couldn't just drive past, particularly as she was on her way home. She put her blinker on and slowed to turn into the small lay by and rolled her utility to a stop.

Mia wound down the window as he walked towards her. He had a strange smile on his face and she had the sudden instinct that she wasn't safe.

'Hi. Can I do anything to help?'

'Mia. How nice.' He smiled that creepy smile again. 'A lift back to the station would be helpful, to pick up some oil, if that's not too much trouble. I'll just lock the car up.' He took his time, while Mia sweltered waiting for him, but she didn't want to get out. Then he walked around to the other side and opened the passenger side door.

She didn't want to look at him as he was getting in, and as soon as he put his seatbelt on she drew out onto the road again.

'Nice little rig.'

'Yes.'

'Mum buy it for you?'

'It was my birthday yesterday.'

'Yesterday, eh? Happy birthday.' There was something very strange in his voice.

She knew he was staring at her but she didn't turn her head. She kept her eyes glued to the road, but she could feel the heat in her cheeks and wished he'd turn away. She felt like saying, 'Can you stop looking at me, please.' But she didn't, so she reached down and turned the iPod player back on.

Finally, he swivelled to look out the window and she let out a relieved breath.

It was only another five kilometres home and she could ignore him for that long.

He reached over and turned the music down. 'Hope you don't mind. Thought we could have a chat.'

She did mind and chatting to him was the last thing she wanted to do. She wished she'd pretended she hadn't seen him and sailed past his broken-down car. Stinker!

'Sure,' she said, refusing to offer anything.

'So where did you and your mum live before here?'

She hesitated, but there weren't a lot of choices. 'Sydney.' She didn't know why she kept it so brief but she did. Before he could ask her to be more specific she said, 'Where did you live?' Not that she was interested. Three kilometres to go.

'I came across from Adelaide. What about your dad? Was he from Sydney, too?'

'My dad died when I was born.' Two and a half kilometres.

'Reallllly?' Patent disbelief.

Now she was getting cross. 'Yes. Really.'

Two kilometres. Seriously, if there'd been a long way to go she would have stopped the car and asked him to get out.

'Did you like it?' If she kept asking him questions she wouldn't have to answer any herself.

'What?'

'Adelaide.' Seriously, if he wanted her to talk to him he should at least listen.

'Adelaide was okay. So just you and your mum?'

'Yep.' Subject change. 'Have you seen that lamb I put back with the mob lately?'

'Nope. They all look the same to me.'

She bet they did. She'd been able to tell he wasn't really an animal person. And thankfully there was the gate up ahead. She put her blinker on and drove across the cattle grid and up the driveway, careful not to stir up the dust and dirty her baby.

Halfway up he said, 'Just drop me here, I'll walk across the paddock to the shed, that's fine. I was supposed to help with the muster.'

She stopped, very happy with that suggestion.

'Thanks for the ride.' He got out and closed the door softly, then waved. She half waved back with relief as she drove away. She was probably being silly.

She saw Lorna sitting on the verandah and the elderly lady still had that sad expression on her face. It just wasn't the old Lorna. She decided then and there that she would try even harder to cheer her up.

After she'd parked her baby in the shed she took the verandah steps two at a time and plopped herself down on the seat beside Lorna. 'Hello, how is my favourite person today?'

Lorna smiled wearily. 'Now that's a lie. I know you idolise Soretta.'

Mia pretended to look around furtively. 'For goodness sake, don't tell her that. She'll be even harder on me than she is.'

Lorna almost smiled. 'A bit of hard work never hurt anyone. But your secret is safe with me.' Lorna looked a bit brighter. 'So how's your new car going?' She frowned. 'And why did you stop on the driveway? I couldn't see that far.'

'The new farm worker broke down and I gave him a lift home. He got out and walked across the paddock.'

'Is he nice?'

Mia was in a dilemma. If she said no, then Lorna would worry, if she said yes, it would be lying, but Lorna would let the subject drop. 'He's okay. What have you been doing today?'

'Sitting here. It's what old ladies do.' Big sigh. 'They sit and rock. All day.'

Mia lifted her brows. 'So you don't even need a rocking chair to rock?'

Despite herself, Lorna's mouth twitched. 'Minx.' She grimaced. 'That did sound self-indulgent, didn't it?' She checked her surroundings before lowering her voice. 'Lachlan and Soretta have been taking it in turns to mind me and have only just left together to go over to the sheep yards because they knew you'd be home any minute. I hate that I'm a nuisance.'

'You're not a nuisance. How about I mind you now, and you can help me with my homework. If we get it wrong we can just say it was your fault.'

This time Lorna laughed out loud and Mia felt the warmth of affection growing in her chest. She really was becoming fond of this pseudo granny they'd adopted and it was sad to see her so down on herself.

'We need to update our webpage, too.' Lorna would love this and she'd been meaning to tell her since she'd found out this

morning. 'I had a look at the Paypal account that goes straight into the FDS fund and we've hit our first thousand dollars. We got an email from the director to thank us.'

Lorna brightened visibly. 'A thousand dollars?' Awe spilled from her voice. 'For auctioning a photo of Dr Morgan?' She smiled the best smile Mia had seen since she'd come back from the gymkhana with Soretta on Sunday.

Mia nodded. 'And we have eight hundred likes on the website. Two hundred on your photos on the camel.'

'You wicked child.' Lorna stood up and waited until she was steady before she moved. 'I'll be back.' She waggled her finger at Mia. 'Don't go away. I'll just have a look and see what other photos we have and you can put them up.'

She turned away with purpose and Mia could hear her muttering to herself. 'A thousand dollars for the flying doctor. Now that's wonderful.'

The dogs started barking and Mia looked up to see Daphne's car climbing the hill to the house. There wasn't much dust because of how slowly she was driving, but Mia knew Daphne could gun it down the hill if she needed to get to town fast.

Lorna wasn't the only one she was appreciating more each day, too. Mia remembered how Soretta had described Daphne's heroic actions the day she'd saved Lachlan's life and that was just one instance in a year filled with rescue missions that the flying doctors attended each year. She found herself more invested with Lorna's fundraising for a cause that deserved the support of everyone in Australia.

And this was what her mother did? Indeed, all the women in the house were inspiring. Not the least her own mother, now that

she was being forced to look at her through the eyes of the other women.

Soretta had given her a huge lecture when she'd said something disparaging about her mother's ability to be busy all the time, and that had resonated with an uncomfortable perception that she hadn't made it easy for her mum in the past.

In fact, she had the sneaking suspicion that she'd been a brat, and vowed to make it up to her. Soretta hadn't ever known her mother, her gran had apparently been the maternal support, but then Soretta had lost her as well. Mia was beginning to appreciate just how lucky she'd been to have had her mother all her life. And it was about time she stopped focusing on the fact that she didn't have a father. Though she was close to her grandad, Soretta didn't have one of those either.

Daphne arrived on the verandah carrying two bags of groceries. Mia stood up. 'Sorry, didn't see you've been shopping.' She took one bag from her and opened the door with her other hand.

'Thank you, Mia,' Daphne said. 'What were you doing sitting there all by yourself?'

'Lorna's gone to get some more photos and we're going to update the webpage.'

Daphne stopped and studied her. 'How is she?'

'Okay.' Not a lie.

'That's good, then. Your mother was worried. We all are.' She smiled. 'How did your car go on the way and back from school? Better than the bus?'

Mia laughed. 'Just a bit.' She didn't mention Joseph to Daphne either. She might later.

They put the groceries away together and Daphne lifted the lid

for tea on the verandah. Everyone's home tonight for a change.'

She laughed. 'You sound like you're getting used to the new extended family.'

'Yes, well, I like that they've taken at least some of the load off you.' He patted her shoulder again. 'And you're happier, too. And yes.' He shrugged. 'I like them all, a lot.'

Impulsively she hugged him. 'And they even pay to stay here.'

'Can't say that's been a bad aspect. Come on, my little business-woman. Delegate the work and come back with me.'

There wasn't a way to say no to that. And she didn't want to.

on the beef and mushrooms she'd had simmering all day.

The aroma filled the room and Mia's tummy rumbled so loudly Daphne laughed. 'We could have a taste now if you like.'

Which was how Lorna caught them spooning a small serve of beef bourguignon into two saucers.

'Ah ha!' Lorna said. 'Do you realise that Lachlan and I have had to inhale that aroma all day and not lift the lid?'

Daphne reached for another saucer. 'Shhh,' she said and ladled a scoop out for Lorna and handed her a spoon. The three of them tasted and sighed with unanimous pleasure. 'This will tide us over until they all come in at tea time.'

Over the hill at the yards, Soretta wiped the sweat from her forehead. She paused in thinking about paddocks and sheep rotation and watched the new man, Joseph, herd the sheep, and she could see that he seemed to have the knack for keeping them in line. He'd come in later than expected with some car trouble and she had to admit it was easier now that he was here.

She still wasn't sure if they wanted to keep him. Granddad didn't seem to mind the man, apparently he knew a bit about metal detecting and they'd had quite an animated conversation about the pros and cons of finding precious metals with different kinds of devices. It wasn't like she had to deal with him socially because he seemed to like keeping to himself. She didn't think he'd been to the house once since the first day she'd interviewed him.

She let the thoughts go. They were nearly finished anyway. She wanted to separate the younger ewes and lambs from this mob and move them to the best of the minimal feed that was left. If it didn't rain decently soon they might still have to sell half of the mob. Klaus was working on the other side with the dogs and her grandfather was working the gates.

She'd heard Mia come home so there was no rush to get back to Lorna. Apart from being quieter than usual, she thought Lorna was pretty good today. Her grandfather had shared some of his experiences on Saturday and she'd seen he'd been genuinely upset at Lorna's distress. It must have been disturbing for everyone and she was a somewhat glad she and Mia had missed all the drama.

She looked across at the man opening the gates. Her granddad seemed happier now and being back with the sheep was good for him. Especially since they'd had another few mils of rain last night. There'd been no more silly talk of selling Blue Hills.

'That all of them?' She heard her granddad's voice and she snapped back into sheep mode. Saw that he was right.

'Yep.' The younger ewes were in the left yard and the older in the right. 'We'll take the younger ones up first.'

Her grandfather opened the left gate and the milling sheep streamed out. Klaus climbed onto the four-wheeler and was onto them with the dogs circling the pack, and the mob started up the hill towards the new paddock. It would take at least an hour to walk them there, but he'd return more quickly.

'Going back to the house?' Her grandfather had crossed the yards and appeared beside her.

She smiled up at him. It was so good to see he had his spring back. 'I'll just wait till the mob get through the first gate and then I'll let this lot out.'

He touched her shoulder. 'Joseph can do that. Why don't you come back to the house a bit earlier than usual? You could join us was emotionally drained from the phone calls and her heart went out to the people who had actually had to deal with the events as they happened, let alone Daphne, who had flown out and retrieved most of the wounded.

When she came in from the last flight, Daphne's shoulders were bowed and her face shone pale in the afternoon sunlight. Plus, she was on call again that night so she'd planned to stay in town at the old townhouse.

Rex followed her, telling Morgan that he was taking her home to his place for a bit of spoiling. 'They can ring her there.'

Billie decided there was a 'don't ring her there' in his voice and watched with a touch of wistfulness as they waved goodbye. Daphne even winked.

Billie's lips twitched. It was so good to see. Mia was staying over at Trent's parents', a lovely couple who had come out one day to Blue Hills for afternoon tea, and everyone had liked them. Now with Daphne away, the numbers would be down at home tonight.

She checked her computer screen, straightened her back off the chair and stretched, then glanced again at the clock. Another hour and a half until she knocked off.

'Would you like to come back to my place for tea tonight?' Morgan had come up behind her where she was sitting and she jumped. That made her cross. Normally she could feel when he was near. An indication of how drained she felt today.

'Because you feel sorry for me?'

He raised his eyebrows. 'I don't feel sorry for you.'

'Well you should,' she said unreasonably, and to make it more annoying he smiled.

'Cranky pants.'

And you're not getting into them. Thankfully, she didn't say that out loud, but even in her thoughts the words didn't have much conviction. 'Sorry.'

He put his hands on her shoulders and squeezed once, then stepped back, as though the action was out of bounds. 'If you come back to my house I'll massage your shoulders.'

OMG. Not an opportunity a single lady like herself could possibly pass up. Nobody rubbed her shoulders and today was the perfect day to be spoiled a little. 'You're on!'

An hour and a half later she drove into Morgan's spare car space. She'd rung Lorna to tell her not to save her a plate for tea. There had been an inquisitive archness in Lorna's comment and she smiled at the memory. Lorna was getting better. Thank goodness for that, and she hadn't mentioned leaving for twenty-four hours now.

Billie stopped and waited for Morgan to unlock the door. Now that she was here, she felt a little self-conscious as she preceded him past the front door and into the lounge room. They hadn't discussed their sunset jaunt at the station, and apart from the occasional tension when she found Morgan watching her at work, their relationship had remained tenuous. Until today. Why today?

She stopped in the middle of the room and tried to think of something to say apart from, *So, when are you going to rub my shoulders? And do I have to take my top off?* 'It's nice and cool in here.'

The sliding curtains were open and the afternoon sun was still high, but the tinting on the windows kept the temperature down substantially from what it was outside.

'The air conditioner is on a timer. It came on at five pm. One of

the things I love about this flat.'

Oh. 'There goes my tinted-window theory. I was going to tint my windows if I finally bought a house.' What was with her sudden need to fill the room with words?

He put his hands on her shoulders and gently pushed her down into a seat. 'Hold that thought. I'll just change and be back in a flash.'

She raised her brows. Looked up at him hovering over her while he waited for her response. She fought against the feeling of being small and fragile. Pretending she was very relaxed, she managed to make a joke. 'You're going to come back and flash me?'

He shot her a grin. 'It could be arranged.'

She had a sudden vision of him doing just that. 'Ah, no thanks. Too much of a good thing and all that.'

He nodded sagely. 'I can see how it could be.'

Then he was gone and she sagged back in the chair as if someone had untied the knot of her internal balloon. 'Crikey!' she muttered. Maybe she'd ask for one of those manly T-shirts he seemed to have in abundance to change into herself and get out of her uniform. It would probably smell fabulous.

Then he was back and she forgot what she'd been thinking. He had on one of those shirts she wouldn't mind sniffing, beneath which a nice expanse of torso rippled and tightened like the sensations in her belly. His strong legs extended from loose shorts and his quite beautiful feet were bare.

She resisted the impulse to fan her face. Apparently the air conditioner had stopped working.

He put out a hand to help her up and her fingers were lost in his. Up she sailed. Talk about a rollercoaster of sensations.

'Come through to the kitchen. Sorry I keep leaving you while I change.' He shrugged those truly delightful shoulders. 'Maybe I've lived too long on my own and have a routine.' He smiled ruefully at her. 'I like to strip off work with my clothes.'

She could picture that. Mmmmm. She followed like she was on a string and sat on the low-backed stool at the breakfast bar that he pulled out for her.

Maybe she should say something. 'I might have to leave a sarong in my glove-box if we keep doing this.' She glanced down at her work trousers. 'I'm at a disadvantage.'

He looked her over. 'Believe me. You're not at any disadvantage.' The tone of his voice made the room feel even warmer.

Her cheeks must have hinted at this because he turned to the fridge and brought out a bottle of juice. 'Would you like a cool drink?'

'Thank you.' He poured her a glass, half of one for himself that he downed in seconds, and then put the bottle back in the fridge. He studied her. 'You do look a little shell-shocked from the day. Let me have a go at those shoulders.'

She put the glass down before she fumbled it and watched, mesmerised, as he walked round the bench, then behind her until she couldn't see him. But she could feel him hovering there. So she dropped her head and waited. Felt the whisper of air just before he touched her and shivered.

When his hands did settle on the apex of each shoulder she tried not to tense. Forced herself to breathe out and droop as his fingers slid slowly along the fabric of her shirt.

'If you took off your shirt I could use some oil.'

'No,' she said in an almost strangled voice. 'That's fine.'

He didn't say anything else and she tried to relax again.

Gradually, as he dug his fingers in gently through her shirt, and then with more firmness, she couldn't help the sag as magic fingers began to work on releasing the tension.

An involuntary groan escaped as he kneaded a particularly tense section above her left shoulderblade and he slowed, dug deeper, around and around and around, slow and rhythmic. Like his tongue had been. That insidious thought jerked her back to a semblance of alertness, but too soon she melted like chocolate on the chair again, lost in a cloud of physical sensation.

'You have beautiful shoulders,' he murmured.

'I like your hands,' she muttered thickly.

She heard him chuckle. His big hands slid over and up and along, always moving, never stopping the pressure, so that she was happy just to soak it in for as long as he could keep going.

'Is this okay?'

'Yes,' the word slipping out on a sigh, like she was threatening to slip off the chair.

She could hear the smile in his voice. 'Thank you. I'm thinking I could ask you anything and you'd say yes at the moment.'

'Mmmm. Yes.'

He laughed. 'Then I'd better stop because I'd like to have a serious conversation with you.'

She opened her eyes slowly. Turned her head and watched him walk around the breakfast bar, that lithe easy movement of his a pleasure to watch.

He washed his hands and dried them before he opened the refrigerator and lifted out some cheese and olives. 'I'd better feed you first.' Out came an open packet of tiny crispy Italian bread bites.

Massage then food. She had no issue with that. 'Can I do something to help?'

'Nope. Just relax.'

And enjoy the view? This guy could really tick the boxes if she let him. And that was the problem. Could she let him? Or would they both retreat if she did? These were all good questions that she realised she would have to answer soon.

His tone was serious. 'The more I get to know you the more I want to know.'

Her shoulders felt so good. 'There's nothing to tell.' Except she loved the way his hands worked.

It came out of nowhere and she wasn't prepared. 'Tell me about the man who was Mia's father.'

'Sorry?'

'Mia's father?'

The room became suddenly claustrophobic. 'What about him?'

'What was he like?'

What could she say? Nice one minute, an emotional blackmailer the next. 'Hard work. And in the end too hard to stay around.'

'So an amicable separation?'

Amicable? The hard lump of a sarcastic snort lodged in her chest. She'd escaped in the night and never looked back. Just the little issue of Mia thinking he was dead.

'Why are you asking this?'

'I want to know.'

'Why?' Because she didn't want to talk about it.

He looked at her and she could tell he was turning cold, but she couldn't help that, and she got it now that she wasn't good

at sharing stuff. So she was shutting him out because she didn't want to go there. They could be friends, maybe lovers, but she didn't want to be accountable to any man and that included talking about her past because he felt he had a right to know. He didn't have that right.

She'd managed this on her own for seventeen years and she could manage for the next seventeen. No guilt. Well, maybe some guilt, but she didn't need to be reminded about it.

'I have this feeling I'm missing something. Something I should know.'

She should probably tell him. She'd told Lorna, and Daphne a bit. Not the lot. Why couldn't she tell Morgan? 'Nothing you should know. Very boring.'

She looked at the slate of the kitchen island bench, suddenly fascinated by the swirls of different coloured minerals.

'Billie?'

'I just don't want to talk about it.' She could feel the wall growing like Jack's beanstalk shooting up between them. She had the suspicion he was watching it grow, too.

He said unexpectedly, 'When my fiancée left me standing at the front of that church I discovered things that I could've helped her with if only she'd let me. But she shut me out.' He ran his hand through his hair. 'Maybe we could've saved the trauma of her imploding and running away if I'd known more about her life before we met. I don't want to make that same mistake.'

'I'm sorry. There's nothing to tell.' They both knew she was lying. She looked around for her handbag. He'd gone ahead and ruined the night. Or they both had.

She stood up. 'Thanks for the massage.'

'You don't have to go. I was going to make dinner.'

'I can't give you what you want, Morgan.'

'It's not hard. Just talk to me. If you need protection I can do that.'

What did he know? He couldn't know. Nobody knew.

'I have no idea what you're talking about.'

'Don't shut me out, Billie.'

She found her keys. 'I'll see you tomorrow.'

All the way home she was asking herself why she couldn't have just told him the facts and admitted she'd made a mistake that had resulted in Mia thinking her father was dead.

TWENTY

The next evening everyone was waiting for the rain to come. The previous night they'd had a sprinkle so light it had only made Soretta kick the dirt as she went across to check the troughs.

Not fair, Sorretta thought. It was raining so much in Adelaide that they'd called off the cricket, and that was only four hours away. It had looked promising all day, but the disappointing and dry electrical storms set everyone's teeth on edge.

Then they'd heard that an hour and a half across the border they'd had a deluge. So far there was none at Blue Hills. The heat increased the pall of anxiety in the homestead and the air seemed to palpate with tension.

Grandad looked as edgy as she felt, as they watched the sky because the house water tank was almost empty. He'd gone into town to order another tank just in case the heavens opened, which they had the money to do now, and Klaus had started up the old bulldozer and scraped the empty dam another few feet deeper in case they had a storm burst they could capture.

Billie had offered to pay the water carrier to bring a load for the house, but it wasn't just the house that needed water. Soretta was praying the water table they were using from the bores to keep the stock alive would hold up. They'd certainly given it a run over the last months. She knew everyone felt it was so close to rain that the waiting was torture, made worse by hearing that it was raining everywhere else.

She glanced across at Daphne who looked jumpy. Soretta knew she was on call tonight, but knowing Daphne, she'd be more worried about Rex than herself, flying with thunder and cumulonimbus everywhere.

Lorna had started talking about moving out to a retirement village to save water now, because one less person using the tank might help.

And to top it off, Mia had let slip she'd picked up Joseph and how uncomfortable she was every time he spoke to her. Of course she'd instantly fired him. And maybe she had been a bit harsh when she'd told her off for not saying anything earlier.

Another rumble of far-off thunder reverberated through Soretta's nerves and the whole house simmered with the strain.

An hour later Billie wandered outside. The clouds had slipped away again and the air hung still as the scorching afternoon sun hit the top of the gum tree outside the back door before it plummeted behind the hills.

Billie needed air, a release, and then she heard that bird she and Daphne hadn't been able to identify, and jumped on the excuse to be diverted.

Finally she saw it. Sitting at the top of the tree, singing exuberantly to its intended mate, and she pointed the video on her phone to capture it for proof. They'd be able to have a good look later

when she googled it and the birdsong would help.

Another movement caught her eye and she blinked, discerned the outline of a man walking towards her across the yard, but the sun was in her eyes and she shaded them.

Adrenaline tingled her skin and whipped her head up.

Jock. After all these years. As if she'd conjured him by all the thoughts she'd been having lately. So he'd found them. Her heart sank, almost with relief. At least she wouldn't have to worry anymore.

Then he spoke softly. 'Do you have a secret, Williamina?' Deceptively mild, the words floated in the hot air with a hint of derisive amusement. All she could think about was the whereabouts of Mia. Whether it was at all possible to keep her daughter out of sight from this man.

He stepped out from behind the bush and his classic good looks, far from attracting her, made her physically wince at her own stupidity. She couldn't believe she'd ever been so blind not to see through him. She knew what that full mouth hid. How those eyes were constantly sizing up what could be used to his advantage.

A man who had started from a privileged family, had burned chance after chance until his family had cut him adrift, had lost job after job, never able to see anything good, could only inhabit the negative world he created for himself and his status as victim of that world.

She didn't know what had happened in his past to form him that way, but she knew nobody could help him until he woke up to himself. She'd chosen not to let him spoil her life like he'd destroyed his own.

Years of dissolute living had left marks on his face. There were traces of weakness he couldn't hide behind his white teeth.

Her voice was stark. 'How did you find me?'

'Honey, I've been here for a week. Just didn't know it was you over here at the homestead.' His voice purred, 'Pure divine intervention.'

'Hardly divine.'

'Luck, then.' He shrugged and smiled lazily. Confident now he held all the power. 'I met a man in a pub.'

'Your whole life begins and ends in a pub.'

He stepped closer. 'Nasty. But in this case I'm delighted I met that particular man in a pub. Not only did he suggest I do some prospecting up here, but I found you as well. My dear old girlfriend.'

'Ex.'

He ignored her comment. 'Not only have I found my girlfriend but I've found out she's a mother.'

She jumped.

'You are a mother aren't you, Williamina? The mother of my daughter. Such a sweet girl. Exactly the right age to mean she's mine as her birthday was last week.'

Her heart sank. 'You've spoken to her?'

He laughed and it chilled Billie's soul. 'Her? Still afraid to say her name to her rightful father?' He smirked at her. 'Yes, my daughter, Mia.'

'You're not her father.'

More smirk. 'I think the mirror might tell you differently.'

She lifted her head and spoke evenly. 'You lost any chance when you threatened me. When you turned into a man I couldn't trust.'

His eyes flashed and she saw the glint of him turning and it was as plain to see as a bolt of lightning illuminating a dead tree.

'I was drunk. You got it wrong.'

He'd always been the victim, Billie thought. It was always everyone else's fault except his that his life wasn't what he wanted it to be. Billie had moved on but she wouldn't forget those seams of narcissism and violence that could never be cured by anyone but himself.

She almost felt sorry for him. But not quite.

She'd hoped her daughter would be spared this exposure, but it seemed it wasn't to be. Finally, she could accept that it had to happen one day. That she couldn't protect Mia forever from the truth. All she could do was hope Mia was grown up enough to understand why she had excluded him from both their lives.

'Don't you think I should be introduced to my daughter?'

Footsteps fell behind her and she knew with sickening despair who it would be. 'Mum?' Mia looked between the two of them. 'What's Joseph doing here? Soretta fired him.'

'His name's Jock.'

'Ah. The princess.' Jock smiled. 'Your mother knew me as Jock.' Billie wanted to slap him for the hurt he would cause Mia. But anything she said would only incite him more.

He went on. 'Oh yes, I'm leaving. Now I've found the person I've been looking for.'

Mia looked from one to the other. 'What do you mean?'

'Your mother.' He gestured grandly towards Billie. 'My old girl-friend.'

Billie shook her head. 'I walked away from you years ago.'

'You ran away.'

'Yep.' Fatalistically, Billie said what she should have told her daughter. 'As far and fast as I could.'

Mia was staring at them in shock. 'And me?'

He laughed. Held out his hands. 'You're my daughter.'

She looked at Billie with a world of hurt in her eyes. 'My father is dead.'

'Your father was dead.' Jock laughed. 'But now I'm alive.'

Mia threw another glance at Billie, pleading for her to dispute it. 'Mum. Him? Is this true?'

Mia was looking at her like she'd been stabbed and Billie felt the pain slice into her heart, but the stakes were too high for this to come out the wrong way. She would win this battle no matter what.

She lifted her chin. 'Genetically. But never intentionally.'

Mia whispered, 'All these years you lied to me.' Billie saw the hurt. Winced at the damage she'd caused when all she'd wanted to do was protect her.

Now she met her daughter's horrified eyes. 'I made a mistake trusting him once. You didn't need to make the same mistake.'

Mia gave her a long hard look that made Billie cringe from the contempt it held and then turned slowly towards Jock. Looked him up and down. For one horrible, interminable moment Billie thought Mia was going to choose to go with him. Find out for herself.

Jock smiled and held out his hands. 'Come to Papa.'

Mia shook her head at her mother, before saying, 'You might have made a mistake but what makes you think I would be so stupid?' Then to Jock, 'Get out of our house and leave my mother alone!'

Billie was almost as shocked as Jock. But not quite. She saw his face change. Saw the lack of control and rise of violence. She stepped forward and pulled Mia behind her, ignoring her resistance with a strength she didn't know she had.

'Get inside.' She pushed Mia towards the house, before turning back to Jock. 'And you get out.' There was steel in her voice. She would never be afraid of this man again.

She realised, too bloody late, that it was only Mia's distress she'd ever worried about. And finally, she felt the load of guilt and shame and fear of the past fall away like a musty coat she'd been dying to strip off. Hopefully, she wouldn't pay the ultimate price for doing so.

'Yes, get out.'

Lorna's voice rang out over their heads. She stood on the veran-dah behind them. Repeated Billie's words with barely a tremor in the voice that held all the authority of a woman who had faced greater danger than this before.

Stupidly he laughed. 'Spare me.' He looked at Lorna. 'I'll come up there and push you over, you old bag. Then I'll sort out my,' he paused, shooting Billie a death look, 'family.'

'Really.' There was no feebleness in Lorna's response. 'I'd like to see that. And I'd like to see you girls come back up here to me, please.'

Billie backed towards the step, her stomach hollow. Three wasn't necessarily better against him because now she would be responsible for Lorna as well. At least Mia for once did what she was told and scurried back up to Lorna.

'Leave.' Lorna spoke again while they were moving, and Jock laughed.

'What're you going to do about it, old woman?'

He advanced towards the verandah and his sudden menace glinted in the sunlight. Billie drew in her breath and shot a look at Lorna, who for some reason looked relieved.

Lorna's voice was conversational. 'Are you threatening us?'

'Bloody oath I am,' he growled, all pretence of humour gone from his voice.

'Then I'll protect myself and those I love.' She lifted the four-ten shotgun and rested it on the rail.

Jock laughed. 'An old witch with a gun that would knock you on your back if you were stupid enough to fire it.'

'She won't fall over. I'm right here helping her.' This was Daphne's voice. She stepped out of the shadows and hugged Mia into her.

Soretta stepped into Lorna's other side. 'And me.'

Five women. A hundred times stronger than the pathetic man in front of them.

'Get out,' said Daphne and Soretta together.

Jock began to recognise the united steel.

Billie looked down at him. 'Leave. Never come back. Or I will see you prosecuted to the full extent of the law.' She picked up the phone, and let out a sigh of relief that the bird video was still running. She waved the phone. 'It's all recorded.'

She saw it sink in. Saw the colour leave his face as he realised he was beaten. 'Bitch.' He glared pure hatred but it bounced off Billie now, fell harmlessly to the red soil at her feet like a handful of dry dirt that would blow away in the next breeze. Defeated, he turned away.

Soretta pointed in the direction of the gate. 'Get off our land.'

None of them moved until they heard the sound of his car roar into life and the acceleration of anger down the driveway.

Lorna broke the silence. 'Oh my,' she said and began to shake.

Soretta stepped in and relieved her of the gun and Daphne helped her sit down. Daphne swallowed and looked shudderingly at the firearm. 'Is it loaded?'

Lorna shook her head. 'Didn't have time.' Daphne and Billie's breath whooshed out in weak surprise and Mia laughed.

'I believed it was loaded,' Mia said. 'And he did, too. But what would you have done?'

Lorna patted her apron. Shotgun shells rattled in her pocket. 'I have buckshot—loaded with salt. Wouldn't have hurt him but it would've made a big bang.'

As if to underline her intent a huge clap of thunder rattled the windows and into the silence straight after came the *plop, plop* of the first few rain drops.

Big drops. Puffing little columns of dust into the air. Then a few more and finally a steady patter. Then the heavens split open and it started to really rain. Drilling holes into the dirt. Huge sheets of fresh cool water that just got heavier and heavier and louder on the tin roof of the homestead until it drummed like a hundred horses were stampeding across the roof.

It took a few seconds for it to sink in, and then they all turned to stare. Soretta first, then Mia, and they clapped their hands and laughed out loud and stared disbelievingly as it continued to get heavier.

Pathetic men in muscle cars were forgotten in the euphoria of a true rain storm. This was steady, soaking, life-giving rain. A deluge getting heavier. Certainly tank-filling, dam-filling solid rain and the cracked and dry ground drank it thirstily as it went on and on.

'Oh my goodness.' Billie grabbed Daphne and followed Soretta, who ran to the rail as the gutters started to overrun and she leaned over and put her arms out so the water ran down her arms. Then she dashed out into the yard and danced under it. The water poured down her face in tiny rivers, and even through the water Billie could see the stunned disbelief, and the incredulous relief, and the tears of joy.

Billie watched Mia run after Soretta and start to jump up and down, too. Laughing, her daughter's clothes quickly grew saturated and stuck to her, the muddy water splashed over her legs.

Lorna laughed as well and tottered to the rail to grin and reach her hand out into the downpour. 'Oh my goodness indeed.'

Billie felt Daphne take her elbow and they walked arm in arm to stand beside Lorna, grinning at the crazy girls dancing under the opening skies, and Billie realised that because of where she was, because of who she was with, and because of how they had all grown to be a family, she would never enjoy the start of a rain storm as much as she was enjoying this moment.

She tugged on Daphne's arm, took Lorna's thin fingers in hers, and the three women walked down the steps and out into the rain and laughed out loud.

Lorna hadn't been this happy for a long time. The camaraderie, the sheer joy of watching these young women gleefully dance in the rain, their inclusion of her made her cheeks stretch and pull with pleasure, the love she felt lifted her heart and she glanced up into

the falling drops and for a minute she thought she saw Wallace smiling down at her.

Then the pain came from nowhere. One minute Lorna was grinning with the rest of them and the next she staggered. She felt Billie's hand slip free as something in her chest crushed any chance of drawing a breath and the fog wasn't the rain on her Dame Edna glasses. No! She was happy. She didn't want to leave yet, Wallace.

Then the world began receding, rapidly, the sounds drifting away, the lightness of floating, and the last thing she saw as she slipped away was Billie turning towards her, saw her mouth open to ask a question, but then Billie was gone . . .

Billie saw Lorna's face go white, felt her fingers slip, begin to fall, caught her just enough to lower her gently to the ground to frantically feel for a pulse.

Cardiac arrest? It didn't matter, she told herself, treat it as if her heart has stopped.

'Daphne,' she shouted over the roar of the rain. Daphne was beside her in an instant and they straightened Lorna on the ground and began to compress her sternum there in the rain and mud and madness. One two, three . . .

Soretta and Mia turned, shock slackening the smiles from their faces and the two girls fell to their knees beside them.

Billie panted, 'Phone for an ambulance. Get my bag.'

The girls bolted up and away.

As Billie compressed her chest Daphne counted. 'Twenty-eight, twenty-nine, thirty.'

Billie said, 'Breathe,' and Daphne did for Lorna. Twice.

'One, two, three . . .' There was no time to get Lorna out of the rain, and bizarrely they carried on in the torrential downpour, crawling around in the mud to change places every two minutes, to save their strength. To stay efficient. Working like the team they were as they waited for reinforcements.

Fleetingly, Billie wondered if they were being selfish, if Lorna wanted to go, but that wasn't her decision to make. 'If you wanted to go why couldn't you have gone in your sleep,' Billie grunted spasmodically as she compressed the frail chest a third, and every thirty seconds Daphne inflated the lungs and she tried not to think about who it was beneath her hands.

'Come on, Lorna,' Daphne's fierce whisper was lost in the noise of the rain on the roof.

Then Mia was back with Billie's doctor's bag. She fell again to her knees beside her. 'I'll do that, Mum. Take the bag.' Billie blinked. Her baby was far from a baby as she elbowed her out of the way and began to compress Lorna's chest with efficient strength.

Mia glanced at Daphne and asked if that was right. Adjusted her hands and kept going as Billie switched modes and unzipped the bag, began to draw up the adrenaline, and squinted at the dose through the rain in her eyes.

Soretta arrived back. 'The ambulance is on its way. Ten minutes.'

Billie nodded. 'We can do this for ten minutes if we have to.' She hoped they wouldn't have to because the longer it went on the less chance of success they had. She held her hand up for them to stop for a second, and they all paused, mud-splattered comrades amidst the falling rain, the thunderous noise on the roof, the swishing of the trees as the storm built, but that was nothing to the

shock of disaster to one of them and the angst of the unknown. Then Billie bared the frail chest, pushed aside the wet lace singlet, and injected the adrenaline straight into Lorna's heart. They all held their breath.

Until Lorna drew one. Lorna's chest rose in a wheezing gasp and then another and they sat back on their heels, and Billie fell across Lorna's chest and then hurriedly lifted off her and tried to contain her relief. Daphne had her hand over her mouth, and Mia and Soretta began to sob in great uneven gasps.

Lorna struggled to rise and Daphne wiped her eyes and gently pushed her back. 'No. You darn well stay there, young lady,' she hiccoughed and sniffed and Soretta picked up the umbrella she'd forgotten she had and opened it over their patient.

Lorna said softly in regret, 'I liked the rain on my face.'

Much later that night, after Lorna had been settled into hospital for observation, Billie tried to insist the others go home, while she decided to stay nearby in the townhouse, in case Lorna needed her overnight. But there was another reason she wanted to stay. She needed to talk to Morgan. Man, she needed to talk to Morgan. But would he want to talk to her after they way she had walked out of his flat?

His response was curt when she rang at first but she persevered.

'Would it be possible for you to come out and talk to me tonight?'

'It's late. It's pouring.'

'I know.'

His voice was cautious. 'If you need me to.'

She didn't want to use the Lorna card. That wasn't fair. She wanted him to come because she asked him – not because he felt sorry for her. She closed her eyes and tried to banish the picture of her hands on Lorna's chest in the rain. If she didn't she was going to cry. She tightened her hand on the phone. 'I need you.'

There was a short silence. Then, 'I'll be there in fifteen minutes.'

'I'm not at Blue Hills. I'm at the hospital. Lorna had a heart attack.'

'I'll be there in two.'

He wasn't much longer than that. Morgan came striding up the corridor of the hospital towards the intensive care unit like a hero in a movie and Billie wanted to throw herself on his chest. But they were all sitting outside the doors on the waiting room chairs with Lorna's son and daughter-in-law.

They'd all seen Lorna briefly though they weren't encouraged to stay. Mia and Soretta had refused to leave until Lorna was pronounced stable enough to fly to Adelaide for specialist assessment. They'd find out soon if that was going to happen. So Morgan and Billie left to find a private place to talk.

Which is how they came to be sitting in Morgan's car in the dark, where nobody could hear them, with the lightning illuminating the night sky and the steady rain splashing off the bitumen of the road and pouring along the gutters.

She told him the details about Lorna, about the resuscitation and her transfer later when she was stable. He didn't know anything because the locum doctor had the phone. Then she told him about Joseph. She kept nothing back like she had for the others.

'And that's why I didn't want a relationship. I judged badly last time and it wasn't just me if I stuffed up again. Mia had to be safe,

had to come first. But she's older now, independent.' Billie paused, took a breath, held it. 'And now that I've met you I feel differently.' Billie let her breath out. There. She'd said it. Or as close as she could go without some encouragement from him.

So now all she could do was wait for his response and the tension was ramping up again inside the car.

Morgan shook his head. 'You didn't trust me enough to tell me you had a psychopath on your tail?' Her heart sank.

She'd known this was going to be a sticking point for his pride. She could see and feel his big, muscular silhouette vibrating with the need to protect and she couldn't change the cold hard fact that she hadn't let him support her. His protective streak wasn't a bad thing. She might even grow to like it if he gave her the chance. 'He wasn't quite a psychopath.' She thought about the beaten man being turned away by five strong women. 'And he's gone now. It wasn't your problem.'

He shook his head again in the dim illumination from the street lights still diluted by the rain. She could feel him building that wall between them again. 'What if I wanted it to be my problem? What if you keep other things from me that I think I should be a part of? That's my dilemma. That's why I kept pulling back, and now you're confirming how much you kept from me.'

'We'll work on that. I'm telling you now.' Hopefully, they could progress. Billie crossed her fingers in the dark, not game to touch him yet. 'Your real problem is that I'm planning on staying here for a long while. I want to give us a chance.'

'Are you?' A car drove past and she caught the glimmer of a smile illuminated by its headlights before he hid his face. *Good timing, car.*

Billie prodded. 'What about you?' She saw his head turn to pick her features out in the dark and felt his hand rise to touch her cheek.

'Oh, I'm planning to stay, too.' He paused. 'Permanently.'

'Really?' Some of the tension seeped from between them, through the rivulets of rain on the glass and out into the wild weather. The storm was calming inside the car.

She felt the slow release as his shoulders came down. Felt the wall shimmer and crack and disintegrate into scattered remnants around them until a different kind of tension began to rise. The kind he seemed to be able to switch on for her with just a look.

'Now that is a problem we should talk about,' he said, reaching for her.

EPILOGUE

A week later Lorna was discharged from the Mica Ridge rehabilitation ward. She'd been transferred and flown back from Adelaide, where she'd undergone a single bypass for the clot that had stopped her heart, and apparently her cardiologist was still shaking his head that she'd survived.

Before she'd left on the air ambulance with Hector and Michael, Lorna had made them promise not to spend money on flowers. 'If you want to spend money then donate it to the Flying Doctor Service and send me the receipt. That would make me happier.'

As the news had flown around town, helped by Mia's posting on their website, the two thousand likes on Facebook, and the flurry of tweets, the donations to celebrate Lorna's survival had topped two thousand dollars. More than Morgan's photo, Mia kept reminding him.

That hadn't stopped the array of floral arrangements that had filled her room when she arrived back at Mica Ridge, though none of them had been bought from the florist. All the flowers had come from gardens and rose beds and homestead patches arranged with love and admiration for a tough old bird who'd given everything for so long.

When they picked Lorna up, none of the homestead girls stayed home, so it was a bit of a squeeze with Billie driving, Daphne, Soretta and Mia in the back and Lorna in pride of place in the passenger seat, sitting sedately as if she hadn't caused anyone a minute of worry.

Soretta spoke for all of them. 'I never thought I could've forgotten it was raining, not after the drought, but I did. I swear that night you scared the living daylights out of us, Lorna. We love you. Don't do it again.'

'I promise,' Lorna said meekly, and a collective sigh of relief filled the car.

ACKNOWLEDGEMENTS

To the readers of my last book, *Red Sand Sunrise*: you were so enthusiastic and generous with your support and encouragement I have chosen to write again about the incredible people who carry our agricultural heritage through tough times. This topic was particularly poignant because, as I wrote this book, outback Australia was suffering the longest drought in one hundred years. Families had to ship their animals, watch dams dry completely, look for other ways to make ends meet or just walk away. There is such strength in their connection to the land and mateship for each other—I loved writing about these outback heroes who deserve to be celebrated, and the nurses and doctors who fly out to care for them.

It was such a great relief when the drought broke in western New South Wales as I finished the book and I could write the rain scene I had wanted so much for the real people out there. Distressingly, Queensland is still waiting for rain. May it come soon.

To Penguin Australia, and my wonderful editor Sarah Fairhall who flew up from Melbourne to launch my first book, and is always available in my moments of doubt with her full attention, faith, and excellent suggestions. Also, to my copyeditor Alex Nahlous—love your work—and to my publicist, dear Maria Matina, who is such fun to work with and who helps readers find me with her boundless enthusiasm.

To my agent, Clare Forster, who does all the tough stuff and is always looking out for new writing adventures for me. You are a champion.

To my writing family, of whom there are many, including Carol Marinelli, Trish Morey, Kelly Hunter, Anne Gracie, Barbara Hannay, Linda Brumley, Alison Roberts, Meredith Webber and Lillian Darcy. And to my good mates Bronwyn Jameson, and Annie Seaton, as well as many other writing colleagues who share the highs and lows of writing, including Eloisa James who saw the beginning of this book.

To my midwifery friends, who laugh when I go off on another research trip and wonder out loud if I'll find my way back to work, and who drive miles for my book launches. And especially to Rae, who helped me find a bolt hole when I needed a quiet space to write. You are all true friends.

To the wonderful Jillian Thurlow, who so kindly gave me an insight into her journey as a flight nurse and the details of the ins and outs of transferring patients by air. You are a star. Thank you.

I'd sincerely like to thank the people I met in Broken Hill, who were so inspiring. Thank you Kym and John Cramps for the sheep discussions, the glorious sunset tour at Mount Gipps Station, your generosity in answering my questions over the next few months and your warmth and sense of humour. Also, for letting me take over your shed for my ABC Radio interview while you all listened inside.

To Billy and Elaine at the Outback Church Stay, Broken Hill, who could not have been more generous with their time and kindness.

To Rae and the Broken Hill Tourist Information centre who sent me the newspaper clippings from the Barrier Truth, and to the reporter from the Barrier Truth who opened doors for me.

To the staff at the Visitors Information Centre at the Royal Flying Doctors Broken Hill, and Steve Martin, the General Manager at RFDS centre, who shared so much of his time and experience.

To Silver City Scenic Flights for the aerial tour of Broken Hill and the surrounds.

And to my new friend and reader, Fiona Austine, who grew up on the land and worked on far-flung stations in her school holidays —and said I got it right.

And finally, to my husband for his endless patience as I wander vaguely off into my writing world and for organising and sharing my outback adventures. Thank you, Ian, my rock, my biggest fan, my love and living proof that there are strong, heroic, honourable men in my town too.

From the internationally bestselling author Fiona McArthur comes a heartfelt story of family ties, the power of love and the passion of ordinary people achieving extraordinary things.

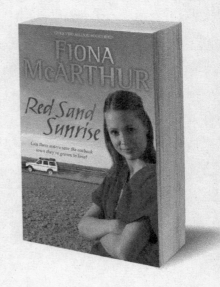

When the father she barely knew dies suddenly, midwife Eve Wilson decides she owes it to him to go to the funeral and meet her stepfamily in Red Sand. She doesn't expect to be so charmed by the beautiful remote township in far west Queensland – or by local station owner, Lex McKay.

After disappointment and heartbreak in Sydney, Dr Callie Wilson doesn't hesitate to move home and spend some time with her grieving mother. When she is approached to oversee the establishment of the area's first medical clinic, it seems the perfect opportunity. And Callie is keen to involve Eve, the sister she's just getting to know.

It seems fate is intent on bringing the three sisters together when Melbourne-based obstetrician Sienna Wilson is sent north to research the medical mystery affecting women in Red Sand. And when disaster strikes, they must each decide if being true to themselves means being there for each other . . .

'A book that you just have to devour in one day.'
NEWCASTLE HERALD

'Being present as the midwife at a baby's birth is one of life's glorious adventures.'

Nineteen Australian midwives share their incredible stories with passionate midwife and bestselling author Fiona McArthur.

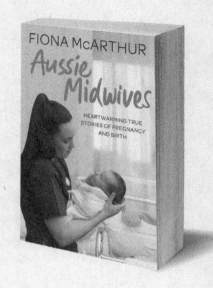

Midwives play a vital role in supporting women through some of the most challenging and rewarding moments of their lives. These remarkable people watch over births across Australia from the remote outback to busy urban hospitals.

Meet Annie, working on the tiny island of Saibai where mothers arrive by dinghy; Kate, a clinical midwifery consultant, who sees women with high-risk pregnancies; Priscilla and Jillian, who fly thousands of kilometres to get mothers and babies to hospital safely with the Royal Flying Doctor Service; and Louise, who gives impromptu consultations in the aisles of the local supermarket.

Funny one minute and heartbreaking the next, *Aussie Midwives* explores the emotion and drama of childbirth, and the lasting effect it has on the people who work in this extraordinary profession.

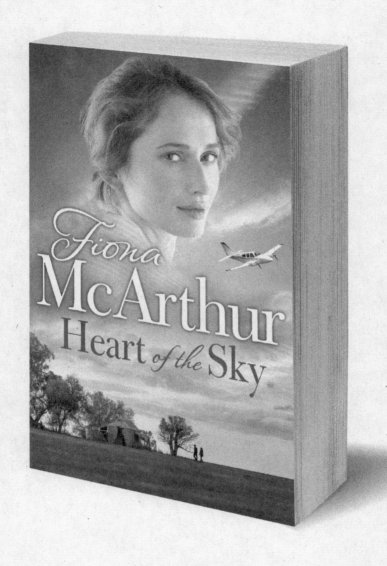

Coming soon from Penguin Books